THE TRIALS
AND TRIBULATIONS
OF LUCAS LESSAR

THE TRIALS
AND TRIBULATIONS
OF LUCAS LESSAR

SHAUNA SELIY

BLOOMSBURY

First published in Great Britain 2007

Copyright © 2007 by Shauna Seliy

The moral right of the author has been asserted

Bloomsbury Publishing Plc, 36 Soho Square, London W1D 3QY

A CIP catalogue record for this book is available from the British Library

ISBN 978 0 7475 9196 2
10 9 8 7 6 5 4 3 2 1

Typeset by Westchester Book Group
Printed in Great Britain by Clays Limited, St Ives plc

The paper this book is printed on is certified by the © 1996
Forest Stewardship Council A. C. (FSC). It is ancient-forest friendly.
The printer holds FSC chain of custody SGS-COC-2061

FSC

Mixed Sources
Product group from well-managed
forests and other controlled sources

Cert no. SGS-COC-2061
www.fsc.org
© 1996 Forest Stewardship Council

www.bloomsbury.com/shaunaseliy

For my family

We're troubadours
because we've learned
from the burrs of plague and war:
life on earth is
brief, keen, incendiary—

     —Cyrus Cassells
      "Guitar"

PART ONE

CHAPTER 1

I WAS GREASING THE cookie sheets, watching my grandmother and her sisters do shots of whiskey and feed each other moonshine cherries, when Zoli came into the house, pressed his hand against my throat, and whispered that he would kill me dead if I didn't tell him where my mother was.

My grandmother put her drink down and said, "What in the hell are you doing here?"

They both worked at the Plate Glass and he had rough hands like she did, covered with cuts. He pressed hard on my Adam's apple. I couldn't swallow.

He nodded and said, "Christmas, Slats. Just having a conversation with Lucas." The Plate Glass was closed for the holiday, but he was wearing their deep-blue uniform. It was stained and dirty.

"A conversation with Lucas?" my grandmother said. She got up from the table. "That should be rich. He won't cough up more than two words a day for me." She walked over to the chopping block, where she'd been carving the stems out of peppers, and picked up a knife.

In my ear, Zoli said, "Tell me where she is, you little fairy boy." I was still holding the stick of butter I'd been using on the cookie sheets. I dropped it.

Slats walked to the sink, turned on the tap, and ran water over the knife. Her sisters were quiet. They were all in dresses with aprons over them. We were in Great-grandfather's kitchen. It was 1974, the year I turned thirteen, the year my mother disappeared.

The knife Slats was cleaning was big, with a wooden handle. She shut off the faucet and pointed the business end of the knife at Zoli. Some of her sisters yelled, some of them scattered.

She said, "You listen, you crazy son of a bitch. Get your hands off him."

He loosened his grip on my neck but pulled me closer. "Is Mirjana here?"

"She sure as shit isn't," Slats said.

"Where is she?" he said.

"California," she said.

"California?" I said.

Zoli took his hand off my neck and moved it to my shoulder. "Where in California?"

Slats said, "What are you gonna do, go there? Might as well be Arabia."

All of Slats's brothers came into the kitchen. They were big. They wore flannel shirts, jeans, farming boots with thick brown soles. Zoli picked me up under my armpits and held me in front of him. My feet were off the ground. I heard the metal click of the screen door and then we were outside. It was still bright daytime. We fell back off the steps and hit the ground. My head knocked on his chest bones. His belt buckle dug into my back.

The great-uncles were on us. I tried to get away. Zoli crossed his arms over my chest and held on to me. The great-uncles couldn't pry me from him. They kicked him. They got on their knees and landed punches on him. I caught a fist on my arm. Red and black flannel covered my eyes, scratched my face. Great-grandfather's dogs barked and growled. They shoved their noses through, trying to get a piece of us. I shut my eyes against their hot breath, the snap of their teeth.

Slats yelled after her brothers to be careful of me. She called for the dogs to come to her. Zoli kicked and squirmed but didn't punch back. He turned us over, pressed my face in the cold grass and said, "I know you know where she is." His head cracked against mine; he'd taken a boot. He said, "Mirjana, Mirjana," soft and sad, as if he were praying to her or to me or to God. I felt his knee on my shoulder and everything got lighter. He was off me, running.

Slats's brothers ran after him. He got in his green Skylark with the black top and tore away up the drive, disappearing in the tunnel of trees.

Everyone said my mother looked like Hedy Lamarr. The way Zoli looked at her, you'd think she *was* Hedy Lamarr. He liked to say it was against the law to be as beautiful as she was, and then he'd pick up the phone and pretend to call the police or the fire company. Sometimes he did call the police or the fire company.

He thought the two of them should get married, but she didn't think so. She told him she'd stay a widow until she stopped dreaming about my father, and that she would probably never stop dreaming about my father. One of the times Zoli proposed, he took her out behind the Plate Glass and set up a sheet of blue tinted glass between two trees. They watched the sun go down behind it. When she said no, he spread out his arms and walked through it.

Slats said he was a gypsy with no sense. My mother said he just didn't understand some things. Love, she told me, didn't have anything to do with walking through a piece of glass.

In the kitchen, Great-grandfather passed around a bottle of pear brandy to Slats's brothers. He raised his little fist in the air, smiled, and said, "Such unkind boys I have made!"

He had a visitor with a long black coat. The man took the brandy and passed it to me.

Slats said to him, "He only just turned thirteen, Eli. Maybe next year."

"Let's see young Lessar's chest," he said. I didn't remember seeing him before, though everyone else seemed to know him. I wasn't sure how he knew my last name. He had the same accent as Great-grandfather, but not as thick. And while Great-grandfather had only two hairs left, he had a full head of it, all snow-white.

"No one's looking at his chest," Slats said.

But they were all staring at me, expecting something. I unbuttoned the top button, the second button.

Eli said, "Look, young mister. If you drink this, it will make your hair here." He pointed to his own chest. He said, "Like this," and opened his collar to show me the big white tufts. "And you'll grow very fast, faster than regular boy."

Slats said, "I have food to cook. Don't destroy him." She turned away from us and went to the stove.

I took the bottle. Great-grandfather made the pear brandy himself, using fruit from his own tree. In the spring, when the buds came out, he would put bottles on them so that the pears would grow inside the bottles. People in the family thought the pear brandy could heal you. When the animals were hurt,

Great-grandfather poured it on their wounds. My mother drank it when she felt a cold coming, though she didn't like the taste of it. She'd had me rub it on my gums once or twice for toothaches, but I'd never swallowed it down whole before.

I lifted the bottle and took a long drink. It was sharp and bitter, but I didn't cough or spit. Eli made a big circle with his arms and took a deep bow, as if he'd just done a magic trick. Everyone clapped.

When they turned away from me, I touched the skin over my heart; it was still smooth.

My mother had been gone for two weeks. Slats had been staying with me at my house, where we waited, without saying so, for her to come back from wherever she'd gone to. Since Great-grandmother had passed on and Slats was the oldest of the daughters, she was boss of Christmas Eve dinner. So, even though I didn't like going to the farm, she made me go up there with her to get ready for it. For days, we'd been boiling things and cutting things and kneading things. After the dinner, everyone would eat and drink and go out to the barn at midnight, because at midnight on our Christmas Eve, the animals could speak. Neighbors called us "hard Russians," since we didn't have the Pope, and we took our Christmas on the seventh of January.

Great-grandfather's house was big and pale white and on the rim of a cupped valley. The front door and the mailbox faced a long driveway lined with oak trees that led to the county road, but I'd always thought of the kitchen and the dining room as the front of the house, because they were usually crowded with people, and because their windows faced the valley. No one ever sat on the wide front porch, or used the front door; they always came up the short stoop of concrete block steps on the side of the house, into the kitchen. There was a table in the kitchen with silver legs and a yellow Bakelite top. At Christmas, we pushed the table against the wall so people could get in and out of the room easier. But they liked to congregate there, and if Slats didn't chase them away, they'd stay all day, talking and drinking.

Slats had four sisters and five brothers. Each of them had five or six sons and daughters, and some of those sons and daughters had children. Usually, at Christmas Eve, I would have run around the property with the other boys looking for animal skeletons, or I would have stayed in the house with them staring at the gun cabinet and trying to get at the liquor. But that year I kept close to Slats, her purple dress with the flowers on it always just in front of me.

She complained a fair amount about all she had to do, but everyone knew she liked being in charge of the kitchen. Usually she got her hair done once a week, always on the same day, at the same time, and it was always the same color, a kind of reddish brown. But she'd gone on a different day to get it done specially for the party, and she'd been sleeping on a pillow shaped like a horseshoe to keep it looking right. She'd dressed up too. Most of the time she wore plain skirts, or jeans, and big shirts with milky mother-of-pearl buttons that used to belong to my grandfather. In the kitchen, she'd stop what she was doing, every so often, and fix her lipstick in the reflection of the silver-plated fan cover that hung over the stove.

A few times, in the days leading up to Christmas, I forgot about my mother altogether and it was just regular life, just shaving a carrot with a blunt knife or pouring honey out of a jar for the *kutya*. Then someone would say, wasn't that Mirjana's recipe, or sweater, or plate, and I'd come up out of the dream.

* * *

Close to dinner, Slats made me help her set up card tables in the living room and drag in a picnic table from outside so there would be enough room for everyone. She didn't want people in chairs eating over their knees like gypsies. She set down plates and I followed her with silverware. I said, "How'd she get out there?"

"Out where?"

"California."

"Oh that," she said. She picked up a plate and polished it with her apron. Then she kept going around the table.

When we were through, she grabbed my arm and led me outside. It was getting dark. She pulled me toward the barn, her heels wobbling in the mud and stones. We weren't wearing coats. She let go of me and rubbed her arms to keep warm.

We went to a part of the barn I'd never been to, a floor up above the cows and goats and sheep. It was dark there. The only light came through the spaces where the wood didn't fit together. I heard her feeling around on the wall for something, then she opened a hatch and suddenly we had a view of the whole farm. I could see the pond at the bottom of the slope the barn was on, the hay field up to the left, and over on the right the old cornfield where Great-grandfather had an idea once to dig for oil, and then to dig for water—it was all pocked with holes and craters and looked like the front of the moon. By itself, between those two fields, in a clear patch of meadow he never opened for grazing, was the pear tree. It was winter, so the branches were bare. There were bottles scattered around the bottom for when the buds would come in the spring. The last sunlight of the day shone off them.

We stood there for a while looking at everything. Slats said, "California is more like something to say when you don't know the answer to a question. It's not so much a real place, like this here."

*   *   *

When we'd all settled around the dinner table and it was time for Great-grandfather to tell his story about coming to America, like he did every year, and for everyone to toast him with his pear brandy, he didn't do it. He looked around at all of us, his shot glass shaking a little in his hand, and apologized for landing us in a country of disappeared women. He turned and looked only at me, and then he put his glass down and started eating his dinner.

We dipped bread in honey to remember that life is sweet, and then we dipped it in garlic to remember that life is bitter. There was *kutya* on the table, with honey and crushed poppy seeds, to eat for good luck and deep sleep. There was hay under the table so that people would think about Jesus in his manger while they were eating. I didn't think about Jesus. I thought about how Zoli used to say he would string me up if my mother kept denying him. I thought about the three miners who got killed by the blackdamp in the explosion that took my father. They didn't get cut up or burned; they died from the inside out. When there's a fire or an explosion in a closed-in place like a coal mine, the air isn't any good for breathing. If you're down inside and you hear a big booming noise, you can make a run for it. If you get out with only a little of it in your lungs, you'll probably be okay, though you might come down with some pneumonia. But the mouth of the mine is usually too far away, sometimes a mile, and the blackdamp gets all through you and chokes you.

They found two of the miners in a dinner hole sitting with their pails on their laps, sandwiches still in their hands. The one I thought about most, though, was the one they found on his knees, his hands together in a prayer. I'd always thought my father had it the worst of them, but I was starting to think that the guy who was praying did. That guy knew what was coming and knew he couldn't do anything to stop it.

*   *   *

After dinner, Great-grandfather asked me to walk his friend Eli home.

Eli said to him, "No, no. I don't need ambassador."

Great-grandfather said, "Lucas will see you to there. It's late. Cold. He is company for you."

In the kitchen, Great-grandfather buttoned my coat to the top and kissed me on both cheeks. Usually, he wished goodbye to the great-grandchildren by patting us each on the head as we trailed out of the house behind our parents. I wasn't used to being so close to him. He had a liquor smell coming off him, and sharp stubble on his cheeks. I backed away. He said he trusted me to take care of his friend. In my ear, he said, "Don't let him wander aways from you in woods. Get him insides his house."

Slats was surrounded by sisters; they were deep in with the dishes. I was nervous and I must have looked it, because Benci, the oldest and biggest of the great-uncles, said to me, "Don't worry, Lucas, that Zoli won't fuss with you no more. He won't come around here again."

Another great-uncle said, "Not after that beating."

Benci smiled.

Outside, I looked at the parked cars and up the road for the Skylark and was glad for not seeing it. I followed close behind Eli. We walked up the driveway toward the county road. A few of the dogs walked alongside us for a while and then trailed off. Eli walked leaning over as if he had a cane, but he didn't have a cane. His bones poked at his coat. Whenever he said anything to me, he called me Luca, and there was no correcting him. After a long while, he turned off the driveway onto a grazing field. There wasn't anything around, no houses or cars.

At the end of the field was a set of woods. He stopped, pointed at the wall of trees, and then stepped into them. The ground was thick with bushes and twisted vines and the trees were packed close together. I couldn't imagine there was any kind of house in there, but after a while of picking our way through, we got on a skinny path that led to a shingle brick shack with one window. He fished a big skeleton key out of his pocket. He opened the door, walked in, and switched on the light.

I stuck my head in the door. "This where you live?"

"You could say this. Is like living."

There was paper everyplace—pinned up to the wall, spread out over the chairs and tables. There were books on the floor, piled under the furniture and against the walls.

I looked at the papers that were tacked up. From what I could tell, they were hand-drawn maps of coal mines. There were so many of them and they were tacked up so close to each other that you couldn't see the wall behind them. "What are these for?"

"I was engineer, in mines," he said.

"Which mine?"

"*Mines*, I said. Many."

"You been in King?"

"Of course, I was been everywhere, through all of seam. It was my job to understand if we dig here," he put his long fingernail on one of the drawings, "what will happen to over here," and he moved his hand to a different part of the drawing. "Maybe rocks are falling down, or ceiling, or whole place. Always something wants to come apart."

He took off his coat. He had a map of the bituminous fields tacked over the fireplace with the Pittsburgh seam colored in yellow and red, like a gash. He had stacks of papers all over. Some of these were drawings of mine tunnels, some had numbers scratched over them. And there were just regular maps, of the county, of Pennsylvania, of other states—West Virginia, Ohio, one of the long stretch of California in light yellow. While he was hanging up his coat, I shoved the California map in my jacket.

He said, "If you make so tremendous a hole in the ground, there is big pressure, Luca." He lifted up his arms and pretended to be pushing down hard on something with both hands. "Everything will make some movement, you know, try to make hole go away."

The navigators who worked for Christopher Columbus were Croatians from Ragusa. My father liked to tell me about this. All of his people were Croatian. He was born in Banning, but he didn't learn English until he went to the first grade. He would say I might think my homework was a heavy chore, but going to school for him was like going to a new country every morning. He told me that navigating was a science, but it was also sorcery, because it was looking into the future. What was up ahead? Islands with friendly people? Storms with waves big as mountains? Without the Croatian navigators, my father said, there would be no coal mines in America because there would be no America. So it was our own fault we had to work them.

Every morning when he was getting ready to go into the mine, my mother would lodge a piece of cotton between his pinky toe and the one next to it. This way if there was an accident, we could know him from his piece of cotton. But the real reason she did it was to make sure nothing would happen in the first place. To her mind, if she spent the morning preparing for a disaster, there wouldn't be one.

The fireshot that exploded next to him was so strong that pieces of his bones got lodged in the coal wall. They had to mine those parts of him out with picks.

My mother never dreamt about my father, even when he was alive. That story was just something she cooked up to say to Zoli, because it was hard to argue with the widow of an exploded miner when she said something like that.

My dad used to say King mine was a mine fit for a king. He rode the mantrip down into its pit every day. He was navigating his way through the seam with fireshots.

"Fire in the hole," he'd shout.

Boom.

I found the path out of Eli's woods back to the field. I heard something move behind me, a click, and then there was a bright flashlight shining at me. Zoli's hands were on my collar. I kicked at his legs. "I don't know where she is."

He had a good grip on me. I couldn't get loose. He said, "You couldn't live without her for two seconds. You know where she is."

He pulled me across the field to his car. He smelled like gasoline. He opened the driver's door and pushed me across the wide vinyl seat. He pressed the boxy orange flashlight against the side of my head. "You ready to tell me where she ran off to?"

I pressed my teeth together. I shoved my hands under my legs and leaned forward so he wouldn't see I was shaking.

He held the flashlight there for a while, and then he leaned back against his door, rested one hand on the steering wheel and the other on top of the seat behind me. "Are you gonna tell me?"

"Smells like gas around here," I said.

He nodded toward the back. I turned and looked. There were two metal containers on the seat. I said, "What's all that for?"

"Gasoline's for burning."

"Burning what?"

He shrugged. "None of your beeswax." He tapped his fingers on the steering wheel and scratched his neck. He usually had his brown hair and sideburns kept neat, but they were getting away from him, and hair was growing in splotches on his cheeks and all the way down his neck. He said, "Thick as thieves, her and Slats. Pair of thieves, those two. Maybe Slats wasn't shitting me—maybe she is in California. Slats knows. If she told you she don't know, she's lying." He looked out the window, then back at me. "Think she found some old Russians out in California to have a Christmas with her?"

He kept staring at me, waiting on me to say something. He had heavy black eyelashes and sad-looking brown eyes. It didn't matter what he was doing—he could be laughing with my mother, or making a sandwich, or saying something to scare the crap out of me—half the time those eyes made him look like he was about to fall over crying.

He said, "I bet she did. Probably not having a thought in her head about either one of us. Having a warm drink someplace, eating that *kutya* mush."

He leaned over, opened the glove compartment in front of me, and took out a pack of cigarettes. Taped inside the glove compartment door was a picture of my mother holding a bushel of tomatoes. She wasn't looking at the camera. She was looking just to the side of it, smiling to herself like she had a secret.

He closed the glove compartment and started taking the wrapper off his cigarettes. Before he finished opening them, he breathed out a long sigh and dropped them on the seat between us. He said, "You're gonna have to tell me where she is. I miss her too goddamn much."

"I don't miss her," I said.

He reached out, picked me up off the seat by my shoulder and pressed me against the window. "Don't disrespect her, you little shit. Think you're something else, huh, like Slats and her brothers? They'll learn their places."

I could feel his fingernails through my jacket and shirt. I said, "She's staying in an old hunting camp around here."

He opened his hand. I dropped back on the seat. He turned on the car and said, "Then that's where we're going. I knew you knew."

I pointed him around the barn and over to the woods behind the old cornfield where Great-grandfather had tried digging for oil. I wasn't sure there was a hunting camp, but I thought there might be some little place like Eli had.

Zoli parked the car and pulled me across the seat out his door. He had me hold the flashlight up to his face so that he could fix his hair in the window reflection. All the windows were lit in Great-grandfather's house. Sounds came up from it, not separate voices, but a kind of hum, people talking and laughing.

Zoli took the flashlight and I showed him into the woods. They were just as much a mess as the ones where Eli lived, vines and brush everyplace. I kept saying, "There's a path around here somewhere." I picked through the bushes pretending I was looking for it.

"Jesus Christ, Lucas, come on, hurry up."

"I think we went into the wrong place. It's down a ways. We have to go back out."

We made our way out of the woods and stood on the edge of the old cornfield. I said, "I don't think I can find it without the flashlight."

"How long has she been staying back there?"

"Since she left, couple of weeks."

He handed me the flashlight. I aimed it in front of me and bolted across the field, dodging the craters, jumping over the deep holes. He yelled after me. I kept running. I heard a thud behind me and his voice got muffled. I stopped and listened for him. A high-pitched bird noise came up out of where he was. He'd fallen into one of the craters.

I dropped the flashlight and walked the rest of the way back to the house.

Inside, they were all lit up like lampposts, singing and talking too loud. Benci was asleep under the dining room table, hugging a bottle of something, hay stuck to his shirt. Great-grandfather was in the kitchen singing some sad Russian song. One of the great-aunts stood in the door watching him, translating it into English for no one in particular.

I know now that I should have sent the great-uncles out to find Zoli. Maybe if I had, they would have stopped him, and none of what came later would have happened at all.

I didn't tell them, though. I wanted to look at the map of California I'd taken from Eli. I went upstairs to an empty bedroom. The bed was piled high with coats. I unbuttoned my jacket and started to take it off. I smelled gasoline on it and remembered the canisters in Zoli's car. I opened the window. It took a few minutes of looking into the dark before I could make out the Skylark. It was parked next to the pear tree with its doors hanging open, the lights on inside. Zoli was standing next to it. I saw a flash of metal. It took what felt like minutes and minutes more of staring into the dark before I could understand what he was doing. He was swinging a can back and forth, throwing gas all over the pear tree.

I ran downstairs and yelled for everyone to go outside. They stopped their singing and eating and drinking and everything turned quiet and it was just my voice ringing through the rooms. I wasn't saying anything about Zoli or gasoline or the pear tree—I was shouting for my mother over and over.

Slats went for the door. We all followed her into the cold and ran together, the ladies in their heels, the men in their boots. When we got to him, Zoli was standing in front of the tree holding a lighter. He threw it behind him and the grass caught and the bottles at the foot of the tree exploded, and the whole thing went up in red and blue and purple.

CHAPTER 2

G REAT-GRANDFATHER GOT THE IDEA for the pear tree from Slovenian monks he met on his way out of Europe. He was walking. He was headed for the sea. He wandered into the monks' monastery, and then into their arbor. It was full daylight. There was something in the arbor that made him think he was dreaming—the trees were shining. It seemed to him that the monks had performed an act of magic possible only because of their relationship with God—they had wrapped the pears in glass.

He and the monks hunted for a common language. They discovered that one of them could speak a little Russian. So he learned how they made the pears grow that way and how they made their pear brandy. They shared a bottle of it with him and he said it was the finest brandy he'd tasted. As he drank, he marveled at the fruit lodged in the bottom of the bottle. Before he left, he took an unbottled pear from a tree, ate it, and kept the seeds.

He sailed to America on a boat called *Philadelphia*. Somewhere in the Atlantic, he gambled away almost everything he had. He arrived here only with what was in his pockets—a little money, a list of names and addresses, the pear seeds.

He came to Banning and rented a room in a farmhouse. He got work in the mine. Secretly, he planted the pear seeds in a field he could see from his window on the second floor of the farmhouse. He didn't know who owned the field, but he liked the way it sloped down toward a pond at the bottom of the valley. He collected empty bottles for the day when the pear tree would grow large enough, would bear fruit, and he could put them on the buds. He learned in a book that it could take eight or nine years for fruit to come from a tree grown with seeds. He decided that in eight or nine years he would buy the farmhouse and the field. And after eight years had come and gone, he bought them.

Sometimes when I'm falling asleep, I taste the fire. I was close enough to get it in my mouth. It tasted like smoke and gasoline and live things coming apart from burning.

Since it was winter and the grass was dry, the fire spread quickly. The great-uncles who were chasing after Zoli had to give up on him to chase after water. I might have been the only one watching when he got in the Skylark and drove off. I felt that was the only way I wouldn't be afraid of him—standing in front of a house full of knives and guns, surrounded by people protecting themselves and me.

The headlights threw an arc of light against the woods and I saw a slip of white. I thought it was one of those bone-colored trees, but then it moved. It was a person, a man, stripped to the waist and all pale, like a fresh ghost. I opened my mouth to tell them to look, but then the man walked out of the trees toward us and I saw that it was Great-grandfather. I closed my mouth.

He got closer to us. Other people caught sight of him. "Dad?" someone said. "Grandfather?" someone said. He got down on his knees, dug his hands into the ground, and started shoving fistfuls of dirt and grass into his pockets. The great-aunts and great-uncles circled him, but it seemed like he couldn't hear or see them. He took some of the dirt and grass out of his pocket and put it in his mouth. Slats grabbed my arm.

"What's he doing?" I said.

She put her hand on my back and pushed me in front of her. "In the house. In the house."

Inside, she shoved my head under the faucet to get the smoke smell out of my hair. She put a towel on my head and pressed down. "You don't need to worry. He's going to be all right," she said. "What do you think, some Zoli can ruin him? Your coat stinks. Give it here."

I went to one of the empty rooms and sat on the bed. Slats stood in the doorway holding my coat. "Go to sleep," she said. "Okay? I don't want to catch you staring out the window. Like I said, you don't need to worry about him. He's a grown person, a couple of hundred years old."

"Who said I was worried about him? I just want to know why he was putting dirt in his mouth."

"Get under the blankets." She turned out the switch. The white walls caught the shadows and light from outside.

"I thought you were going," I said.

"I'm going. I'm going," she said, but she pulled a chair over to the window and sat down. "If your grandfather was still living, he would have chased that Zoli off a long time ago and none of this ever would have happened."

"Wouldn't have happened either if you hadn't told him to start coming around."

She held her hand up like a policeman stopping people at a crosswalk. "You don't want to get yourself into a battle of the wills with me. What was I supposed to do about her? Nothing? It's not my fault he turned out the way he turned out."

A few weeks after my father got taken, my mother fell into a long sleep. There were other women in Banning who had husbands or sons dead from the mines or from the war in Vietnam. I saw them almost every day, walking around, buying groceries, awake and talking to people. I thought that I'd just have to wait and then my mother would be up doing errands like them, instead of asleep with Slats and me sitting on either side of her in bed, reading her the paper.

He'd been gone for half a year by the time she worked up to taking a walk in the afternoon. She'd go over to Slats's and sit on her porch swing. I was in school and Slats was working, so for a while neither of us knew she was going out there. Later, she told me that it was easier for her to be awake at Slats's. At our house, all she wanted to do was close her eyes. Slats lived right across the road from the Plate Glass, and my mother would sit there and listen to the goings-on in the factory—the machines grinding and screaming.

One afternoon, Slats had to carry a broken sheet of glass outside and she saw that someone was on her porch. She walked halfway across the street, squinted, and it seemed to her that she was seeing a person brought back from the dead. She shouted. Her arm shot up in a wave. My mother waved back.

Slats looked out the window for her from the Plate Glass the next day, and the next. She kept coming. Slats wanted to talk to her, but she could never leave during those hours in the afternoon. She grabbed Zoli as he was leaving one day—his shift let out before hers—and asked him to walk over to say hey to Mirjana and see if she needed anything. He started to visit her every day. I heard her tell Slats about how quiet he kept on the porch swing, as if they were in some kind of church. She liked that.

Outside, the great-uncles were shouting, Benci's voice above the rest of them. Slats said, "It's times like these I get to missing your grandfather so much it feels like a sickness, like a flu. I did have a dream just a few nights ago that he *was* still living. He came in the bedroom and asked me for a hammer. I said to him, 'It's up in the attic,' and then he went up there, and hearing him stomping around, I remembered it wasn't in the attic at all, it was out in the garage. I woke up feeling terrible about making him go all the way up there. You know how it is, got to climb the ladder and undo the latch and push up that door—it's a labor. I didn't think it meant anything, but maybe it meant something."

"Meant what?" I said.

"That something was going to happen," she said. "Why aren't you sleeping?"

"Because you won't shut up."

"When he was in the Navy, he worked on a ship, your grandpa. He was a flagman. He made messages with semaphores and—"

"I know. I know what he did."

"He still does it, sends signals, sends them to me. Of course I can't always understand what he's trying to say. It comes through confused, in some kind of code."

"He tell you in a code my mother went to California?"

She turned away from the window and looked at me. "I think I liked it better before, when you were acting like a mute. We were getting along then. I told you already about California. It just came out of my mouth. It doesn't mean anything."

"Zoli says you know, and that maybe it's true, about California."

"Oh, she isn't out there. But if he thinks she is, that's fine by me."

"You know where she is then? How come you been telling me you don't know?"

"I didn't say I know where she is. I said I know where she isn't."

"How can you know where she isn't if you don't know where she is?"

"Who are you now? The Federal B.I.?"

She turned back to the window and after a few minutes of quiet, said, "Your grandfather gave me a sign the night your mother was born. He was away with the Navy, on a ship someplace. I was living by myself in the row houses—"

"Zoli said you and her are thick like thieves. Says you know."

"I'm not listening to you," she said.

"I'm not listening to you either," I said.

"I was too pregnant to sleep or go anywhere. One night I get this idea to waddle out to the picnic table across from the houses. While I'm sitting there—and it's late, dark—some kid, blond and waify, comes and sits on the sidewalk and starts pounding on something with a hammer. Usually, I would have said, 'Hey, kid, what are you doing? Cut it out.' But I couldn't manage it. I got all mesmerized by that hammer going up and down, up and down. Then the kid turns to me and says, 'Oh, hi Mrs. Jankovic. Hi.' And the hammer hits the thing and the thing goes ba-boom, blows up loud, real loud. His mother comes screaming down the road. Kid was okay, but he could have gotten his arm ripped off. He was beating on a blasting cap he'd found by the mine."

"That's no sign," I said.

"The blasting cap going off, that was a sign if ever there was one—my water broke at the sound of it."

The house turned noisy. Downstairs, people were walking in and out of the rooms. Slats said, "Maybe that's why your mother is the way she is. Her being so good-looking always set her apart a little, but, you know, starting out with a blasting cap like that might do something to a personality."

I heard Great-grandfather getting carried up the stairs and falling into his bed. I finally fell asleep, and it was maybe the heaviest sleep of my life. I felt like I was dropping through deep water.

My dad used to tell me about this B-25 bomber that crashed into the river up in Pittsburgh when he was a kid. Most of the crew made it out alive and they pointed right to the place where the plane went under the water. But even after dragging the river a couple hundred times, they couldn't find the plane. They never did; it's still under there, even now. Whenever my father talked about it, he always seemed so surprised at the way it had vanished. Going down into that sleep, I understood, in that way you understand things when you're falling asleep, half dreaming, that they hadn't found the plane because it was still going, dropping and dropping, on and on. I'll explain it to him when I wake up, I thought. I'll tell him they have rivers running underneath the rivers there, always more and more dark water to move through.

I slept until the sound of shoes knocking down the stairs woke me. I opened my eyes and sat up. The room was empty and everything was quiet. It was still dark. I thought I might have imagined the sound, but then I heard a door downstairs open and close, and cold air blew through the room. I got out of bed and stood on my bare feet on the wood floor. Coming the rest of the way out of that sleep was like swimming up through layers and layers of warmth. I wondered if steam rose up from my shoulders and back like it did from the great-uncles when they worked the fields in the cold. I could feel, maybe for the first time in my life, the heaviness of all that I needed to do just to stand up, my bones holding together and balancing on top of each other.

I walked down the hall to the room where Slats was staying. I thought it might have been her going down the stairs, but she was in there asleep. I went to Great-grandfather's bedroom. The door was open and the light from the hall shone on his white sheets and blankets. He had a wide bed with tall, spindly wooden posts at each corner. It was the only bed like that I'd ever seen and I always thought of it as a bed for a king or a president, or someone like Great-grandfather who owned a lot of animals and fields. There was grass and dirt scattered over the bed and the floor; it must have fallen out of his pockets. He was gone.

Downstairs, everything had been cleaned up and cleared away, and everyone had left. Except for the buzzing of the freezer and the wind knocking against the windows, it was quiet. I looked out the window. I didn't see the Skylark, but I still didn't want to go out there. The dark looked big. I kept thinking about Great-grandfather, though, walking in the cold, no shirt on him.

I took an old coat from the closet, pulled it on, and stepped outside. There was no fire anymore, but the air still smelled charged with it. The lights above the barn doors had burned out, or someone had turned them off, but a dim light was on inside. I headed toward it. The animals were making a racket. A few dogs were just outside the barn doors looking in. When they saw me coming, they shot off a round of barks.

I found Great-grandfather standing in the middle of the barn with a sack wrapped around his naked chest. He was talking to the animals, addressing them. He picked up a hen and whispered in her ear, put her down, and then he leaned over Valentina, his favorite goat, and said a few things to her.

It wasn't like other years. Other Christmases, talking to the animals was a good part of the night. People would carry drinks to the barn, sing pieces of songs while ice knocked against the insides of their glasses. Great-grandfather would tell us how fortunate we were that this was all we had to do to make good luck for the farm. He'd had a neighbor in his village in Russia who'd had to walk the whole perimeter of his fields on stilts every Christmas Eve to make sure he'd have a big harvest. Then Great-grandfather would talk to his animals and they'd talk back and he would translate for us. He said the animals answered in a language only he knew. His translations were always about how good crops were on their way, and good weather, and good health. Then it would be over and we'd go back in the house and have the rest of the night of people singing and drinking and telling stories.

He squinted at me. "Benci? No. No. Lucas. Of Mirjana."

"Hey," I said.

"That coat you wear, was used to be Benci's coat."

A cold wind blew through the barn, lifted up some dust, and scattered it. I said, "We should go inside."

"I was conversationing with Valentina." This was a regular-looking, gray goat with white patches and long ears that flopped down on the sides of her face. He had three other goats besides Valentina, five Polled Herefords, a handful of Suffolk sheep, and a set of dogs. They were all mild-mannered, and they stuck close to him, especially the dogs. I could never tell the dogs apart from each other or even tell how many of them there were. It was more like they were a part of him than that they were separate animals. When he walked the property, they'd swirl around him like a wide cape. But Valentina

27

was the only animal on the farm with a name. Even the dogs went nameless; he called each of them and all of them together *sobaka*, "dog." He gave Valentina a name because he thought she was the smartest of his animals. He named her after the famous cosmonaut, the first Russian lady to make it up into space, Valentina Tereshkova.

He said, "I was telling to Valentina about *Tot-to*, about *dedushka*. When I was small, *Tot-to* makes steps creak. He lived under there, under stairs. I can't run down without mother yelling at me to be careful of him."

Dedushka meant "grandfather," but I didn't know the other word. I didn't know one bit what he was talking about. "It's real cold," I said.

He touched the sack he had wrapped around him and pulled it tighter.

The light came on outside of the barn and we both turned toward it. Slats was standing by the doors blinking. "What's all the excitement?" she said. "Jesus, Dad, what is that you're parading around in?"

He looked down at the sack and shrugged. He went on talking to Slats, mostly in Russian. He said that word again, *Tot-to*. He looked up at the ceiling and held up his arms. The sack fell down around his feet. I could see his whole white chest and his skinny arms. I looked away.

Slats said, "Seems some people can't hold their liquor, even after a lot of years of serious practice."

She took one of his arms and wrapped it around her, behind her neck.

"You do the other side," she said to me.

I shook my head. I didn't want to touch him, his white skin hanging off him.

"Can you open the door for us? Or is that too taxing?"

Upstairs, I stood out in the hall while she put him to bed.

She said to him, "Look at me tucking you in, just like you and *mamushka* used to do me."

He started shaking. Slats held his hand and said, "Person could probably get themselves dead if they stood outside long enough in a piece of sack, Daddy."

He said a few things back to her. I heard Great-grandmother's name—Katalin—but the other things I couldn't understand. "What's he talking about?" I said.

"We need a person can translate the language of the inebriated. Come in here, feel his hands."

"I don't want to."

"They're freezing." She rubbed the blankets to warm him up, but he kept shaking. "I'm going to make a hot water bottle for him. Don't let him wander out of here. Who knows where he'll end up next."

"What's *Tot-to*?"

She looked at me for a minute like she was sizing me up, deciding what kind of answer to give. "It just means 'that one.' It's like when you say 'that one, over there.'"

After she was gone, he lifted his hand out from under the blankets and waved for me to come into the room.

"I'm all right out here," I said.

"I'll say to you what is *dedushka*, what is *Tot-to*. At night, when you hear bottles knocking on pear tree, it's him making sound. When they break, him also. When he is angry with us, he spoils pears and bottles. When I am young as you in my farm with father and mother, *Tot-to* lived inside with us, under stairs. But when I come to here, he takes up living in pear tree. From there, he can see everything, good things coming, or bad. Bad luck he can see, and if he wants, he can stop. Is protector of us." His breathing got deeper and slower. He closed his eyes and pulled the blankets close around himself. "You are understanding me?"

"Sure," I said. "I guess."

"Now that tree is broken, *Tot-to* will leave us here." He reached up and rubbed his fingers together like he was feeling the air between them. "This is why everything is now turning so cold. He is warmth for us. But now he pulls away, like ship."

Something about that gesture of his, rubbing the air between his fingers, made me feel like someone had dumped ice down my shirt. I went to the room I was sleeping in and sat in the chair Slats had pulled up to the window. When she came upstairs, she cursed at me for leaving him alone, and went off to bed.

People were always doing different things to stay safe in the mine, carrying pictures of saints or coins they thought were magic, or wearing special belt buckles. Putting the cotton between my dad's toes was my mother's way of protecting him. I had my own way. Most nights when we went to the Croatian Club and there was a band, a man sang, but every once in a while this woman was there. I don't know if she even lived in Banning. I never saw her anywhere else but the club. She would just sort of appear and sing this one song, always the same Croatian song, "Samo Nemoj Ti." The song didn't have a lot of lines, just a few that were repeated over and over. The refrain, "*Ti si rajski cvijet,*" meant something like, "You are a flower from heaven." But it wasn't the words of the song I liked so much; it was something the woman made in the room with her voice. It was like a kind of big net, but it didn't fall over us, not that kind of net. More like it went through us, knotting us all together so that no one could leave the dance hall, or the club, or the town without the rest of us. "*Tebe ljubiti ja neću prestati,*" the song went. "I'll never stop loving you."

Though my mother favored the trumpet and flugelhorn

blasts of Balkan brass bands, she would dance or sing along to just about anything, but not this song. She said she couldn't take it. So we would, all three of us, sit together and watch other people dance. I would think the song was doing something I couldn't do—keeping my father safe from falling slate and poison air.

I thought maybe Great-grandfather's idea about the protector that lived in the tree was something like that. From the tree you could see to all corners of the property, just like from nearly anywhere on the farm you could see at least a slip of shining bottle, a spray of leaves. And the tree was noisy sometimes. When the windows were open and it was breezy outside, you could hear the bottles knocking into each other.

I went downstairs. I wasn't sure what I was going to do, but when I got to the dining room, I knew. I took a plate out of the cabinet, shined it with my sleeve, and set it down on the table. Though we hadn't had to that night, if someone in the family or a close friend had died during the year, we set out a place for them at the dinner table on Christmas Eve. Some years there was more than one place. I always thought it was spooky having the empty chair with the plate and silverware set out, like inviting a spirit to the table, but Great-grandfather said we had to "for to show respect, and for to be with them one more time."

I got a fork, a spoon, and a knife. I got a shot glass too, though I knew my mother didn't go in too much for the pear brandy. I set the place for her and sat down next to it.

She left me a note before she went away. Written in the empty space between two stories in the newspaper. *Keep things right like your dad would have said to, at school, I mean, and whatever else he would have told you if he was still here. Don't come looking for me. I'm going to be far away from here anyway. For a*

CHAPTER 3

M Y MOTHER WASN'T the first woman to disappear from Banning—that was Mrs. D'Angelo, the policeman's wife. This happened a couple of years before the fireshot blew out next to my father. Everything was regular then, though it wasn't until everything changed that I knew that. My father went into the mine in the morning and came up out of it in the afternoon. All I knew of Zoli was that he worked at the Plate Glass with Slats, and he didn't wear plastic safety goggles like the rest of them. He wore old glass goggles attached to a leather cap, like a pilot from the First World War.

Mrs. D'Angelo and her husband had come up to Pennsylvania from an old coal camp in West Virginia and moved into the empty house across the street from us. They only lived there a year or so before she slipped away. The night before she left, we had our first deep drop into that winter's cold. I was in the kitchen working my math. My mother came in the house smelling of cold. She said, "I just saw one of the phony deer on the Markovics' lawn shake with a chill and fall over. It's freezing out there."

Marko Markovic and my father were best friends. He and his wife ran the Croatian Club. He was the bartender. She was the cook, and their son, Walter, who was in my grade, helped them out. Their house was next to the D'Angelos'. Both of their backyards faced the woods that belonged to the Bluebird mine. The Bluebird pit was back there with its mouth sewn shut. They'd closed it a long while before I was born, because of a slate fall. Most of its buildings had fallen down, but its toadholes were still there, and its coke ovens, and all of its old boney. Boney is the bones of the coal—ashes and spent coal. Bluebird had the tallest boney piles in Banning. Sometimes when the sun was going down behind them, they looked like small volcanoes ready to open up and take the sky apart.

My mother hung her coat and hat in the closet. She said, "You shouldn't go out in that cold tomorrow. We have to be careful of your sensitive teeth."

I didn't have sensitive teeth. When she wanted company, she'd keep me home from school, and after my dad left for work, we'd go to Brilliant and have lunch in the department store cafeteria, or we'd go to the movies. There were no restaurants or movie houses in Banning. We used to have all that when the mines were running, but the only working mine left by then was King, and people were always saying its days were numbered. The buildings were still there for the movie houses and the restaurants, but they were empty. We had a grocery store, and a drugstore where you could get magazines and cigarettes. We had the Croatian Club, and the big windy hall where the Slovenes held their dances. If you were after something else, though, you had to drive out on the snaking road lined with old coke ovens to Brilliant.

I said, "These teeth are hurting me already," and closed my math book.

My mother opened the newspaper to look for a movie. She said she'd been visiting with Rose D'Angelo across the way. She said, "Sometimes a person gets more than they signed up for." I didn't know if she meant Rose D'Angelo or herself, or if something in the newspaper had her thinking about how things were for people out in the world in general.

Going to sleep, I thought about how the next day I'd be sinking into a movie seat while everyone else was at school. My father hadn't come home yet, the Markovics were still at the club, and Mr. D'Angelo's carport was empty. My father had been telling me, for as long as I could remember, that when he was away I was to take care of my mother. He smiled when he said it, and I think he meant it as a joke. The idea of me looking after another person must have struck him as funny. I could hardly take care of myself yet. But I always took it seriously, and nights like that, when it was just me and my mother and Mrs. D'Angelo home in our houses, I figured myself in charge of things.

My father woke me up the next morning. He pulled aside the curtains and pointed out the window. "It's a damn handsome layer of snow, isn't it, Lucas?" He turned to look at himself in the mirror above my dresser. "I can't do a thing with my hair today," he said, smiling. He had wavy black hair that grew down to his collar and that he parted to the side. It often fell down in front of his eyes, though, like it was that morning. We had the same blue eyes, he and I; everyone said so.

I got up and looked out the window. The snow rose up in a wave to cover our picnic table benches, and in another wave against the piece of fence that held our grapevines. It was falling still.

"If you help me get the car out, I'll give you a ride to school," he said, and left the room without waiting for an answer.

I put my school clothes on so he wouldn't be on to us. I went outside. Usually our snow was heavy and wet and turned to slush when it hit the ground. But that morning the flakes flew away from each other, stayed whole, were sharp to the touch. They stung my face and the bottoms of my ears sticking out of my hat.

My dad and I were shoveling the drive when Mrs. D'Angelo came out of her house. Sometimes her light brown hair was twisted up on top, and sometimes it ran loose all the way down her back. That morning it was loose.

She walked across the road toward our house leaning forward, pulling her bright green coat collar up to her face. She walked by like she didn't notice us, even though we were making plenty of noise, and went into our house. My dad was singing one of his Croatian songs. Mrs. D'Angelo wouldn't have been able to understand him; she couldn't speak anything but English. When she came to the Croatian Club with us, I used to stay near her and change things from Croatian into English for her.

My dad opened the garage and started up his car. He wanted to make sure he could get it out before he ate breakfast. While he was warming the engine, Mr. D'Angelo came across the road in his policing outfit, blue stripes on the sides of his pants. "Lucas," he said. "Seen Rose?"

My father had been complaining lately about the way I looked away from people when they talked to me. He said it made me seem like I'd been raised by beasts in a dark forest. I forced myself to look at Mr. D'Angelo and concentrate. He had short red hair, and his cheeks and chin were always shaved clean, like he'd just taken a razor to them. He was harder to look at than most people because of the things people said about him. They said that down in West Virginia he carried a switch he'd made from the skin of a striker he'd drowned in a mine pond.

I said, "She went into our house, Mr. D'Angelo."

"What's she doing in there?"

"Probably having a coffee. They like a coffee around now."

He stared at me until I started feeling nervous with that answer. I said, "Pretty much everyone does."

That didn't help change his expression. I looked down and started shoveling again. I wished that we didn't have any police in Banning. A lot of people thought we shouldn't and that we only had them because the other towns did. People liked better to do their own policing. When Mr. D'Angelo was sent to look into a burglary, or a vandalism, or a killing, people handed him a tough time, lied to him, turned quiet at his questions. Most of the time they weren't staying quiet to protect anyone in particular; they just wanted to keep the law in their own hands, and out of his.

He spent some time walking back and forth between our place and his car. I kept working at the snow. He made up his mind and got in the car. When he pulled away, snow sprayed up from under his tires.

My dad backed out of the garage slow and careful and left the car running. He stepped out singing to me, "Hey, hey, Lucas. Need a ride to school, Lucas? In my fancy aquamarine car, Lucas?" I was supposed to sing back. But I just said, "No, I don't think I do." He pinned my arms to my sides and lifted me off my feet. We'd shoveled the snow from the drive into a big pile. I was expecting him to push me into it headfirst, but, instead, he set me down on top and planted a kiss in my hair.

"I'm going to have some breakfast," he said. He went in through the garage and pulled down the door. The gears on the garage door were rusted and usually they made a big grating noise, but the snow had a way of making everything quiet. I hardly heard my mother when she said, "Lucas, get off there. Your pants will be soaked through." She was standing at the bottom of the porch steps with Mrs. D'Angelo. I rolled off the pile of snow and walked over to them.

Mrs. D'Angelo pulled a cigarette out of her coat pocket and put it in her mouth. She didn't light it. It wasn't that she was so good-looking—her eyes were deep-set and ringed with dark circles—it's more that when she was standing in front of me, I couldn't remember what other people looked like. She stuck her long, pale hand inside her coat pocket, pulled out another cigarette, and held it out to me. I didn't make any move to take it. My mother nodded at me, impatiently, to go ahead. Mrs. D'Angelo still hadn't lit hers, and she didn't take out her matches. She pretended to take a puff and then blew out a long breath above my head. On account of the cold, it trailed away from us like smoke. Once, at a wedding at the club, she spent a good part of the reception tying the stems of cherries into knots with her tongue. When she was through, she arranged them on the table, in a display.

My mother and I started back toward the house, but Mrs. D'Angelo stood still with her unlit cigarette in her mouth, staring after us.

"Mirjana," she said to my mother, "soon?"

My mother nodded. She took the cigarette I was holding and then tugged me inside. We were in the hall kicking the snow off our boots when my father came out of the kitchen and said to me, "Let's go."

My mother said, "He hasn't eaten yet and his pants are soaking wet."

"Are your pants wet? What kind of operation are we running here?"

My mother said, "I want to take him. And I want the car. I'd like to go for a drive and see the snow."

"A drive to see the snow?"

"That's right."

He moved in close like he was going to kiss her, but he stopped and said, "Except for the fact that you look a little like Hedy Lamarr, I don't think I've ever seen you before."

We dropped him off at the mine and drove away in the direction of the school, but after a few minutes we switched roads and went to Mrs. D'Angelo's house. She was waiting inside her living room, looking for us out the window. When she came out of her house, I saw that she'd changed her hair; it was wrapped up in a bun on the back of her head. She was still wearing her green coat and she had a bag tucked under her arm, a traveling bag.

Before she got in the car, I said, "Where are we going?"

My mother told me to get into the back seat. When I got back there, she turned around and looked at me. "We know how to have a secret," she said. "Me and you. We know."

We were sitting in a cafeteria someplace in West Virginia, my mother and Mrs. D'Angelo drinking coffee, when she told us that Frank kept five shotguns in their pantry. Mostly she was a quiet person, and had a careful way of waiting to say something, but she was talking so much that she hardly had a chance to drink her coffee. "He always says he won't tell me where the cartridges are so that I won't go out on some kind of spree, like Bonnie and Clyde. But it wouldn't be like that, it'd just be me. Well, maybe I'd pick someone up along the way." She looked at me and said, "A handsome someone, like Lucas here."

I felt a powerful heat in the back of my neck.

She said, "Mirjana, isn't it something how on Jimmy those blue eyes are so sparkly, but on Lucas, they're all broody and dark."

My mother was sitting next to me in the booth. "Look here,

L," she said, and turned my face toward her. "They are not broody," she said to Mrs. D'Angelo.

"They are too," Mrs. D'Angelo said. "Like the water back in the Bluebird mine pond."

The waitress came over and refilled their coffees. Mrs. D'Angelo waited for her to go away, then said, "I bet Frank won't tell me where those cartridges are because he's worried I'll blow off his head one morning while he's frying an egg."

My mother laughed a little. "Oh, Rose." She put her arm around me and scratched the back of my head. She did this when she was bored or when she was nervous, or when we were out someplace with my father and she wanted to go home but couldn't say so. Later, when Zoli was around and she did this, it meant it was me and her against him.

Mrs. D'Angelo said, "That's usually how it happens with people. Frank will tell you, it's the people closest to you, the people who supposedly can't live without you, will do the cruelest things—cut you into bits and put you in a teapot . . . I can't figure it out, how it happens . . . When it comes for you, though, love, the bad kind, maybe even the good kind, if there is such a thing, you do get a close-up look at what you're made of. Most people probably aren't real happy with what they end up seeing . . ." Her voice trailed off and she stared at the table.

My mother stirred her coffee. I watched Mrs. D'Angelo hold on to her thought. In the back of the restaurant, a waitress dropped a tray. The cook shouted. People at the next table helped each other with their coats and the air stirred around us. Mrs. D'Angelo shook her head a little, took a sip of coffee. She said, "Frank will tell you about the things he's seen, the things that happen to people. I mean, if you got the fortitude to pry the words out of him, he'll tell you."

My mother nodded and went up to the register to the pay the bill.

It was just me and Mrs. D'Angelo at the table. I looked around. The restaurant wasn't as nice as the ones in Brilliant. I'd never been in West Virginia before. It had taken us an hour or so of driving to get there. Mrs. D'Angelo lit another cigarette. She said, "So how about it, Lucas, you and me? We'll steal Marko Markovic's Nash one night when they're at the club," she blew out a long puff of smoke, "then we'll light out for the territory."

The heat on my neck moved up to my face and set off a buzzing in my ears.

She said, "Oh come on, I know you'd like to go out for a ride in that pretty black car. See some of the country."

"Okay. I'll go," I said.

She laughed and raised her eyebrows. "I think you might do it. I think you just might."

My mother came back to the table and rested her hand on Mrs. D'Angelo's shoulder. She said, "Girl at the register told me the temperature's going to drop again tonight. Snow could make the roads slow going."

Mrs. D'Angelo looked behind me out the window and said, "What's the gal at the register know? Weather isn't her line of work."

My mother picked up the pack of cigarettes and studied them. She said, "I'm just saying. It's not too late to, you know, go home, make it for another day."

Mrs. D'Angelo tapped the pack of cigarettes in my mother's hand, and said, "You can have one, Mirjana. Go ahead."

"You know I don't smoke," my mother said. And she didn't, but she sat down and lit one up.

Mrs. D'Angelo pulled a sour apple hardtack candy out of her purse and gave it to me. I bit down on it and the candy cracked. She put her hand against my chin and said, "You'll break your teeth." She held her hand steady. I didn't move until she let go.

She raised up her arm and waved to someone outside. There

were people walking up and down the sidewalk, and cars on the road. I couldn't see who she was waving to.

She said, "He's here, Mirjana. He showed."

My mother nodded. "Tell him to come inside and say hi."

Mrs. D'Angelo stood up, smoothed out the front of her dress, and pulled on her green coat. She said, "I don't think so. He's out there in his car. It'd be a to-do."

My mother said, "Come on, bring him in. Let me have a look."

She shook her head and said, "Thanks for the ride, Mirjana. Thanks for all you did for me."

She leaned down and kissed me just next to my mouth. Her lips were wet with coffee and lipstick. She held them against my face longer than I was used to people doing. She had a deep cigarette and perfume smell all through her hair and her coat. When she pulled away from me, it was like being inside a cloud.

After she walked away from the table, I said, "Where's she going? Who's out there?"

"She's making her way, I guess," my mother said, her voice all soft and full of air.

"Making her way where?"

She watched Mrs. D'Angelo walk out of the place. She said, "We know how to have a secret?"

I nodded.

"You aren't to tell anyone that we came down here today. It's just us that knows about this. I can't be sure, but I don't think Rose D'Angelo will be around town anymore. And you can't say to a soul that you saw her here. Not your dad. Not Slats. Especially not Slats. She can talk, my mother, can't help herself." She pulled her purse close to her and snapped it shut. "Now I'm going to the ladies' and then me and you are going home."

I went outside to see if I could get a look at the man

Mrs. D'Angelo had gone off with. I walked to the end of the block looking in all the parked cars. Then I saw, on the next block, a flash of Mrs. D'Angelo's green coat. I ran after her, my shoes slipping on the snow. When I got close enough, I saw that she was by herself. I stopped running and watched. From the way she was walking, sort of slow and distracted, I got a feeling that she wasn't going anywhere in particular, that maybe there was no man in a car. She was alone.

All of a sudden, I couldn't think of anything but Marko Markovic's Nash. On nice days, he was always polishing it, and it would shine in the sun like a piece of wet coal. My mother said that car was the love of his life. But he never took it anywhere, it just sat still in the driveway all the time looking nice.

I turned around and walked back toward the restaurant. Mrs. D'Angelo's sour apple candy had melted, but the taste of it was still in my mouth.

Later that night, we drove to the Croatian Club. Usually we walked, but my mother said her bones would break if she had to walk in that cold. When we got in the car, my father said he didn't want to go to the club right away. He said he wanted my mother to show him where she'd gone out driving to look at the snow. He was eyeing her when he said it, suspicious, and it made me nervous, but she said, "Okay, doll," without showing a flicker of worry.

She guided him around, down one street and up another. It was a good trick. She picked nice-looking roads, big spiny trees leaning over them, branches heavy with snow. With the moon out as big as it was, the branches seemed to glow. I got an idea that the thing that made a person grow up was how many secrets they had, how big the secrets were, and how good they were at holding on to them.

A cop car came up behind us flashing its lights.

"Is that for us, Mirjana?" my dad said. "Lucas," he said, "look and see if that's for us."

My mother said, "Just pull over, Jim. If he doesn't want us, he'll pass us up."

"I wasn't speeding."

"There aren't any other cars out here, Dad."

We pulled over. The cop left the lights on and they flashed into the woods on both sides of the road, lighting up the snow-covered mountain laurels and white sycamores. He didn't come up to the driver's side like they always do. Instead, he knocked on my mother's window. She rolled it down.

My father leaned over and looked up at the cop. He said, "Oh Jesus, Frank, you scared the hell out of me. Mirjana, it's just Frank."

She stared ahead at the road.

"Frank D'Angelo," my father said to her, as if they'd been arguing about who he was and my father was insisting on it. I sunk down a little in the back. My mother blinked at the lights swinging through the car.

Mr. D'Angelo leaned down so that his eyes were level with my mother's. He looked at her for a long time, and then said, "You seen Rose?"

My father nudged her shoulder, but she didn't say anything, just slowly shook her head. My father said to Mr. D'Angelo, "Everything okay, Frank?"

Mr. D'Angelo said to my mother, "You haven't seen her then?" This time his voice was harder.

My mother didn't say anything, or move. My father seemed like he didn't know what to do. He said, "Mirjana?"

Mr. D'Angelo said, "There was a bag. She took a bag."

Nobody said anything. My father looked down. My mother kept staring ahead. The lights from the patrol car were swinging through the windows and passing over us, and the inside of the car seemed to billow out like a sail. I realized that my mother's skin was running pale because she was afraid, something I'd never known her to be.

I leaned forward and said, "I seen her."

Mr. D'Angelo and my dad both looked at me, but my mother didn't turn around.

"On my way home from school," I said. "I saw her walking down at the creek."

My father nodded and said, "All right then, Frank?"

Mr. D'Angelo didn't answer.

My father said, "We're on our way down the club. If we see her there, we'll send her home to you. Maybe she went for a drink. Nice night for a warm drink."

Mr. D'Angelo held on to the car door for a while, then let go and walked to his car. He turned off his flashing lights and pulled onto the road away from us. My father asked again if my mother had seen Rose. She said no, just for coffee that morning. He put the car in drive and we got back on the road.

Without taking her eyes off my father, my mother reached back and put her hand on the side of my face. I had a wide scar under my right eye, a patch where my skin was whiter. My mother always claimed it wasn't a scar. It looked the way it looked, she said, because she'd kissed me there so often that the skin was wearing away. It was true that whenever she kissed me goodbye or hello or for just no reason, for as long as I could remember, that was nearly always where she landed the kiss. Just then, she ran her finger over the spot.

When we got home that night, I saw that Marko's black Nash was sitting where it always was, just a little ways in the drive, close to the road, as if he might pull out at any minute and go off somewhere. After my parents went inside, I walked across the street to take a closer look. Its shiny black paint showed through the places where the snow wasn't thick on it.

I wiped the snow off the windows and looked at the brown seats, the polished steering wheel. I hadn't told my mother that I'd seen Mrs. D'Angelo walk off alone. I think I had an idea that I would get in the Nash and go out driving until I found her in her green coat. The two of us would light out for the territory, like she'd said, and then come back to town. I tried the doors, but they were locked, or maybe they were frozen. My hands stung touching the handles.

I hadn't believed my mother when she said that Mrs. D'Angelo wouldn't be coming back to town. It wasn't that I thought she was lying to me; it was that I didn't understand yet that it was possible to put a few things in a bag and walk away from everything you knew, and just keep walking. My mother, though, I guess she knew.

CHAPTER 4

A FTER CHRISTMAS, Slats made us switch from sleeping at my house to staying at hers, where she said she had easier access to the things she needed to fend off Zoli. She borrowed a six-inch hunting knife from one of her brothers and stowed it under the couch. I could see it shining when I pulled my shoes out from under there. I started out sleeping on that couch, but after she caught me two nights in a row trying to slip out to go back to my house, she took up the couch herself and put me in her room.

Her bed had a white lacy cover that looked like it should have been wrapped around a box of Kleenex. Next to it was a TV stand that, instead of having a TV on it, was covered with figurines of St. Francis. Slats was tall as could be, with real long legs—that's how she got that nickname—and she had a heavy way of walking. When she was going from room to room, the St. Francises clinked together. I tried to space them apart so they wouldn't do that, but the tray was too crowded. The window above the bed faced the Plate Glass. I didn't like sleeping at her house in the doily bedspread next to the St. Francises, but I liked the noises the machines made at the Glass, their humming and screeching. When they were running a big order, they kept at it all night. Maybe it was because of the things that were happening then, or maybe all thirteen-year-olds are like this, but I liked it best of all when things broke; the noise of glass shattering would ring out over the street. I'd stand still waiting and hoping for more of it.

After she moved us around, Slats started locking the windows and pushing chairs against the doors at night, to keep me inside, she said, and Zoli outside. But Zoli didn't show at the Plate Glass when the holiday was over; day after day, he missed his shift and never called in to say why. Slats seemed to favor him disappeared, but I would have liked better to know where he was.

"If he's not coming to the Glass, where's he at?" I asked her.

"He's just laying low. Hiding out in his place. He's probably more scared of us than we are of him."

"I'm not scared of him," I said, but I was thinking about him out in the Skylark, circling us and circling us, gas cans rattling against each other in the back, packs of matches sliding across the dash.

About a week after Christmas, Benci came into Slats's kitchen and after saying his hellos, fell quiet and stared at his shoes.

"What's the matter with you?" Slats said.

He looked up and said, "Daddy's still in bed."

"From this morning?" Slats said.

"No," he said, "from Christmas."

"What's wrong with him?"

"I don't know. Can't get him to say anything that makes sense."

"Is he feverish?"

"I ain't no doctor."

"No kidding."

Benci looked at his shoes again.

"Was he hot?" Slats said.

"I tried to get at his forehead, but he wouldn't let me."

"Well, is he not making sense in his usual way or is he not making sense like his brain's boiling over?"

"He says to me, 'Benci, I got a ghost trapped in my lungs.' I says to him, 'You mean you got a cough or something.' He says, 'No cough. Ghost.' I don't know. Maybe you could go up there and have a look at him."

"We got our own problems here," she said.

He looked at me, then back at Slats. He stared at the floor some more, waiting for her to say something, but she didn't say anything. He said, "Come on, you know Daddy won't listen to no one but you. He thinks you're the only one with sense."

"Well, he's right."

After he left, Slats called the farm. She waited a long time for an answer and then hung up. "We should take him something to eat, I guess," she said. She took cans of soup out of the cupboard and looked through the refrigerator. "How are we living like this? All we have is Kool-Aid, ketchup, and beer. Like a pair of bachelors. I guess we do have one bachelor in the house now, young though, a starter kit."

"I'm one of the tallest in my grade."

"Did I say anything against you and your great tallness?" She picked up the phone and called again, waiting longer this time. "Daddy, you okay?" she said. "Is that right?" She waved her finger in circles by her ear, letting me know she thought he was saying something crazy. "I know. I heard from Benci you aren't feeling too good." She listened for a minute, then said, "Me and Lucas will be by." Worry passed over her face. "No, Dad, not *Lukacs*. Lucas, Mirjana's boy, Lucas." Then he said something that made her laugh. "No, I don't know how Benci got so heavyset. You're right, it's an actual mystery. See you soon, all right. *Do zavtra*." She hung up the phone and said to me, "Well, I don't think he sounds all that bad."

"Then why'd he call me *Lukacs*?"

Lukacs was how you said my name in Hungarian, Great-grandmother's language. It sounds like "Loo-katch." Great-grandmother and Great-grandfather's first son was named Lukacs. He died from catching a fever when he was just a baby. After he went, they had a few more sons and daughters and tried to forget about him. But when they were lying in bed listening to the noise of all their babies and growing kids, they would always hear a hole of quiet where Lukacs's yelling should have been. Then they had their biggest baby yet, a fat boy who screamed so loud when he was born that Great-grandfather had to stuff newspapers in his ears. They thought he was too tough and big and loud to get cut down by a fever, and they missed their Lukacs, so they brought out his name and gave it to that baby.

All of my mother's growing up, this second Lukacs was her favorite uncle. Even though he'd started out big, he turned out skinny. She told me that when he stood up straight, or curled over laughing, you could see his ribs, even through his clothes. When she got married, since my grandfather wasn't living anymore, and since she loved this Lukacs so much, she had him walk her down the aisle to my father. I've seen a picture of this, Lukacs with his skinny neck and bright eyes, next to my mother with her secret-keeping smile and dark eyes.

Like the first, the second Lukacs was prone to fever. He beat them back one by one. He killed off a few by sitting in a bathtub full of ice, others by sitting in the freezer room at the butcher. One winter he caught hold of a terrible one, and he fought with it by walking around in the snow in just a T-shirt and jeans, picking up snow and melting it on his burning skin. He was near the barn where Benci was working, and he shouted up to him, "I'm going out to the fields to find colder snow."

After a while, they all went out looking for him around the barn and the house. I guess they hadn't known how far he was willing to go looking for cold snow. When they finally did get to him, he was miles and miles away from the farm, deep in the woods. If he was living under a curse, maybe he outsmarted it, because it wasn't fever that killed him, it was cold.

The first Lukacs had been dead for a long time when I was born, and the second for just a year. He was still heavy on my mother's mind. As soon as I was born, she said I would be named after him, but with regular American spelling, like a regular American. Changing the spelling, she was sure, would change the luck. I don't know what it means in Hungarian, but in English it means light. Not light like a feather, light like what comes off stars.

There were a few pictures in Great-grandfather's house of that second Lukacs. Tucked in the corner of one of the bigger photographs of him was a baby picture of the first Lukacs. Sometimes when there was no one around, I'd have a look at them. I'd think about how the second Lukacs and I had to haul around that dead baby's name. I'd wonder what it was like to be so hot with fever that you had to walk in the snow until you froze to death.

At school, our teacher, Miss Staresina, changed our seats around depending on how we did on our tests; high scores sat you up in the front rows, low numbers landed you in the back. In her note, my mother had told me to look after my school-work, but after our Christmas, I made steady progress away from the front, where I'd been sitting for most of my life. I'd usually worked hard because I had my father's reputation to look after. There was a picture of him in a glass case in the entranceway at school. The first time I noticed it, I thought it was me. There was my black hair swooping down in front of my eyes. I looked at it for a while trying to figure out when it was taken, wherever was I that someone was handing me a trophy? Turned out it was my dad winning at a quiz show. The smartest kids from all the schools—Banning, Mineral, Brilliant—used to go to this quiz game. My father was the only person from Banning to ever be smart enough to make it the whole way to getting the trophy. From my first days in school, even in the first grade, people expected things from me because of him. If I didn't turn in my work, or if I did a poor job, teachers would say, "Your daddy would have been able to do that in no time."

After what happened in the mine, they stopped mentioning him. Instead, they gave me long worried looks like they thought I might come apart if they said one wrong word anywhere near me. If I showed up without my homework, they said it was no rush, I should take my time. They hardly said anything when, after Christmas, I started my slide to the back of the room.

A kind of wide berth started to spread itself around me. I'd seen other people get set apart because of a sharp turn in their luck. Mostly people were all right, but they had their own husbands and brothers and fathers in the mine and they had to be careful about what their luck knocked up against.

I found that from the very last seat in the room, I had a good view of the Plate Glass. On a day when I was nearly pressed against the window, Walter Markovic leaned back from his desk and said to me, "Lessar, what are you staring at?" Walter was permanently in the back of the room. I don't think he had much time to study. Most days he went straight to the Croatian Club after school to help his parents. There was a cot under the bar that I think he slept on some nights. My father and his father, Marko, had always tried to make a friendship between me and Walter, but it never took. As far as I knew, Walter wasn't a real friend of anyone's; he was always off on his own. There were things about him that made you want to stay away—he smelled like old sauerkraut and cigarettes and stale beer. With his dirty yellow hair and skin pale as chalk, he looked like maybe he had something you didn't want to catch.

"I'm looking for Zoli," I said. "You seen him?"

"I saw him in the Monkey Dumps sitting on an old couch."

"Today?"

"No. In the summer."

"Jesus, Woj."

"What?"

"I'm not looking for where he was in the summer."

He shrugged. "You asked me if I seen him, and I'm just saying, I seen him."

At lunchtime, I slipped out of the school and headed toward the Monkey Dumps. It wasn't really a dump, not the regular kind with a scrap heap and piles of trash. When the coal companies mined their pit on the surface, instead of tunneling underground, they scraped away the topsoil and rocks with a dragline and dug right into the seam from the top. The dragline made a kind of mountain range of dug-up earth. When they were through with the land where the Monkey Dumps were, the company moved away and left the piles behind. Trees grew on the heaps, and eventually a whole woods. Some of the trees had those long thick vines a monkey might swing on. There were no real monkeys there, of course, just those vines putting you in mind of them.

It wasn't hard to find the couch Walter was talking about. It was big and brown. It sat at the edge of the dumps, looking down over the gully where Zoli's house was. Most people wouldn't think of sitting on it; it was damp and dirty. But I could picture Zoli there, surveying the mountains of junk around his place, landing his empty stare on whatever unlucky thing happened to pass him by.

After my mother started with Zoli, she kept working her way out of her long sleep. He seemed to help her do that, but then something else happened—she started having trouble sleeping at all. She said she'd stored up so much sleep that she didn't need much rest anymore. After a few weeks of it, you could see her reserves were spent. "Go back to sleep," I yelled out to her one night from my room. She came in and said, "He's mad at me."

"Who?" I said.

"Your dad. I had a dream and in it I could hear his footsteps. All these years of not dreaming about him. He must be mad at me."

"Why?"

"There was a blind corner in this old house I was standing in, and I thought I heard him coming, walking around that blind corner. I know what his boots sound like. 'Jimmy?' I said. 'Is that you?' Then I woke up. I'm afraid if I go back to sleep, he'll come the whole way around the corner."

"How do you know that means he's mad?"

"It's because of Zoli."

"He's not mad," I told her. "He's dead."

I looked down into the gully. I didn't see the Skylark. Zoli didn't go anywhere without that car. He'd get in it just to drive from the Plate Glass twenty feet across the street to Slats's house. I walked down the hill.

There weren't any lived-in houses down there besides his, just a couple of empty places with their porches so tilted that they looked like ships on a rough sea. He had an old company-owned one-story house, only there wasn't a company anymore. Their open pit had made the Monkey Dumps. Maybe someone in his family had worked for them. If you lived in a company house and the company was running, they'd usually send someone out to paint it every so often and make sure it wasn't falling down. But since they'd called it quits, Zoli was on his own. The paint was coming away in fat peels. There was a big cushion of dead grass in the front yard. Zoli was always saying that if my mother married him, we could all live in there together. He'd fixed it up himself, and he thought he'd done a good job of it. The way he talked about it you'd think it was the nicest house in the county.

I'd been inside two or three times and I knew that he always went in through the back. I walked back there and tried to look in the windows, but they were all curtained up. I'd never seen them like that before. I twisted the doorknob. It was locked. I tried it again. I studied it for a minute, to see if there was some trick to how you turned it. There had been a couple of times when I'd watched Zoli from the car while he'd gone inside to get something. I didn't think that door was ever locked. He always walked right in.

I remembered a night in the back seat waiting, his headlights against the house, my mother's shoulder, her looking out the window, him walking into the house. "I hate him," I'd said to her all of a sudden, for no reason really that I could point to just then. "I hate him more than anyone."

"Oh," she'd said, "I'm sure there's other people hate him more. Girls, most likely. He was always a heartbreaker."

"Are you kidding me? He's awful-looking."

"Not really, honey. Not to girls." She turned around and looked at me. "Don't waste your bitter on him. He's harmless."

* * *

CHAPTER 5

IN THE SLATE FALL that made the Bluebird people shut down their pit, back behind the Markovics' and the D'Angelos' houses, two miners who hadn't heard the top talking soon enough got buried so deep that the company couldn't dig them out. They're still under there. People used to say that if you lay down next to one of the toadholes and put your ear over it, you could hear them. They were two gypsies, people said, tricked into working, and their sad gypsy songs came out of the ground. Other people said they were two men who'd been in love with the same woman, and they did nothing but shout at each other.

The morning of the slate fall, a miner, early for his shift, saw a woman with dark hair walk out of the pit. In those days, a woman in the mine was the worst luck there was. He thought he'd imagined it, but going down in the lift, he couldn't shake the picture of her. He made up a story about not feeling too good, and instead of working, he went home. Later, when the ground shuddered, he was the only one in town who didn't run out into the street to see what had happened. He already knew.

Some people had the gift like him; the rest of us had to pay close attention—search our dreams for clues, keep our eyes ready for signs. My father said his only gift was for remembering the lines of songs without trying to. My mother never claimed to have the gift either, but from time to time, she knew things. One night she and I were driving back to our house from Slats's when a piece of silver on the road caught the light from our headlamps. We slowed down, then stopped. It was a hunting knife lying flat on the road. "I'm taking that," I said. I got out of the car. She came after me. I was reaching down for it when she grabbed my hands, kicked the knife off the road, and told me to get back in the car. I said I would just come back and find it later. She didn't say much when we were driving, only that something was wrong about that knife, and we needed to get home as fast as we could.

"What's wrong with it?" I said.

"I don't know. Something about it just being there. I feel spooked."

When we got home, we found my dad sitting on the porch with a bloodied T-shirt wrapped around his hand. He'd been cutting up cabbage and had almost sliced off his thumb. He was waiting for us to take him to the hospital.

When the fireshot blew out next to him, I was at school. I heard a rumble and watched a window rattle in its sill.

There were noises like that all the time in Banning though, and I might have just taken a memory from another day and moved it over to that one.

My mother was at the grocery. She only had a few things to buy, so she was holding them in her arms instead of using a cart. When she was in line at the register, she saw a flicker of light in the corner of her eye, like a firefly, and then everything in front of her went black. She fainted, dropped her packages all over the floor. In her whole life, she'd never fainted. When she came to, everyone in the store was standing around saying her name, trying to help. She got up, left everything on the floor, walked out the door and up toward the King mine. Then she heard the boom. She ran the rest of the way, even though she knew there was no sense in running.

My father told me that years after the company had shut the Bluebird mine, he and Marko decided they were going to settle things about those two trapped miners. They wanted to know for certain—was there gypsy singing? Was there shouting? They were still in high school, and one day after classes were over, Marko tied a rope around my dad's leg and lowered him, headfirst, into a toadhole. He took a flashlight with him and wore his father's old mining helmet strapped around his chin. He hung down there for a long time. Word spread through town about what they were up to, and a crowd gathered.

When Marko pulled him up, my father didn't want to tell them what he'd found out—he kept his mouth shut. He'd thought the scare was going to come from the ghosts yelling, or whatever they were doing, but what he found scared him much more—there wasn't anything down there at all. No one fighting. No one singing. Nothing to see. Nothing to hear.

Slats came home from the Plate Glass, stopped up the sink in the bathroom, and soaked her hands. She cursed the whole time. She cleaned her cuts every day so they wouldn't get infected. Most of them were small, invisible from a few feet away, and she painted them over with iodine. The white basin had a pink glow from all the years of her rinsing her hands and spilling the iodine.

"Hey," she said. "How about sitting in here and making conversation with me. Distract me from my tortures."

I didn't answer her.

When she was through, she piled food in the trunk to take to Great-grandfather at the farm. She came back inside and told me to get in the car.

"I'm not going up there," I said.

"Why?"

"I have to go over to my house to get something."

"Get what?"

"Something."

She kept staring at me. "What kind of something?"

"I don't know."

"I don't want you going over there without me. Just come up the farm."

"I don't like it up there."

"No sense in liking or not liking—it's the farm, our farm."

"It's not mine. I hate going up there."

"I didn't mean it's ours, like it's yours and mine. I mean, the family, all of us." She drew one of her long sighs and went outside. I heard the car start up, the tires rolling over the gravel. Right away, though, she cut the engine and came back in the house. "You don't have to get out of the car. Okay?" she said. "You can listen to the radio or do your schoolwork, or stare at your face in the mirror. I just want you to come with me."

"I'm not going."

"All right, all right. We'll stop over at your house first. Okay? Just for a minute. We can't loiter over there. We don't have the time."

"You got the key? Let me see the key."

"Jesus H. Christ." She held her keys out.

We got in the car and started out on the road toward my house. Slats said, "He's old, you know."

"Who?"

"My father."

"How could I not know he's old? I got eyes don't I?"

"But you don't know what it means. You don't know. Think you know things, but you don't."

"I know things. I know Zoli's not doing what you said, hiding out in his house. It's all locked up. He's driving around looking for my mother. Probably he'll find her. Maybe he already did."

"He won't find her."

"Who knows what he'll do or has already done to her if he found her."

"He won't find her."

"How do you know?"

"He just won't."

"You know where she is then?"

"I didn't say that. I just said he won't find her. And quit asking me that. I told you already, I don't know."

"You do too."

She hit the brakes and took a sharp turn onto a road that cut through the Banning mine woods. "What're you doing?" I said.

She didn't answer me.

"This isn't the right way. Where are you going?"

"I'm going to see my sick dad."

"You said we could go to my house."

"Well, you're stubborn and I lie."

We didn't talk the rest of the way.

The Banning mine was the mine our town was named after. It had been shut down for years and years. They'd grown their own timber, and their woods were a little ways off from where the mine was. Since they'd used sycamore to hold up the roofs in their tunnels, their company woods were thick with sycamore trees. On a quick look, these woods seemed just like a regular patch of forest, but when the car slowed down to take a corner, you could see it wasn't quite right—it was too organized. All the trees were about the same height, and they grew in straight rows, like pews in church.

Closer to Great-grandfather's, the houses started to thin out and everything opened up like a book, just fields and animals and loose woods with trees all different sizes and not even two of them lined up straight. Then we got to Great-grandfather's farm, with the house and the barn and the pond, and the pear tree—still standing, but black, with pieces of glass shining like little lights along the ground.

Pulling in the drive, we could see other things weren't right besides the tree. The barn door was swinging open and shut. When it opened, I could see Valentina, the gray goat, jerking around, and then bolting back in surprise when the door swung toward her. She was trying to knock her way out. The dogs ran barking up to the car. Slats pushed them away, but they kept after her. "Find them something to eat," she said, shoving at them, trying to get to the house.

I went inside the barn. Except for Valentina, all the animals were gone. I saw that they were scattered around the fields, hunting for food. I fed the goat. I filled a bucket with feed to take up to the other animals. I thought Valentina would follow me, but she went back to pressing her head against the door.

When the animals saw that bucket, they made a run for me. Two goats jostled their way through the sheep, climbing and bucking at them. The cows slowly waded through the crowd. The goats started in on the hem of my jacket and my pants pockets, their eyes wild. They tore the bucket away from me and knocked it on the ground. They nosed up under my jacket and chewed on my shirt. It was as if someone had replaced all of Great-grandfather's nice animals with a whole different set of fierce ones. "Get off me," I shouted.

Eli must have been walking nearby and heard. He came out

to the field, took my arm, and pulled me away from them. We left them fighting each other and tearing up the bucket. We walked back to the barn, and when we got there, I sat down on a bale of hay and opened my jacket. Half of my shirt was missing. "Jesus. They ate up my clothes."

"Ha. They're smart, you know. They make a food out of anything. We are lucky they don't eat two of us."

He put out feed and water for them, and threw down some straw. To the animals, he called out, "If you are behaved and leave Luca alone, you are invited. We have food for you." They didn't come. He called out to them again, this time in Russian. We waited. First the goats and then all the rest came into the barn and ate.

Valentina was bucking against the door, trying to get out. He stood by her for a few minutes, his hand on her head, then he led her away from the door. "You are such good animals," he said. "You make me regret I was never farmer." He propped open all the barn doors, and it filled with air and the last of the day's light.

"You didn't like being an engineer?" I said.

He sat down next to me on the square of hay. "What's to like? When I went into mine my hair is heavy black, as the sky at night." He touched his white hair and said, "And when I come out, it's this."

We watched the animals for a while. He nodded his head back toward the house, "Our old person friend is not doing so good."

"He has a cold or something."

"He isn't been coming out here, you know. I think you better look after farm for now."

"Me? The only reason I'm here is Slats tricked me. I don't like it here."

"She so smart to trick you?"

"She's not smart. She just . . . you can't believe nothing she says." I saw that his fingers were all blackened at the tips. I pointed to them, "Is that from being in the mines?"

He spread his hands out in front of him. "This? This is from charcoal, from drawing. A kind of mine, but all its tunnels are in here," he said, and tapped his head.

"You draw with charcoal?"

"Why pay money for pencils when the whole forest is full of free branches."

"You draw with branches?"

He hunted around on the ground, picked up a twig, and took a flame to it. He smudged it out on the ground before it burned up. The floor of the barn was mostly dirt, but there was a slab of concrete under one of the hay piles. He pushed it aside and drew for a few minutes. Because of the way he was leaning over, I couldn't see how the drawing was shaping up. After a while, he stepped back. There was a small ghost of a face. It looked just like me.

"Hey, that's good," I said.

"You think is good? Must be then." He took a quick bow and made like he was tipping a hat at me.

"Where'd you learn how to do that? Someone show you?"

He looked at the twig in his hand and shrugged. "Myself shows me."

"You didn't learn it in school? Or your dad showed you how?"

"My father? No, no. He didn't show me. He was a sort of crazy person. He wasn't like your father, working hard. I teach myself."

"You knew my dad?"

He nodded, "Some little." He pointed to the picture of me. "The animals will have you as foreman now, and they need to

64

grow comfortable to your face. They can look here at drawing and make examination of you."

"Benci will do it. He'll take care of them."

He shrugged, handed me the stick he'd drawn my picture with, and left.

Closer up, I saw that the drawing looked more like some combination of me and my father than a picture of me, a kind of guess at what I might look like someday. I got down close to it and wrote my name on the concrete: Lucas Lessar.

I heard Slats coming. I buttoned up my jacket so she wouldn't notice that I'd had my shirt eaten. I threw straw over my picture. I didn't want her seeing it. She came into the barn, sat on the hay bale, and didn't say anything for a long time, which wasn't like her; I knew from staying at her house that she even talked when she was alone.

She said, "He's so skinny, if I held a light up to him, I could see straight through him. You should have come inside."

I pulled some hay out of the bale and twisted it around my hand.

"He would have liked you coming in. How come you didn't?"

I didn't answer her.

"You're holding a grudge? Well, sue me. I didn't feel like going over to her house. All their things. I miss her too, you know. Miss both of them." She got up and walked out of the barn.

I followed her. I said, "If you miss her, how come you aren't looking for her? I mean, we should try to find out where she is."

"Look for her? You can't do that. You hear me? In her note, she asked for you not to. She said for you not to do that."

We got in the car and she started it up and switched on the headlights. They lit up the grass and the trees just in front of us, and they were powerful enough to shine some light out toward the pear tree. She held her hands in front of the heater and rubbed them together like she was standing in front of a fire.

She took a long look out the window. She said, "You know, when we were kids, we weren't allowed to climb that tree, or throw balls or sticks anywhere around it, because of the bottles mostly, but he would yell at us to be careful of That One too. That's what he was talking about the other night, that word he kept saying. He was talking about that thing he thinks lived inside that tree—*Tot-to*. It wasn't like a good fairy; you could make it mad and then it would get after you." She turned toward me and said, "Can you imagine the kind of mind that makes up a guardian angel you have to be afraid of? That's the kind of mind my father has. He'd tell us it bit off fingers if it got mad. You wouldn't know you'd disturbed it, you'd just wake up in the morning with no fingers. Of course nothing like that happened. We all still got our fingers. And no good things happened either. I mean, think about it. We aren't getting any extra help up here. What about poor Lukacs wandering around in the snow getting himself frozen? Zoli setting things on fire? Any protecting spirit worth its salt would have pitched in a little more."

The car was finally warmed up. She put it in gear, but before we pulled away, she put her hand on my arm and said, "He's not sick from some spirit going away, or some ghost stuck in his lungs, like he thinks. Nothing's in that tree but sap, seeds, whatever it is they have in trees. He's sick from drinking too much and staying out in the cold and not eating. I'm going to feed him and make sure he stays warm and out of the liquor cabinet. He's going to be fine. He's going to be running laps around us." The more she went on about how good things were going to get, the tighter she squeezed my arm. "And you're going to help me."

"Let go of me," I said. "You can take care of him yourself."

She squeezed my arm tighter. "You ever think of who'd be feeding you if it weren't for me?"

I pulled my arm loose.

"It's not right to say that, but you're making me." She put her hands on the steering wheel and squeezed it tight. "This is how it is—I'm all you've got. Unless you want to go live with the nuns in the mission, you're helping me."

CHAPTER 6

I N THE WOODS all around Banning were left-behind blasting caps, lamps, hard hats, signs in ten different languages
saying Danger, saying Watch Your Head. Abandoned block
ovens and beehive ovens, empty boiler houses, washhouses,
lamp houses, and machinery sheds. Pieces of mantrips, machine
loaders, coal cutters, and pickaxes. Sometimes filing cabinets,
chairs, blueprints, folders full of maps and lists of numbers, big
old heavy black telephones with letter exchanges written on
them. It was as if there were a sea someplace nearby full of all
you needed to make a mining town and that it washed up in
Banning, and then the water ran back to where it came from,
clean and empty.

Banning was one town in a line of towns on a crooked spine
of hills that stretched up and down the coal seam. South of us
was Mineral, then a long space of empty hills, then West Virginia. North of us was Black Lick, where there were no mines
anymore, but instead a giant pale green box of a paper mill;
then Brilliant, where there was everything; then Luna, where a

mine fire had been burning off and on in an abandoned shaft for close to fifty years. When my mother was a girl, she thought the Luna fire was the fire she'd heard about at school that burned at the center of the earth, and that the center of the earth was not far from Banning; it was just up the road, roaring away like a furnace. Past Luna were farms and cornfields, more space, folded hills that hid everything but the top of the choking smokestack of Bedford, the state mental hospital. Past that was Hunker, where there was the county jail and two more glass factories—one plate, one decorative.

The whole way from Mineral through to Hunker, no matter what else was in the towns, or around the towns, there were ovens in the hills, most of them big, empty beehive ovens with dark open mouths. They used to cook the coal in them and turn it into coke. They'd ship the coke to the mills in Pittsburgh or Wheeling, where they used it to cook iron ore and make steel. Once they had steel, they didn't need to turn it into anything; it was just itself, the thing they were after all along.

The day after we went to Great-grandfather's, I cut school to look for my mother. I walked out into the Bluebird woods and climbed up into the boney piles. From the top, I could see the whole town, all of my part of Banning—Mr. D'Angelo's place, the Markovics' house, my house, and Marko's black Nash covered with patches of snow. Past all that was the black roof of the Croatian Club and the Banning boney pile. I could see the King mine tipple and the tops of the trees in its woods. Even from the Bluebird piles, though, the tallest ones we had, I couldn't see beyond Banning in any direction. Where there weren't real hills keeping me from seeing the other towns, there was boney. I couldn't even see the smoke twisting out of the mine in Luna.

It was cold. No one was out. The streets and porches were empty. It seemed that except for those pieces of dust still drifting around Banning that were my father, I was all alone in it. There was a song he used to like to sing when we were doing work in the yard or walking someplace. I couldn't remember all of it. I whispered a few words, just saying them, not singing, because I didn't know the tune the whole way through. I said them first in Croatian, "*Moja mala nosi äzmice*," then I changed them into English. "My love wears boots. They are red all over, red and have beads."

I climbed down off the pile and walked to the mouth of each oven in the hill, my voice echoing back. "My girl wears a vest. So silky and colored and has buttons. So she tells me, come here, my dear."

The ovens were big, had tall ceilings and walls blacked with coal dust. You heard stories from time to time about people hiding out in them. A few draft dodgers had lived in them instead of going to Vietnam before they got rides up to Canada. During the Depression, when almost all the mines were shut down for a while, whole families used to live in them. Sometimes I'd find things they'd left behind: old empty food tins, a piece of baby doll. When Mrs. D'Angelo left town, Mr. D'Angelo looked for her in them. I watched him from our porch.

I worked my way up to the lamp house. I'd been in it a hundred times before, cleaned it out of everything, all its old glass lids and blasting caps. This time I saw a cabinet I'd never noticed before, locked up. I kicked and kicked at it, and worked at the song. I still couldn't get in. I went outside and got a heavy rock and wailed it against the cabinet until I broke through.

Inside there were cans and cans of carbide. Miners used to use carbide to charge their lamps. When you mix it with water the right way, it makes a steady acetylene flame. But if you mix it a different way, it explodes—no sparks or fire or anything, just a big sound. They were made of tin with lids you snapped back to open. When I came across a batch of them, I'd always blow up just one or two and squirrel the rest away in a coke oven.

My mother could hear that sound every time, no matter where she was. She would know what it was, and a lot of times she would know it was me, and she'd come running. If I made a lot of noise out of it, I was asking for trouble.

I'd never seen so many all at once. It was as if they'd been waiting there all along for me to find them. I pulled them out. I was singing pretty loud by then, in Croatian, then in English, and back again, "My girl wears a little skirt. It's red all over, red, and has a lace trim."

I carried the cans farther back into the woods, past the sewn-up mouth of the pit, to a little clearing. Fallen leaves poked through the snow. I thought if I started setting the cans off, wherever she was, she might hear it. She would know it was me. She'd come looking. I opened one, put a handful of snow inside, smashed the lid down, and booked. Boom. Dogs barked, birds kicked out of the trees. In her note, she'd said she was going far away. I looked toward the mine buildings, and into the woods, and up at the tops of the trees leaning against the white undersides of the clouds. The town snapped shut around me. I hardly knew what far away meant. I couldn't picture it.

I pulled up the cap on the second one and did the same, and instead of stopping and putting the rest of them away like I usually would have, I did it again and again. She would come out from the dark line of trees, I thought. I looked for her. I worked at the song until it was past singing, was just shouting. My throat stung with dust. I pulled open another lid, threw snow inside, smashed it down. Boom.

"Cut it out," a lady yelled from someplace far off.

It got so it seemed that every dog in Banning was losing its mind. I couldn't hear anything but the snap of the can opening, my foot going down, the boom, the dogs making a big howling roar.

Someone was saying, "Hey, Uncle."

I opened a can, snap, put snow inside, slammed the lid.

"Uncle, it's me. It's Marko." He put his hand on my shoulder. "I am here." I could hardly hear him. His words were too quiet to deserve answering. I walked away from him, picked up more snow to put in the can. He kicked it over. I grabbed the one next to it. He pulled it away from me. "Lucas!" he yelled.

In my head, there were just explosions. Boom. Boom. The song I'd been singing, low and quiet, echoing underneath. "*Moja mala nosi čizmice.*"

He was wearing a long blue bathrobe, pajamas, plastic slippers. He was shivering. His wavy brown hair was hanging down in front of his eyes. "I already have a headache like someone put a knife in my head, and then you are making so much goddamn noise."

I looked at my hands, cut up from opening the cans, and dirty from the snow and mud and boney. I was shaking. Marko looked at them too. He said, "It's okay, Uncle. It's okay." He ran his fingers through his hair. His eyes were bloodshot. They were usually hazel-colored and kind of blended in with his hair and the stubble on his cheeks, but the red around them had made them turn a deep green. He kept wiping them, like he had something over them he couldn't quite see through. He said, "It's okay. Say some words to me. Make some sign to me so I can see your ears are still working."

I nodded.

"No words, huh. Okay. There's no school today? But Walter's at school." He shrugged.

Marko was named after a Serb prince who lived for five hundred years. He had a Serb father and a Croat mother. Like my dad, he was born in Banning, and he didn't learn English until he went to school. I didn't really notice it until my dad was dead, but Marko sounded like him, the ghost of some other language twisting around in his English.

We were both quiet for a while. The booming echo in my ears slowed down. The dogs were still barking, but fewer of them. He started walking out of the woods. "Come on," he said. "No more explosions. Not today. My head." He stopped and looked up at the trees. "I haven't been back so far into these woods in a long time. A long, long time."

He started walking again. "When we were small, we played a game—Lay Low Sheepy Lay Low—sometimes back here. You know this game?"

I shook my head.

"It's a good game. I played it maybe a thousand times. Jimmy too. And Mirjana. All of us together. There are two teams with captains. One team hides and the other team looks for them. The captain of the team that is hiding draws a map of where his people are for the team that is looking. But what makes the game interesting is that he doesn't write on the map which way is north or which way is south. It's a map, but with no directions. Can you imagine, Uncle?"

I shrugged.

"It's a puzzle. So, the captain follows around the people that are looking for his team and yells out warnings to his team. 'Apples and oranges!' he says if they are far away. 'Lay low sheepy lay low!' he says if they are getting close. When it was Jimmy's team's turn to hide, I could almost never find him. But maybe he was not to be trusted, maybe Mirjana helped him somehow. Always the two of them, like this." He held up his hands and clapped them together.

We were almost out of the woods by then, close to his house. He said, "She wasn't herself after, you know, without Jimmy.

Not herself. I try many times to make her talk with me, but she is not like her old self was . . . One time when we were small, playing that game, I hid with my team in some small cave. Mirjana was looking for us. I had picked this hiding place. And for a long time, I thought she wouldn't be able to find us. But then there is the sound of her feet. We will lose the game when she gets the whole way to me, the other kids on the team will be angry with me for picking the place. But, Uncle, I want to see her. I don't care if I lose the game. I want to see her."

"What for? Why'd you want to see her so much?"

"For a long time, I thought it was the three of us together. Me, Jimmy, Mirjana. I thought it was always going to be the three of us here together . . . But, now there's only me."

We walked around to the front of his house and stopped on the lawn. He said, "You think she left us a map this time, Uncle?"

"A map? To what?"

He looked above my head, behind me. I turned around. There was my house, sitting empty. "A map to where she is."

CHAPTER 7

O NE SPRING, five devils walked out of the woods and into
Great-grandfather's village in Russia. They were all suited
up in good clothes. They found five pretty girls from the village
and asked them to go to a party. The girls thought they were
men, and nice dressers too, so they went along. While they
were walking to the party, one of the girls noticed how the men
had these strange eyes, as if they were lit up from the inside.
While they were looking away, she ran as fast as she could back
to her house. The next day, people from the village followed the
girl out to the place where she'd last seen her friends. Great-
grandfather went along too, even though he was just a boy.
When they got to the place, all they found was the girls' hair, in
a pile.

Great-grandfather told me this story when I was sitting on
the floor in his room, leaning against the wall next to the door.
He was wrapped in blankets and propped up against the headboard. After he was through, he said, "The devils take the girls
and leave us only their hairs. One girl I knew, her braid was

there left behind, so I take. I keep in box. Maybe is still there in mine old house. If house is still there. I didn't take to bring to America."

"How come?"

"Bad things that happen in one place you leave in that place, belongings of bad thing, thoughts of bad thing." He squinted at me. "What? You only believe me if I show you hairs?" He added, "I put her hairs in box to keep safe. They were very beautiful and make long blond braid. She was very pretty, this girl I knew. Always her blond hair is in perfect braid. I find in friend's house one glass box. I take and put braid inside, so I can look at all times, through glass.

"You know, when I tell this story to your mother, she asks me same kinds of question. Why I don't have glass box to show her, she wants to know. She was my first grandchildren. When she was coming to here, I tell her these important things all the time, like I'm telling you. But she is like it here very much, hard to keep her still for listening. The pond, she wants to swim into, the silo she wants to climb up . . . When your grandmother says to me that Mirjana is disappeared, I looked in these places for her. She wasn't swimming in pond or climbing corn silo since she was been ten or eleven years olds. Still, I was looking for her there."

Neither of us said anything for a while. Outside, I could hear the dogs barking at something, then the cows answering them. Great-grandfather smiled. "Dogs are waiting," he said. "Wondering I am where?" The windows were closed, but from his bed, he called for them, "*Sobaka!*" They kept barking. "I will soon again be to walking with you."

"They can't hear you," I said.

"Of course they can hear me. Even I don't speak, they can hear me." He coughed a little and twisted around and around in his sheets.

He looked hard at me, waiting for me to say something. He said, "You have fear of me, Lucas?"

"What? No. I'm not afraid of you."

"Why you sit so far aways then? I can't hardly see you. Get chair. Sit next here to me."

"I'm okay here."

"Fear of my sickness? My oldness?"

"No."

"Don't be tricked by how I am looking. You should have fear of me. I didn't hardly need tools when I worked in mine. No pick! No shovel! Who cares! To me is like picking up feathers. If it is me against you, I am strongest, you know."

"Are you kidding me? You're so skinny, I could probably pick you up with one arm."

"Ha! Come over here. Try! Ha!"

I stayed where I was.

"You miss school to sit here?"

"I go there first before I walk out here," I said.

"What they teaching you there?"

"Regular things. Math. History."

"That everything?"

"Mostly."

"You have homeworks?"

"No," I said, though I did have homework. I just didn't have any plans to do it.

He said, "I think school is not teaching enough to you. My story about girls is to teach you something—to be careful to make sure you are person who gets away. She is very smart one, girl that sees they are devils and runs home. And for her smartness she is get to be alive." He coughed more, louder this time.

"You want some of this cough syrup?"

He waved my idea away. "I already said to your grandmother and to Benci and now to you. It's no cough. It's ghost come to

79

take up living in my lungs. Medicine, thank you for it, but it can't give me help."

I read him the directions for the syrup and the advertisement on the box.

He said, "After my pear tree is burn, I am here alone, everyone gone. In my bed going to sleep, I see one ghost standing against wall. His face is to wall, but sometime he turns just some little, and I see he looks at me from corner of his eyes. I see side of his face. And I know it's this man from Banning Two. I used to know him. He was always difficult, hard on me. When *Tot-to*, when *dedushka*, was caring about us and saving me from bad luck, he always kept this ghost away from me. But now what does he care."

There was no such place called Banning Two. The Banning mine had only had one main entrance. I'd been to it a hundred times. Bigger mines than Banning could have two or maybe even eight or nine entrances. Sometimes towns sprung up around each main entrance; this had happened at Brilliant, and there were two Brilliants. The first one was bigger and had been there longer, so when people said Brilliant, you counted on them meaning the first one. They had to say Brilliant Two if that's what they wanted you to think about. I said, "You just mean Banning. There's no Two."

"When I saw he is in room, I hope I'm dreaming. I close my eyes to make him disappear. I keep closing and opening eyes and always he is there. I become very tired, and fall to sleep. When I wake up, he is go away, but my chest is so heavy I can't hardly sit up. Then I understand that he crawled into my mouth, into my lungs. And now is like I am breathing black-damp in mine."

He started into a long fit of coughing. It wasn't deep; it sounded more like something tickling his throat than digging into his lungs. But the way it knocked on the bare walls and the thin windows did make it sound bigger, made it echo, like something trapped calling its way out. He gestured that I could open the bottle of syrup. I fed him a couple of spoonfuls. He swung his feet out from the bed and stood up. The blankets fell away from him. His pajama shirt was unbuttoned and it fell open. I saw his skinny chest; it looked like it was caving in. I looked away. He walked slowly out of the room.

"Where are you going?" I said.

He walked to the window in the hall. He shuffled back into the room and looked out each of his windows, stopping, pressing his hands against the glass.

"Maybe it's not best, not always, to be the one that is escaped." He got back in bed and under his covers. "When you close your eyes sometimes after, too many times after, the ones that didn't get away are all there, looking at you. They have a terrible look, so starving for what they want."

"What are you talking about?" I said.

"They want what you have. Tastes on your lips, sunshines on your eyes, food, drinks, other peoples' skin to touch. Like that."

He closed his eyes and seemed to be falling asleep. After a while, the sound of him toiling away at his breathing was all through the room. Tunnels of air passed by me, as if he were pulling all the air from all corners of the farm into his lungs, and still, I got the feeling it wasn't enough.

CHAPTER 8

INSTEAD OF GOING TO SCHOOL the next morning, I walked over to my house. I tried to pull myself up by one of the windowsills, but my fingers were freezing. I couldn't hold on. I dragged a concrete block over from the driveway, set it up under the window, and used it like a step.

As soon as I was inside, I knew I wouldn't find anything, no map like Marko said.

There was a light on in the bathroom. "Hello?" I said. "Hello?" I stood still waiting for an answer. Water dripped someplace, a window rattled. "Mom?" I went from room to room pushing open all the doors. "It's Lucas." In the bathroom, I switched off the light and for a second everything was dark. Just then, the phone rang and I felt like someone had grabbed hold of all my nerves. I switched the light back on. I went to pick up the phone, but then thought it might be Slats. Maybe one of her friends had seen me. I let it go on ringing.

There was stuff scattered all over the house, as if someone had run out to get something and would be right back. It didn't smell that way though. It smelled close. I cracked open the window above the sink in the kitchen.

In the living room, my mother had a little desk where she sat to write letters or pay bills. I sat down in the chair and pulled it in to the desk. That's how she always sat, like she was going to lock herself into that spot until she finished her paperwork. I opened all the drawers. Scissors, scratch pads, pencils. There wasn't anything much. She liked to keep it clean. Even when she wasn't sleeping at all and the dirty dishes were stacked everywhere, that desk was still right and cleared off. Tucked between a cup of pencils and the lamp there was a big envelope. I pulled it down. *For L*, it said, in my mother's handwriting. I tore it open. Inside there was a picture of me on a pony. I looked about five or six years old. It wasn't a picture I remembered seeing before. I shook the envelope and then took it apart at the corners. There wasn't anything else in it. The phone stopped ringing and a heavy quiet fell on the room.

I moved to the couch and sat down. I turned the picture over. On the back, she'd written, *J and L at county fair*. I turned it over and looked at it again. Her note wasn't right. It was just me in the picture—my dad wasn't in it at all.

The phone started ringing again. I gave up thinking it was Slats. She didn't have that much patience. I picked it up and before I even had a chance to say hello, he started talking, almost shouting. It was Zoli. "Hey. Mirjana. Hey. You finally picked up the phone. I been calling there like every day about thirty, forty times . . . Don't hang up, okay? Just, don't hang up . . . I kept picturing the phone ringing and then picturing you picking it up, and then when I say something, hearing my voice makes you smile. It's nice to see you smile, even if it's only in my head. Still seems to do me good . . . You still there? You smiling yet?"

"No," I said.

Away from the phone, he said, "Fucking Christ," then back into the phone, "She there?"

It was different from when he was standing in front of me staring me down; I wasn't afraid of him over the phone. "You think I'd tell you?" I said.

"You'd better tell me."

I didn't say anything, but I didn't hang up. I could hear a television. "Well," he said. He took a long breath and then his voice changed, nearly back to the voice he was using when he thought he was talking to my mother. "How you been making out?" he said, like he really wanted to know the answer.

"Where you calling from?"

"Why? You worried about my phone bill getting too high?"

His words sounded muffled. "You chewing tobacco or something?"

"Cotton. One of Slats's brothers knocked my mouth pretty good, loosened up a tooth. I think it was the big one, Benci. He's got a fist wide as a car door. I lost it all the way yesterday."

"He knocked out your teeth?"

"'Tooth,' I said. One."

"Ha."

"You think I won't tear your whole mouth out from your tonsils next time I see you?" He was back to his regular-sounding voice. The hair on the back of my neck stood up. He said, "You in that house by yourself? I always thought that place was a little creepy, you know, after what happened to Jim. You and your mom should have moved in with me. I mean, maybe then, things wouldn't have gotten all—"

"You at your house?"

"—a mess like they got. Because, I don't know, I been out here driving around looking for her and . . ."

"And what?" I said.

He didn't say anything for a while. "I don't know, Lucas . . .

Sometimes I get this weird feeling that maybe there ain't no her to find . . . It's like she turned to vapors or something. How's something like that happen? And I start thinking about . . . Remember when that guy from the mine in Brilliant piled a bunch of dynamite in his bed all around him and blew the whole second story off his house?"

"What about it?" I said. I was too little when it happened to remember, but they still hadn't torn the house down. You could go and look at it. Rain falling into the rooms.

His voice turned almost to a whisper. "Not that way. She wouldn't . . . Slipping away, kind of quiet, that'd be more her style, maybe walk into the creek and swim under the ice, or swallow a bottle of pills and go to that meadow she likes and—"

I pulled the phone away from my ear and slammed it down on the receiver. It started to ring again right way. Once I got outside, I ran and ran. The phone kept ringing. I could still hear it halfway up the street.

I slipped into school after lunch. No one seemed to notice I'd been missing. Miss Staresina announced that she was getting married. All the girls crowded around her desk asking her questions. Walter turned around and whispered, "My dad said he caught you trying to blow up the woods. He thinks you're about to lose your head."

I didn't feel like talking. I still had Zoli's voice humming in my ears.

"I told him you didn't have too much of a head to lose no more, that Staresina stuck you in the last seat, behind me."

I didn't say anything.

"He says that's all the more why we got to look out for you. Like me and him go over and take a look at your house every couple of days. Make sure it's still standing."

I was half grateful to him and the other half of me, and I couldn't say why, wanted to leave the room and tear both of our houses down. "You don't got to do that," I said.

"We don't go inside or take nothing. We just look around. Hey, when you were back by my house trying to blow up the woods, did you see how I hosed down that patio and made a slab of ice? Like a rink. I'm going to train on it, speed skating."

"How'd you get skates?" I knew the Markovics didn't have two sticks to rub together.

"You've got a couple of problems if you're me and you want to be a hockey player—no rink and no skates. The worse problem is not having the ice, right? So I already fixed that one. I can make skates or steal them or slide around in my shoes."

"No wonder you're always stuck back here with the people who can't hardly read."

"You're behind me now, Lessar. That means you're dumber than me."

"If I was dumber than you, they wouldn't let me in the building."

For the rest of class, Walter drew pictures of skates he said he could make with tin scrap from one of the broken-up tipples. I pulled out the picture I'd found in the house. I searched all through it, looking for some trace of my dad. Behind me and the pony there were some trees. I didn't see him back there standing in them. I turned it over and ran my finger over my mother's note. *J and L at county fair.*

At my dad's wake, our house was the brightest I'd ever seen it. Before, you could see that the place was worn-out from all the years of miners living in it and casting coal dust on everything. After the accident, and before my mother went into her long sleep, she took down the curtains and scrubbed the walls and floors. I noticed at the wake that the floor wasn't the dark brown I'd always thought it was; it was lighter, almost yellow.

I noticed it because Slats's sister Kaya was standing on it in blue shoes in a pool of light. She was singing a song. It was hard not to look at Kaya when she sang, because her voice didn't fit the way she looked. She looked pretty much like she'd always been happy, but her voice was the saddest thing I ever heard come out of a person's mouth.

She'd learned a couple of songs in Croatian in honor of my father's passing. I half expected to see him peeking in the door trying to get a look at who was singing, because he would have liked the songs and he would have liked the way she sang them. "Where is that angel noise coming from?" he might have said.

I looked out the window. It was bright out. My eyes blurred with bare branches and sunlight and snow. I closed them and put my head down on my desk. I fell asleep and walked right inside a dream. Great-grandfather was standing at the classroom door in mining clothes, big boots, a hard hat. He waved to me to follow him. I got up out of my chair and went to him. He led me out to the King mine. It was a slope mine—you didn't need a lift to get down into it—so we just followed the sloping entrance down into the deeper partings. He pulled a loose match out of his breast pocket and lit it by scraping it across the rough surface of his palm. We passed the second room on the right, the third room on the right, R2 and R3, rooms my dad used to work. We went farther and farther into the mine, but instead of things getting darker and darker, everything got brighter and brighter.

We turned into one of the rooms off the tunnel. Great-grandfather got down on his knees and dug his hands into the coal. It moved away from him as if it were soft, like ashes. He pulled a box up out of it and dusted it off. It was a glass box, and inside was hair. The box was just like he'd told me, but the hair wasn't a thick blond braid; it wasn't in a braid at all. It was loose and a little wavy and dark brown. I opened the glass door and took the hair out of the box. I looked at it for a while, the strands of it twisted through my fingers. I brought it closer to my face so that I could smell it to be sure, and then I was sure. It was my mother's hair.

CHAPTER 9

WHEN THE ARCHANGEL MICHAEL booted the devils out of heaven, the ones that fell into the woods turned in to *leshie*, and the ones that fell into ponds and lakes became *vodianye*. The ones that landed on houses and barns turned into *domovye*, or what some people called *Tot-to*, That One. The way Great-grandfather explained it, all the other devils, the ones who didn't fall the whole way to the earth, were flying through the sky above us, winged, on fire, ready to make trouble. He said I might have heard their wings brush past me; that maybe it was one of them who rigged the fireshot so that when my father lit it, he came apart.

The *leshii* took charge of the animals and trees of the forest where he fell. He wore regular clothes, except he never wore a belt because at any minute he might change shape; he could shrink down as a seed if he wanted to, and then the next second he could be towering over the trees. He carried a whip. You know those wrinkles on the caps of mushrooms? Great-grandfather said those were from a *leshii* taking a whip to them. If you wandered into his woods he might make noises that sounded like someone calling for you, and pull you off your path until you were so far lost you would never get found. But every so often, he did a good turn, made the path through the trees that took you home safe. The thing was, though, you never knew what he was up to, never knew if you were being led home, or led farther away.

The *vodianoi* never did a good turn, his only business was drowning people. Great-grandfather would never let anyone swim in the pond unless he was right there to watch and make sure they were safe. He said the one in his pond was long and blue and naked and part-man and part-fish. He didn't do anything but lie at the bottom of the pond, and look up through the water hoping to see someone touch the surface so he could pull them down, and stuff their lungs with water.

Tot-to, That One, protector of the house and farm, didn't even have a body. He was just there—you just knew. He made sure you knew. The *Tot-to* at the farm had it in for mirrors and goats. When he had anger to unleash, they were the first things he went after. Great-grandfather said this was why I kept finding Valentina bucking at the barn door or gnawing at the fence, she was trying to escape. And it was also why he'd woken up to find all the mirrors in the house turned over and the one in the upstairs bathroom cracked and looking like a field of spiderwebs.

"Did you see what *Tot-to* did in night?" he asked me.

I was setting a steaming bowl of water on his lap. "You got to put this towel over your head and lean over this bowl. Slats says."

I walked around the house to see what had happened. When I got back to the room, he said, from under his towel, "I didn't do. I swear. I go to look at my handsome face in bathroom this morning and I see That One has been at work on his revengence."

He took the towel away from his head and handed the bowl back to me. His skinny arms shook and the water splashed everywhere.

"Be careful. You know who'll have to clean that up? It's not you."

He shrugged and frowned.

I said, "So, what do you want me to do? Turn those mirrors back the right way?"

He threw his arms up in the air. "He'll just do again. And too I think he must know I hate to have everythings be so much quiet because the silence here, Lucas, you should hear at night after you and your grandmother leave, so much quiet, is like already I'm in grave, that quiet. I was wrong about *Tot-to*. I thought he was just to going away, but since we let the tree where he was living get burned, I think first he wants to visit us with griefs."

I went from room to room and turned the mirrors back. They were mostly light slips of glass hanging from nails and all I had to do was flip them over. In the front room downstairs, there was a heavier mirror with a thick wood frame. It was nice-looking and would have been the first thing you saw when you came in the house if we ever used the front door. It was a full-length mirror and too heavy to hang from a nail, it just leaned against the wall. When I turned it over, I saw that it had a big crack running from top to bottom. I stood away from it and looked at my reflection. One eye was higher than the other. I looked like someone had split me in half and put me back together not exactly right.

I leaned in closer. I took a long look at the white patch of scar under my right eye. I ran my finger around its edges.

Upstairs, I asked Great-grandfather, "How'd that big mirror get turned around?"

"You think I did, don't you? How could I? I can't do nothing but sleep and choke on this ghost."

"It doesn't make sense."

"You think there's someplace where things are making sense?"

"No place where you are."

"Ach. Go take some raisins from kitchen and bring to Valentina. Carry happiness to at least some one person."

Outside, I noticed that he was right about the quiet. It was always quieter at the farm than in the part of Banning where the mine was. Even with just King running, pulling coal out of the seam was a noisy business. The sounds of the tipple and the mantrips and all the cutting machines and dynamite didn't reach the farm, wrapped like it was in acres of trees and fields. Usually, the farm had its own noises, animals calling out, tractor engines humming, trees creaking in the breeze. The only sound just then, though, was my shoes hitting the ground.

The animals weren't right either. Benci was supposed to be coming around to check on them, but they were skinny and jittery. When I walked into the barn, they ran up to me and tried to eat their way into the pockets where I'd put Valentina's raisins.

The feed bin and water trough were both cleaned out. I couldn't find any food for them in the barn. I went back in the house and looked through the refrigerator, where I found nothing but all kinds of old soup in pots and jars. Digging through the pantry, I found a box of cereal, some apples Slats had left behind, and a bag of leftover candy bars from Halloween. I unwrapped half the candy bars and carried them and the apples and the cereal out to the animals. I found the hose and got them some water. They ate all the food and drank the water in about four seconds. They went back to watching me, waiting for me to do something else for them. "What do you want from me!?" I said. "Can't you feed your own damn selves like the animals in the woods?"

I went out to look for Valentina. She wasn't working at the fence where I'd seen her other times. I saw that she'd chewed up a good-sized hole there. I climbed through it and knew that meant she could have gotten through too. I walked into the fields along the driveway. When I was close to the county road, a stray dog, not one I thought was ours, came running close, barked at me, then ran off. All of a sudden I understood why the farm was so quiet—the dogs were gone.

I went back to the farmhouse to make sure. They weren't in the barn or anywhere around the house. I didn't see them up in the fields or hear any of their far-off barks. I had a bad feeling that wherever they'd gone, Valentina had gone too.

I sat down on the steps off the kitchen. After a while, the headlights of Slats's car tossed light on the rocks and trees as she came down the driveway. She drove an old Impala she'd named the Lusitania, but mostly she called it Brown Lu because of its color, one shade lighter than milk chocolate. The interior was a cream color with a heavy plastic covering on all the seats that I think she was supposed to take off but never did; she said she appreciated the way it kept things tidy. You weren't allowed to eat or take drinks in it. She had some problems with people even sneezing in there.

She got out of the car and looked at me over the roof. "What'd I tell you about leaving him to his own devices?" She swung her door shut hard.

"He sent me out here," I said.

"Of course he did. He's probably crawled inside the liquor cabinet by now."

"The dogs are gone," I said.

She looked around her feet, where the dogs usually would have been. She looked toward the barn, turned around, and walked out a little ways up the driveway, then came back and stood over me. I was going to tell her about Valentina, but before I could, she grabbed a piece of my jacket and said, low and quiet, "Don't you say anything to him. Not one word. It'll push him over the edge."

She went inside and let the door slap shut behind her. I followed her through the kitchen and down into the basement. "What are you doing?" I said.

She switched on the lights. There were piles of clothes all over the floor. She said, "Will you look at this? He has everything all mixed up. I was just trying to find some clean towels and sheets for him." She walked over to a pile of clothes, picked up a big dress, and held it up to the light. "Oh my," she whispered. "What is this doing here?" She ran her hand over it. "This was my mother's. She wore it all the time." She laid it down, carefully, on top of the pile. "All the time."

"Is she dead?" I said.

"What's wrong with you? You remember her, don't you? You remember when she died?"

"Not your mother," I said. "Mine."

CHAPTER 10

I CAUGHT MRS. D'ANGELO in my dreams that night. She was standing at the edge of the boney pile in her backyard, crushing a cigarette in the snow. "Where you been?" I said. She turned away without answering. I followed her through a field of sycamores. A breeze kicked up. Wide flakes of snow drifted down from their branches. "You seen my mother?" I said. She kept walking without answering me. "She was a friend of yours." The collar of her green coat was turned up around her. She was whispering secrets, too low to hear. I got closer to her. I thought I heard her say a few words of Croatian. I knew she couldn't speak it when she lived in the neighborhood, but I understood, in the way you understand things in dreams, that she'd changed; she'd become a traveler going from place to place in a stolen Nash.

After my mother and I helped Mrs. D'Angelo leave Banning, Mr. D'Angelo looked for her and waited for her. Whenever he saw me, he'd slow down his patrol car and give me a hard stare.

Even after Mrs. D'Angelo was gone long enough that everyone could see she wasn't coming back, he still drove around in the hills looking for her. I'd hear him late at night, or early in the morning, his car door opening and closing. Some nights I'd wake up and watch him out the window. Before he'd go inside, he'd walk up and down the street or sit on the hood of the car.

Then, instead of going to the police station one morning, he took a lawn chair out of their garage and set it up in his back-yard, facing the Bluebird mine's boney piles. He stopped going to work altogether. He didn't seem to do anything but sit in that lawn chair. I'd see him there on my way to school, and on my way back. A few weeks later, two policemen showed up and drove off with his patrol car.

His red hair grew out longer and longer, and his beard grew in. My mother decided he was up to something. "Maybe it's a penance," she said.

"For what?" I said.

"For the sins he did against Rose. Or maybe he really did love her, despite not having a thought in his head about how to let her know that."

"A penance from a priest?"

"L, what kind of priest would tell you to sit in a lawn chair for a penance? I mean one he made up for himself."

"You can do that?"

"I don't see why not. He's the one knows best what he ought to be sorry for and how sorry."

She told me to stay away from him, but whenever I could, I'd go over there and see how close I could get before he noticed me. He stared and stared at those boney piles. I think he was expecting her to come walking over them.

And then, all of a sudden, he went away. Some people said he heard those miners crying in the Bluebird pit and walked over to a toadhole and jumped in. Other people said that he walked into the Bluebird woods, stopped wearing clothes, let the hair get heavy on his chest and back, and took to walking around on all fours.

When he came back a couple of weeks later, though, we found out that he'd just gone to West Virginia to visit a brother. He cleaned himself up, got his job and his patrol car back. Everything was normal again, except that he would still cut me a hard look when he saw me around town. If I saw his patrol car coming, I always ducked behind someone or slipped into an alleyway.

Every so often, I would say to my mother that we should go back to that town in West Virginia and look for Mrs. D'Angelo. She would shrug and say if she wanted to see us, she knew where to find us. But after my father died, there were a few times when she said we should drive down there and try to find Rose D'Angelo and see how she was. We never did, though.

When she stopped being able to sleep, we took to walking late at night all around town. We'd walk past everyone's dark houses, into one of the mine woods, or the Monkey Dumps. She always walked in front of me, guided us. After a while, I noticed that she seemed to be getting smaller and smaller—her coat looked to be swallowing her. High up in the Bluebird boney piles one night, we looked down at Mr. D'Angelo's house. I'd never told my mother, or anyone else, that I'd seen Rose D'Angelo walk off alone that afternoon in West Virginia. It was my secret. My way of keeping her with me, I guess.

We stayed there for a few minutes. Before we walked away, my mother said, "Sometimes I get the strangest feeling that the whole world is emptying out."

The morning after Mrs. D'Angelo showed up in my dream, I walked past the doors of the school and kept going down the hill. Kids pointed at me, saying didn't I know I was headed the wrong direction, saying they were going to tell someone. At the bus stop, I watched them working their way up the hill, slow, carrying bags, some of them holding a smaller kid's hand. The sun leaned over them so that each of them looked like dark comets, and their shadows like long twisting comet tails.

On the days my mother kept me home from school, we nearly always drove to Brilliant, but every so often, if the car was in the shop, or if she just felt like it, we'd take the bus. I didn't remember ever waiting too long for it to come, but that morning, in the cold, it seemed like it would never get there. When it finally did show, the driver opened the door and raised his eyebrows at me. I looked away from him and put my money in the box.

He picked up speed once we got out on the county road that ran flat for a while past the big green paper mill in Black Lick. The driver slowed down and wound up and down the hills, coke ovens pocking all of them. When my father was at the high school, they'd already shut down the Banning and the Brilliant mines, but they hadn't covered the mouths with concrete yet. When he wanted to go to Brilliant, if it was raining, or just for kicks, he and Marko would take a flashlight and walk the whole way there underground, through the mines.

When the bus came into Brilliant, we passed the broken-apart house of the man Zoli had talked about on the phone, the miner who'd done himself in with dynamite. I looked up at the blackened wood, the broken roof. The night before, I'd told Slats what Zoli'd said and she cupped my face in her hands and made me look at her. "Don't you say things like that about your mother. Don't you think them either. You got to trust her. She said she'd come back. She will."

In town, I walked into the department store, straight through to the restaurant where we used to eat all the time. Two waitresses were leaning against the wall by the kitchen talking to each other. I sat down at the counter. Without really looking at me, they put out two place settings and two menus and went on with their conversation.

While I was looking at the menu, an older, familiar-looking waitress came out from the back.

"Oh," she said, when she saw me. She smiled. "Sprung from school again? I, for one, am glad about that. Hadn't seen you two in too long." She looked behind me, must have thought my mother was maybe in the ladies' or still shopping. She whispered, "I heard some talk that she wasn't doing real good, having a hard time of it. Well, you must have been a nice help to her through that?" She smiled and patted my hand. "Sometimes people can't bounce back after a thing like that, but she had you. Lucky for her that she had you. I'll go mix up a coffee the way she likes it."

I put the menu down and walked out, past all the clothes in the department store, and then kept going out the doors and down the street, past the shops and offices.

After five or six blocks going the direction I was, Brilliant ended at the train station. I'd never been inside before. I walked in and sat on a bench that looked out over the tracks, the rail yard, and out toward the roundhouse. I walked around until I found a better view.

Not all train stations had roundhouses, I didn't think, at least not as big as the one in Brilliant. It looked like a kind of gigantic record player. Trains would slide on, then they'd twist the part that looked like a record, and attach the trains to other cars outside of it. I stayed there for a long while watching everything swing around and come apart and then come back together.

When my mother and I didn't have anything else to do and my dad was at work, we used to burn our garbage in the chicken wire can in the backyard, standing close by to take in the good smell of burning paper; we'd go to the drugstore and stand in the aisles eating fireballs and sour belts and reading magazines; we'd walk backward away from our house until it looked small enough to fit in the palms of our hands. She'd ask me about what I'd been learning at school. "Tell me everything, L," she would say to me. Tell me everything.

Sometimes we'd go have a stare at the Japanese fish in the King mine pond, sit by the edge and wait until they'd show us their orange backs or open their round mouths. Behind us, there'd be coal crashing around in the tipple, but we'd lean down close to the water so we could hear the sounds the fish made swishing around. They were so big and their orange had such a shine that when they were close to the surface, they almost lit up the black water.

I went downstairs where the regular part of the train station was. Ticket sellers stood behind glass windows. Above them, there was a black board with white letters listing all the places you could buy tickets for: Pittsburgh, Greensburg, Harrisburg, Philadelphia, and more and more names, places I never heard of, a lot of them not even in Pennsylvania, a hundred places a person could end up.

CHAPTER 11

M ISS STARESINA had us laboring over cranes made out of thin colored sheets of paper. She had an idea that she should decorate the tables at her wedding with them. Mine kept turning out wrong, not looking like cranes, or any other kind of bird. Walter's weren't right either. We both gave up.

Walter said, "I heard these ladies say Zoli must have quit the Glass. They said they thought he was hunting around for your mother."

"What ladies? Did they say where he went to look for her?"

"My dad says they're wrong. He thinks maybe they had to lock Zoli up out at Bedford, pump some medicine into him, make him act like a regular person. He went all the way out of his head when your mom left here, my dad said, grieving. Everyone knows he set that tree on fire. That's crazy, right? What he'd do that for? A normal person would just light up the barn."

"They don't just take people out there."

"How do you think people get out there, Lessar? Someone

takes them. Mr. D'Angelo told me that his patrol car's nothing but a taxi to drive people to the county jail or out to Bedford."

"You talk to him?"

"Of course I talk to him. He's my neighbor. I'm not like you are."

"Like what?"

"Keeping away from everyone."

"What? I don't keep away from everyone."

If you worked at Bedford, you weren't supposed to talk about the things that happened there. And if you went in there, you wouldn't want people to know about it. So most of the stories about Bedford came out around Halloween, usually from some kid at the high school.

There'd be a story about a guy who'd broken loose from Bedford and was coming toward Banning with a sack of knives he'd stolen from its kitchen. Even knowing full well it was made up, I'd still lock my bedroom window for a few nights and jam a chair under my door.

The only person I really knew about who was up there was a guy from Mineral who smashed in his wife's head with a Westinghouse mixer until she was dead from it. He should have gone to jail, everyone said, but he pretended he was too crazy to understand what he did.

I liked the idea of Zoli being locked up, but I couldn't see clear to him being there. "They got phones up there? For people to call out."

"How am I going to know that?"

"What else did they say about him, the ladies?"

"I'm going skating after school. You want to go?"

"Quit saying you can skate. What ladies? Who are you talking about?"

"You don't know nothing about skating."

"I guess I know more than you, since I know you need skates to do it."

"I only asked you because my dad said to, said to look out for you since your dead dad was his good friend and your great-grandfather's up in that old house dying."

Before I knew what I was doing, I stood up and tore him out of his chair and pushed him down to the floor. I pounded hard enough to hear his forehead knocking against the wood. Miss Staresina told me to stop. The other kids yelled at us to keep at it, cheering for me or cheering for Walter. He shook me off and stood up. We faced each other. He made a *tssk* noise with his teeth, and hit me so hard in the stomach that I almost threw up.

Miss Staresina made us clean up all the cranes we'd smashed, then she sent us to the principal's office. The principal told me he knew how things were for me because he was an orphan himself.

"Orphan?" I said.

"I grew up in the orphanage, with the nuns, at the mission."

"The orphanage?" I said.

He let me go and asked Walter in. Even though it was still early in the day and school would be going on for a while, I didn't go back to the classroom. I walked out to the Croatian Club to find Marko.

When I opened the door, Mrs. Markovic was right inside. I hadn't been to the club since my mother left and I hadn't seen Mrs. Markovic since then. Before I could say one word, she wrapped her big arms around me and pressed my face against her neck. She smelled like sauerkraut and cigarettes even stronger than Walter did, but somehow on her it wasn't terrible like it was on him. His smell was secondhand, rotting; her smell was like standing over a pot of fresh sauerkraut smoking your own cigarette.

"I miss you," she said. I don't think anyone had ever said that to me in my whole life. I'd never gone anywhere to be missed. I couldn't help it, my eyes burned and watered.

She covered me with her apron and took me behind the bar. I didn't see Walter come into the club, but I heard him shouting "Hi" to his mother. He said, "What are you doing here, Lessar? You shithead." Mrs. Markovic pulled me into the room-sized refrigerator behind the bar and closed the door on him. She took a towel from one of her pockets and wiped my face. "You can always come to our house and be our own son, Lucas. We will love you equal as we love our own."

Walter shouted at the door, "Lessar, when you come out of there, I'll probably kill you."

His mother smiled and said, "Maybe we'll love you more." She started opening a case of cola. She hummed some song, whispering a few lines here and there under her breath, something about the strongest man in the universe. He ate buckets of iron filings to keep up his strength.

She finished opening the case, put a towel over my shoulder, touched my cheek, and gave me a bottle. "You stay in here as long as you need to." She went out and closed the door behind her.

I heard her cursing at Walter and telling him to leave me alone. He shouted, "All right, Lessar, when you come out of there, I won't kill you, but I'll probably break your bones." She sent him to clean the grease traps.

When my mother and I were driving my father to the hospital the time he nearly cut his thumb off fixing the cabbage, the car kept stalling out. My mother was losing her mind, but he was calm as could be. He kept telling her not to worry. He was stretched out on the back seat holding a towel around his hand. He recited the names of the Croatian saints: St. Nikola Tavelic, St. Ozona Kotorska, St. Augustus Kazotic. Then he went and named the different kinds of tomatoes there were, and corn, and rocks. Whenever he was nervous, he would make lists like that, say them out loud or whisper them to himself.

I sat down on a beer case and started working my way through some of the things I knew. The names of the mines— Banning, Bluebird, Luna, King. The names of the trees we had—shag bark maple, silver maple, mountain laurel. Since I'd stolen Eli's map of California on Christmas Eve, I'd been studying it every so often, just in case Slats had been telling the truth to Zoli about my mother being out there. And I thought of a few things I'd learned from the map—Eureka, Barstow, Redding, Sacramento Valley, San Joaquin River.

The walls of the refrigerator were like slabs of ice, but I didn't want to leave. Something about the lone bulb burning and all the quiet had me feeling better. There was a pile of blankets on the floor. I got off the beer case and went to take up a blanket. When I pulled up the one on top, I saw a flash of skin, a head of hair. I leaned back and tripped on a box. My soda bottle fell and spilled everywhere. The man in the blankets sat up and blinked his eyes hard. It was Marko. "Christ!" I said. "What are you doing in here?"

"Why are you stealing my warmth? How'd I get in here? You put me in here?"

"No."

"You know who put me in here? My wife, who wants to make for me a slow death from being cold."

"My great-grandfather's not dying," I said, sort of shouting.

"Take it easy, Uncle." He ran his fingers through his hair and looked around. "I came in here to get something and then it was so nice and cool, you know. I had a little vodka. Then I was closing my eyes. What was I coming in here for though?" He ran his tongue over his teeth. "Bone dry," he said.

I picked up my bottle of soda. There was still a little left, and I handed it to him.

"*Hvala*," he said. He finished it off and ran his fingers through his hair again.

"He's not dying, you know. He's just got some kind of cold or cough or something." I headed for the door.

He grabbed my coat sleeve. "It's too lonely in here," he said. "Don't go yet, Uncle. Sit some more. It's cold here."

I picked up the blanket I'd taken from him and handed it back. He wrapped himself up and said, "You don't look so good, Lucas. You okay?"

"*I* don't look so good? What about you? You're sleeping in a refrigerator."

"Okay, so we both don't look so good. We are missing our two friends . . . Last time I saw Mirjana she was at the bar with Slats and had a shot of something. Whiskey? Slivovitz? Can't remember. Middle of the day. Place is empty. Just us three."

"When was that?"

"She plays a few times in a row on jukebox that crazy horn music she made me put in there. Songs by that guy from Mineral, Stevo, his brass band. No one plays those songs but her, you know?"

"When was she here?"

He squinted. "Don't remember. I was smoking and Mirjana took my cigarette out of my mouth." He held two fingers out in front of him like there was a cigarette burning between them. "She polished it off herself, didn't give it back to me. But that's okay, Uncle. I don't care. We've known each other since always, me and Mirjana. She can have all of my cigarettes forever."

It seemed like the refrigerator was closing in on us. I opened the door. Mrs. Markovic was lining up a team of whiskey shots for some people from the Plate Glass. I didn't see Walter. I closed the door behind me as quiet as I could manage. I slipped out of the club into the evening air, where the dark was coming with fresh snow. My skin was so cold from being in the refrigerator that the flakes landed on my hands and stayed whole, and couldn't melt away.

CHAPTER 12

NEXT TIME I WENT OUT to the farm I didn't go inside the house right away. I still had raisins for Valentina in my pocket. I'd been carrying them for days. I walked the whole property to see if she was hanging around in the woods or fields. When I was almost through, I ran into Eli.

"You seen that gray goat?" I said.

"Our old person friend always says she is genius animal. Maybe she is away on some intelligent purpose, the wondrous goat Valentina." He walked with me for a while. When we got close to his house, he wished me luck, gave me one of his quick bows, and walked away.

I was close to the place where Zoli had snagged me on Christmas Eve. I walked fast as I could back to the house. It was full dark. Stars and clouds rested on top of the trees. I looked up at the windows of the farmhouse and saw Great-grandfather was pacing back and forth in his room. He passed one window then the next and then he turned and went back again. He was skinny as a rake.

I must have been walking around for a while, because by the time I got to the house, Slats's car was there. I put the raisins in a pile on the stoop for Valentina, in case she came around. Inside, Great-grandfather came down the stairs and threw his arms around me. It was like getting skeleton bones tossed at me. "I thought you were gone away from us!" he said.

"I'm not." I worked my way out of the circle of his arms.

"Maybe better from now on when you get here, you come straight to house, stay in house."

"That's exactly right," Slats said. "He should be staying in here looking after you."

"No," Great-grandfather said, "me looking after him."

"However you want to name it," Slats said.

She made us soup with beans and ham and celery. Great-grandfather was so unsteady that by the time he got his spoon to his mouth, he'd spilled nearly all his soup. He gave up after a couple of spoonfuls.

"What's the matter with you?" Slats said. "Eat!"

"I was thinking," Great-grandfather said. "We must make sure no one drinks pear brandy anymore. Keep it away from my giant sons. Tree can't make pears anymore. So, we must save all there is."

"All right," Slats said. "We'll do that, but you got to eat your soup."

"I look out window today many times. I don't see Valentina. On the other day, did she like the raisins you bring her?"

"She ate them up," I said. I didn't want him asking any more questions about her. I said, "So where was that Banning Two you were telling me about before?"

"Banning Two?" Slats said. "What?"

"I don't know what he's saying about. Maybe your soup is make him feverish."

"You said there was a Two," I said.

"I never said. Maybe you don't hear me right. Maybe I say Brilliant Two, or something other Two."

"No, you said Banning Two."

He started eating and pretended he was too busy to answer me.

Slats said, "You must have misunderstood him. There can't be two of these. There just can't be. I couldn't take it."

Great-grandfather said, "Those raisins she loves too much, Valentina."

"I just saw that Eli out there," I said. "Did he always live out in that shack? How come I'd never seen him before Christmas?"

"You've seen him," Slats said. "He's always been around."

Great-grandfather said, "But sometimes he's not right in the head and goes away for some time. I think he maybe checks himself inside to special place for crazy old mens drunks."

"You mean this house?" Slats said.

Great-grandfather threw her a mean look. "You know, Lucas, I have a few times at parties had maybe one or two drinks extra—"

"Ha!" Slats said.

"Compare with Eli though, I drink dew from blades of grass. He drinks lakes. He has to drink so much more than me because his troubles are many more than mine. This is starting from long time ago. From when he is a boy and lives with his father in Russia and his father is one famous sorcerer. But Eli himself has no abilities, and when he is young man, there is much shame for him and—"

"Stop!" Slats said. "Stop right now feeding him stories." She pointed her spoon toward the window. "You're giving him wrong ideas about what's out there."

"What are you saying? I only tell him truths. It's truth about Eli's father. He was sorcerer."

"Now, Dad—"

I said, "She's kind of right, you know. Every time I look up, you're telling me some crazy story, or walking around in the woods with no shirt on, or telling me something and then saying you didn't tell me, or eating dirt, or—"

"Lucas," Slats said. "Take it easy."

I ate some of my soup. "Why were you doing that?" I said. "Pulling up all that dirt that night. Remember? You were putting it in your pockets and then you were stuffing it in your mouth—"

Great-grandfather looked up at me with his cloudy eyes, and seeing him, looking old and like he might break, stopped me cold. I looked down at the table.

Slats said, "Okay now, let's eat this soup before it turns into ice."

Great-grandfather said, "I was thinking, I want to eat it, whole farm." His voice sounded deadly serious, but he was smiling. "This place, I love so much. And it looks in dangers from fire." He laughed. "Next thing I knows, I'm chewing grasses." He pushed his bowl away from him.

Slats said, "You finish that soup or I'm going to put a needle in your skin and pump it into you."

He pulled the bowl back, grabbed his spoon, and concentrated on eating. He ate almost all of it, then said, "I can be excused?"

Slats inspected his bowl. "Well, I guess. All right."

He started to walk up the stairs to his room. I noticed he was having a hard time standing up. He was leaning against the wall, holding the railing tight. After every step, he stopped and let out a few coughs. He sat down halfway to the top. "This ghost has now moved into my legs. From lungs into legs, that means either next place is out my feet and away, or insides my heart. If it's insides my heart, that will be end of it. End of everythings."

Slats was clearing the table, running water in the sink, but she heard him. "Jesus, Dad. Don't say things like that. You got a bad cold is all."

"I am thinking we should fix up one bedroom for Valentina, keep her inside so she'll be safe from *Tot-to*. Also she'll make good noise for me, keep away all that quiet."

"I am not keeping house for a goat. You can send that idea right back to the central office."

"Is my house," Great-grandfather said. To me he said, "Get her. I wait here."

"You joking?" I said.

"Joking? I might probably be dying. No time for joking. Bring Valentina."

Slats came over to the steps and looked up at him. "If you bring that goat in here, you losing your mind will be official."

"Oh, Raisa, how did you get so much blackness in your heart? Did I give you?"

He hardly ever used her first name. I think it surprised her. She looked at him for a minute, then said, "Okay, the goddamn goat can come in the goddamn house, but just for two minutes. Then she's going outside to the barn. People inside, animals outside, like they do in civilization."

Great-grandfather nodded and waved to me to go outside.

"How am I going to get her to come in here?" I said.

"Take raisins," he said.

I went to the cupboard and got a handful. "She might not want to come in here."

"Where I'm going? I have date? I have appointment?"

Outside, a bright lamp hung over the steps and made a circle of light I couldn't see past. I sat on the steps and started eating the raisins. I ate most of the ones in my hand and took a few from the pile I'd left for her before. I thought of getting a different goat and hoping Great-grandfather wouldn't be able to tell it wasn't Valentina. There was a white one dirty enough to pass for gray, but he claimed that Valentina had special powers and he'd probably test that dirty goat. He said Valentina had smart eyes, like smart people. He said she tilted her head when he talked to her, because she really listened to him and believed every word he said, not like his daughter and his great-grandson.

After a while, the house fell quiet. I stood up, looked inside, and saw that he was still sitting on the steps, leaning against the wall. I thought he might have gotten pulled down into sleep. I sat back down on the stoop and waited for the sound of Slats taking him up to his bed. But then his voice cracked down the stairs and out the windows, "Valentina! Come in! Visit! Lucas Lessar is here. He will make you safe!"

I stood up. "I hate it here," I said. Hard as I could, I flung the raisins out into the dark. Just then, Eli stepped into the light holding a rope. He tugged on it and Valentina came walking around, picking up the raisins I'd thrown. I jumped off the stoop, took the rope, grabbed her by the hair on her neck, and walked her to the door. I'd never been so happy to see an animal in my life.

"Be gentle, Luca. She was journeying far today," Eli said. He had dirt all over his coat.

"Where'd you find her?"

"I found her someplace that is where no animal should go, not goat animal, or young Lessar animal. So you never mind where I found her."

I opened the door and took her inside. Great-grandfather came running down the stairs. "It's you!" he said. Valentina was surprised by the lights and furniture and Great-grandfather making such a racket. She jerked away from me. She ran in fast circles around the kitchen, the rope trailing behind her. Great-grandfather clapped for her, a steady clap, hitting his foot against the floor.

I went back outside to thank Eli. "You coming in?" I said.

"Sounds like party in there."

"You could come in for some soup. You see any dogs where you found that goat? I looked all over. Where'd you find her?"

In the house, something crashed and banged to the floor. Slats hollered. Great-grandfather laughed.

"I will come inside for one soup," he said.

I opened the door for him.

Great-grandfather smiled and kissed Eli on one cheek and then the other. They watched Valentina. They started to clap in a rhythm and then the two of them were all of a sudden inside a song together, and then this strange thing happened— Valentina slowed down just a little and her hoofs hit the floor matching the beat of their song. Slats stopped cleaning the dishes and looked up. "What on earth?" she said.

The brass bands my mother liked weren't the kind with fancy straw hats and candy-striped jackets, or the kind that march around at football games. The one she liked best, Stevo's band, from Mineral, was a mess of flugelhorns and tubas and trumpets, and they played until they were all drenched in so much sweat that there were big puddles on the stage. They played the horns so loud that I'd find myself leaning back against the wall, like the music had pinned me there, like I couldn't move until they were through.

They always finished the night standing shoulder to shoulder with a song that started out slow and quiet. It was almost like they were pulling the song up a hill, or clicking up a spike in a roller coaster. There was even a space of quiet, where they all stopped their horns, and everyone seemed to stop breathing, and then the song rushed along into something so wild and fast that the floor shook.

They came around a few months after my father died, and my

mother said we should go, that he would want us to since we'd been planning on it. We went, and at the end of the night, walking to the car, I couldn't help it—I felt better than I had going in, better than I had maybe even since the wake. I felt so strange and guilty about it, I had to tell my mother. "It's okay, L," she said. She could see I wasn't convinced. "Why do you think all those people were crowding in there anyway?" She put the back of her hand on my cheek. "That's what music is for."

In Great-grandfather's kitchen, I had the feeling—like I did some nights listening to that brass band music—that my heart was a kind of wilderness, some expanse vaster than anyone would ever know the all of, even me.

It was a cheerful tune they were singing to Valentina, and everything in me that was sad and heavy seemed to bolt out like startled deer at each note, each hit on the floor.

CHAPTER 13

I WENT LOOKING FOR Walter in the morning, before school. I found him in the shack behind his house, where Mrs. Markovic sometimes made Marko sleep because he made too much of a mess and a stink to be let inside. I'd watched her put it together herself, her apron pockets full of nails.

Inside, it smelled like liquor and throw-up and sweat, all under a heavy cloud of freshly sprayed perfume. Walter was sitting on a cot reading an old *Famous Monsters of Filmland* magazine and he didn't look up when I came in. I said, "Woj, where'd those ladies at the club say Zoli went looking for my mom?"

"What are you doing here?"

"And who were they?"

"I don't know, Lessar, just some ladies. If I knew everyone's name who came in there, I'd have to have a whole telephone book in my head. They didn't say where he went to anyway." He started reading his magazine again.

The monsters in *Famous Monsters of Filmland* weren't even

famous anymore. The magazines were from when Marko and my father were kids, so they were about old monsters from old movies. Sometimes the magazines had stories about how they made people look like creatures from swamps, or ghosts. Other times there were scenes from the old movies and pictures of all the different kinds of monsters they had in them. In the back were ads for things they sold back then through the mail— pet monkeys and space suits and fake hypodermic needles. For all the mess that Marko sometimes was, he kept the magazines in good shape, all in the right order, by their dates.

There was an old hand-drawn poster tacked to the wall. The drawing was of a guy lying flat on his back on the ground. He had a boulder balanced on his chest. There was another guy standing over him holding a sledgehammer up in the air. "What's this?" I asked.

"It's from a show my dad used to do."

"I never heard of him being in any show."

"He's the one with the rock on his chest."

Under the drawing it said, "Strongest Man in the Universe." I remembered the song that Mrs. Markovic had sung when she'd pulled me into the refrigerator, the song about the man who ate iron filings—the strongest man in the universe. She must have known that Marko was inside the refrigerator, under the blankets. She must have been singing to him.

I said, "No way is that your dad. If that was Marko, they would have called the show Drunkest Man in the Universe." I had my back to Walter and he punched me so hard I thought the shack was falling down. I got knocked into the wall and hit my head.

"Strongest man," he said.

"Christ, Woj. I was kidding."

"We have to go. Staresina'll cut our hearts out and put them in her desk."

"I need to get inside Zoli's place."

"What for?"

"Maybe there's something in there that says where he went looking for my mom. And maybe that's where she'll be too. He could have found her by now."

He picked up his bag of books and opened the door. "You want to see my ice rink?"

I didn't want to, but I followed him out. He'd laid down bricks at the open sides of their patio, and cemented them together. It did look like an ice rink, only it was so small it looked like as soon as you took a step, you'd be at the end of the ice. He still didn't have skates. He was wearing tennis shoes. He dropped his bag of books and jumped onto the ice. "Watch this," he said. He slid fast across it and made turns at all the walls, crossing one leg over the other. I could hardly believe it, but he was skating.

In the afternoon, Benci came to school to take me to the farm. He pulled up to the front door and let his truck run. All the windows in the whole place chattered. Miss Staresina looked out the window, then shook her head. "Crying out loud," she said. "Just a pickup. Thought it was the four horsemen."

"I have to go to the bathroom," I said.

"Congratulations," she said.

I left the room, left the building, and climbed up into the truck.

He looked at the doors of the schoolhouse. "Where's the other kids? They coming out?"

"They let me out early," I said.

"How come?"

"The principal thinks I'm an orphan."

"Oh," Benci said. He wasn't one to make you have a conversation. The truck was so loud anyway, it was easier to keep quiet. Passing the old Banning mine tipple, I saw that it was leaning over farther than usual. It was halfway into a kneel. The next stiff wind that blew through town would probably take it down. I wondered what that would sound like.

When we were almost at the farm, I told Benci the dogs were gone.

"What do you mean?" he said.

"Great-grandfather's dogs, they're gone."

"They're probably just chasing after something. Is his cough getting better?"

I shook my head.

Benci's shoulders slumped down. He was so big, him doing that made the springs on the seat groan and sink.

I said, "He'd tell you he doesn't have a cough though, he's got a ghost in his chest. It climbed in his mouth one night. He said the ghost was some guy he used to know from Banning Two, but then he said there wasn't a Banning Two. You ever hear of a Two?"

"No." His shoulders slumped some more. The seat was down so low by then I had to crane my neck to see out the window.

Great-grandfather and I had tied Valentina to the railing on the stoop by the kitchen. He'd put out a bowl of water for her and big pile of food from the kitchen on a platter. He'd put all kinds of things out for her to eat. When we got to the farm, Benci slowed down and looked out his window at the plate. There was an apple, a couple of candy bars with the wrappers still on, raisins, and a collared shirt.

"What in hell?" Benci said.

"We're low on food for the animals."

"Somebody's been feeding them, though, right?"

"I gave them some apples and candy bars and cereal."

"Candy bars. Good Christ. You should have told me! You'll kill them."

"They aren't killed. They're all right. Go ahead and look."

He hit the brakes and we made a big swooping turn in the drive. I said, "What do you mean I should have told you? How am I going to tell you? You aren't up here."

He didn't say anything. We drove straight away to the feed store. I'd never been inside before. It had high ceilings, long wooden floors, and a million kinds of seeds in packets for every flower or vegetable or fruit you ever heard of. There were books about how to plant everything and take care of every kind of animal. It was so orderly, nicer than the library at school. I ran my hand along the wall of seed packets. I opened one of the books about how to plant vegetables. There were pages and pages of pencil drawings of leaves and different kinds of tomatoes and peppers. I opened another book, this one about trees. There was a picture of a pear tree that looked like it had been torched, only it hadn't been really. It was suffering from something called fire blight, a sickness that blackened its branches as if someone had held a flame to them. The book said that to set things right, at the end of the winter, you had to prune away the parts that looked like they'd really been taken to town. In the spring, you'd just wait and see if fresh buds sprung up, they might, or they might not. There weren't any directions in the book on how to fix a tree that had been burned for real.

Benci was through loading the truck and he yelled for me.

Back at the farm, he lifted the sacks of feed out of his truck and stacked them up on the ground. They were heavy. The farm was stone quiet. We started looking around for the animals. They weren't anywhere around the barn or up in the fields. "What the hell?" Benci said. I showed him the hole in the fence where I thought Valentina had chewed through when she ran away. He said it was much too small for the other animals.

We drove all around the fields looking for them. Though it

was fenced off, we went to the cratered field where Great-grandfather had tried digging for oil and water and looked in all the deep holes to make sure they hadn't fallen in.

"What the hell?" Benci kept saying.

When we got back to the barn, I said, "You think someone took them?"

"Took them? No. It's just, what are we going to do? You can't tell him. It'll kill him. We'll find them. Don't you say anything about it. Don't tell Slats. She'll hang me. She'll hang the both of us."

"What'll she hang me for? You were supposed to be looking after them. And what if he comes outside? He'll see then."

"Don't let him. We got no dogs. We got no animals. Dogs. Dogs are one thing. This is just—it doesn't make any sense."

We checked around outside the barn again. "We have to give him his syrup now," I said. I started to walk up to the house. "For his cough."

Benci didn't follow me. He looked down at the ground and said, "It's real good of you to be in there with him all these days."

"Slats makes me," I said. "Come on, we have to heat up water for him."

"I got to get going back," he said.

"Just come inside and say hey."

"I don't want to bother him. Let him rest."

"He doesn't do nothing but rest."

He looked at the ground some more. "When we were kids, he was—I don't know. I guess I'm used to him cutting a pretty big figure around here. You let me know when he's back to himself. He's talking strange, all that stuff. I don't know. I never seen him so skinny and weak-looking. Even this one time when he got hurt in a slate fall and he got this bad infection in his blood and made me go get leeches. Even then, he looked better than this."

"Leeches?"

"He hates doctors. If he could stand one even just a little bit, Slats would have called one by now. But she knows about him and doctors. This one time, instead of going to the doctor, he sent me out to get a jar of leeches. They got the sick out of him. It fixed him up. Too bad there's nothing like that now. I'd get him whatever he needed."

"Come in and give him some of the syrup."

"You do what Slats tells you. And don't say anything to him about those animals, or about me being out here." He started his truck.

I had to shout for him to hear me. "He knows you're out here. You can hear that truck for ten miles before you see it."

In the kitchen, Great-grandfather was in his pajamas and boots, trying to pull on his coat. He was coughing like a machine gun.

"What are you doing down here?" I said.

He pointed to his boots. They were untied. His eyes were glassy, the blue in them too bright. I walked closer to him. "You okay?" I said. He couldn't get his arm in his coat the right way. He gave up and let the coat drop to the floor. I put my hand on his arm; he was burning up. "I think you should take those boots off and get back in your bed." A cold draft blew through the room. "Why's it so cold in here?"

He didn't answer me or take off his boots. After a while, he said, "They left here, Lucas. My sheeps. My cows."

"How'd you know? You go outside? You're supposed to stay in here."

He sat down.

"They'll come back," I said.

"Where's Benci go?"

"He had to get home. They're waiting on him."

"Weakness."

"Are you crazy? He just lifted about a thousand pounds of feed out of his truck."

"I had idea for us, Lucas. Big idea. Me and you. Together . . . Not good for Benci to be this way. He has to take over this everything, soon, you know, when I'm dressed up in my funeral clothings . . . Big idea I had before. Did I tell you?"

"You can tell me upstairs. You got a thermometer?"

He pointed to his boots again. I made him sit down so I could pull them off. I found a handkerchief and tied it around my face. I was always careful around fevers because of what had happened to the first two Lukacses. I led him upstairs to his room. He'd thrown his blankets and sheets on the floor. I saw why it was so cold in the house—he'd opened all the second-floor windows. After I got him to lie down, I went around and closed them all.

In the kitchen, I filled a bowl with ice and cold water and packed a rag with more ice. I put the bowl on the floor and pushed it under his bed. When I had a fever, my mother always did this. She said the water in the bowl would work its way through the bed and right inside the fever.

He reached out and pulled the handkerchief down from my face. "What I have, you can't catch. It's not sickness."

I pulled it back up. He twisted around, then he closed his eyes and tried to sleep, but he didn't stay down for long. He sat up and stared at me, "We should go to America. Walking to there."

"What's wrong with you? We're already in America. That's your idea?"

"This is here, the place I was going all that time?"

"This is Banning. You're in Banning. You've been here a long time."

He sighed and leaned back heavily into his pillow. "Everythings was happen very quickly to me."

126

I tried to hold some ice against his head. It seemed like heat was coming off of him, all over.

"Then I want again to go. This time, you with me." He put his hand on top of mine. "We going to there together. Not so much lonely this time, because this time with you."

"Whatever you want."

"Will it be beautiful when we get to there? The Hungarians says so, says I won't believe what my eyes see. It's their idea I go to Banning, to here, to Pennsylvania. We leave soon?"

"Sure."

"How soon? Now? Where is my boots? Today we are go there?"

"Not today."

"Tomorrow?"

"All right, whatever you say."

"Tell my boots that tomorrow, we are going. We have to get there. I have to start buying animals, planting things for them."

"Tell your boots?"

"Make them ready."

He made me go downstairs and bring his boots up to him. They were brown and worn and heavy—farming boots. They were clean though; he took good care of them. He pointed for me to put them on the floor by his bed.

He leaned down and inspected my tennis shoes, running his finger along the sides. "Ach," he said.

"What?"

"It's long walk," he said. "Far. You need stronger shoes."

"I could make it okay. These shoes are all right."

"And when we are get to there, you need to buy heavy boots for mine. We have to start digging in mine. Make money to buy farm. Sheep. Goats. In mine, the bosses are make us wear at first painted green helmets. Because we are green! We are as babies. We know nothing."

"All right," I said.

He grabbed my hand and looked hard at me with his glassy blue eyes. "Will it be beautiful when we get to there, like the Hungarians says to me?"

I didn't answer him.

"What about Mirjana? My first grandchildren? She is where? Still disappeared?"

"I'm going to find her," I said. "I'm trying to find her."

"You'll bring her here to see me?"

Slats came in downstairs and up to his room. She took one look at him and set to rooting through all the drawers and cabinets until she found a thermometer. His temperature was sky-high. We packed up more rags with ice and held them to him.

Every so often he'd look at us as if we'd just gotten there and say, "Oh, hi." He tossed around, stared at the ceiling, and coughed and coughed. With him flitting around in his bed like a bird, it was hard to keep ice on him. He said a few more nonsense things. He got out of bed and tried to put his boots on. Slats fought him back at first, but then she let him get up and put them on, and she helped him tie the laces. Since he was hot, he'd pulled his pajama pantlegs up over his knees. His legs looked like little white sticks stuck inside the heavy boots. Walking around the room, he could hardly lift his feet.

Her voice shaky, Slats said, "Try to get some sleep, Dad. Okay?"

I couldn't tell if he'd heard her or not, but after a while he got into his bed, propped his boots up on the footboard and dropped into sleep with his mouth wide open.

I found a big flashlight in the basement and went outside to look for the animals. "*Sobaka*," I called for the dogs, like saying the word would make them turn out of the air. I gave up on them pretty quick and went back inside and fell asleep on the couch.

I don't know how long I slept. Slats woke me up. "Lucas," she was saying, shaking my arm. "His fever's down now. It's fixed. But he's not breathing right. We got to make a mustard plaster."

"It's like the middle of the night."

"He's not breathing right. We got to."

"Leave me alone."

She grabbed my shoulder. I was about to pull away from her, but then upstairs, Great-grandfather let out a round of coughing. "All right," I said. "All right."

In the kitchen, she busied herself with the flour and water and mustard powder. Then the two of us sat at the kitchen table with the light buzzing above, taking turns mixing it with a long wooden spoon. It smelled terrible. She said, "He called up at the Glass today, Zoli. Called the foreman's office."

She handed me the spoon and said, "The foreman wasn't there, but the office girl took a message. He didn't say anything really, just called, and said he'd call again." She spread out her hands in front of her and looked at them. She started to say something then stopped.

"What?" I said.

She put her hands down on the table. Her wedding ring knocked on the Bakelite. "I'm guessing that he's calling in to say his case and that he's going to make up some story or other for himself to see if they'll let him come back to his shift." She looked at her hands again.

"Where'd he call from?"

"He didn't say."

"Maybe he called to quit."

"He can't quit. He doesn't know how to do anything else besides cause trouble, and he's not smart enough to make any money at that." She got up from the table, took a bottle of whiskey from the cupboard, and poured a glass. She splashed some water in it from the tap, then came back to the table. "It's been a long while. He hasn't been to work since the first week of January. We're already most of the way into February. Maybe they won't let him come back to work. Then he won't be able to get a foothold back here and he'll drift away again. He won't have a job anymore . . . or a girl—"

"He'll have a house, though. He still has a house."

She nodded and drank more of her whiskey.

Even though the plaster was ready to go, I kept stirring it until my arms were tired. After I quit, we both sat there for a while under the buzzing light without saying anything. It seemed like the longer we sat there, the more certain it was that he was on his way to us. I could practically hear the dull roar of the Skylark.

Great-grandfather coughed again and Slats and I both sat up straight and looked at each other. We carried the bowl and a cloth up to his room. He was stretched out on top of his covers, his head propped up on the headboard. He didn't say anything to us when we came in, didn't nod or wave.

Slats sat down on the chair by the side of the bed and put the bowl on her knees. She opened out the cloth on the bed to spread the mustard over. She used the wooden spoon to spread it, but some of it got on her hands. "Oh shit," she said. "Jesus Goddamn Christ . . ." She squinted up her eyes in pain. It was stinging her cuts from the Plate Glass. I took the bowl off her lap, and she went to the bathroom to clean her hands and curse.

Hearing her seemed to cheer Great-grandfather up a little. "Ha. She sounds like sailor." His voice was scratchy, quiet.

She stayed there for a long while. I said, "You ever coming out of there?"

"I'm not sure. Ask me something else."

Great-grandfather said, louder, "Where you learn all those swearings?"

"Let's see, one or two or probably all of them from you."

"Not true," he said. "Not one grain of true."

Slats said, "Lucas, I can't be near that stuff. I'm almost killed in here. You're going to have to do it yourself."

"You do," he said to me.

"All right," I said, but I didn't move. I didn't want to touch his skin. He sat up and coughed. He was having a hard time breathing in between.

Slats came into the room. She had towels wrapped around her hands like mittens.

"What if it stings me too?" I said.

She said, "We'll take you to the slaughterhouse and cut off your hands at the wrist."

Great-grandfather said, "She's probably not joking. You hear her swearing in there? She's look like nice person, but her inside, her heart, Lucas, brutal, black as coal." He smiled.

I spread the mustard out over the cloth. She told me how to fold it up so that none of it would touch Great-grandfather's skin—it'd burn him. He unbuttoned his pajama shirt. His skin was falling away from his bones. I folded up the cloth into a square and made sure none of the mix was leaking out. I put the cloth on his chest, under his chin.

Slats told him to breathe in the smell of the plaster, that it would break his cough. He said, "It won't help, but you are manager of me."

He made a big production of it, raised his arms up in the air and breathed in a long, loud breath. His face turned white, then whiter, and then it started up, a coughing that didn't sound anything at all like the coughing he'd done before or like anything I'd ever heard. They were deep noises, almost like a machine was making them, a machine with its pieces breaking apart and coming loose.

"Holy hell," Slats said, "Take it off him."

I leaned over and put my hands on the plastered cloth. My

hand crossed over his heart. I could feel it drumming, banging away, reeling around like a drunk man pounding on the floor of a dance hall.

Taking away the plaster didn't make things better. He coughed and strained for air. He rolled over, put his face down into the bed, grabbed all the sheets and pulled them toward him off the mattress. Slats yelled at me to go to the kitchen and get him a glass of water. Downstairs, his coughing rang all through the rooms, ricocheting off the walls and the photographs and the dishes and the windows.

I went back upstairs with the water. He drank some, but the next cough sent all the water out of his mouth and all over us in a big spray. Slats dried the water off me and him and his bed. He curled up like a baby and coughed, and it seemed like he was crying. "Raisa," he choked out, his voice hoarse, "I have enormous love for you, my first of my daughters."

She threw the towel down on his bed. "Why are you saying that?"

The coughing went on and on. Slats went downstairs to get the whiskey.

I was alone with him. "Lucas," he said, and then coughed for a long time. He grabbed me and said in my ear, "This place . . . My farm . . . "

"Yes?"

He was coughing too hard to talk. Slats came back. In between his runs of coughs, she poured about a whole bottle of whiskey into him. Sometimes he spit it out, sometimes it spilled and ran down his chin. Enough of it got in him that he calmed down some and his coughing started to sound like normal coughing, and then it slowed down and almost stopped. When he talked again, his voice was faint and hoarse, and with every word it got fainter and fainter. He whispered to Slats, "I think I am getting my talking taken away by this sickness,

Raisa. I am through of talking. For my last words, I pick to say that you are the one of them that was what I liked best in all this living, you and my unkind boys, and Mirjana, and all my boys struck down by fever." He looked at me. "My Lukacses."

Slats started to say something to him, but then she ran out of the room.

He stared me down. My heart was pounding against my chest and my neck. He reached his long arms out to me, put his hand on the back of my head, and pulled me toward him. "This place. Make everything that is disappeared come back to here. To this place." He kissed my forehead. "Make farm again to be what it was." He kissed both of my cheeks. "Animals, dogs, grasses, sunlights." He kissed my hands and leaned back against his pillow.

I thought of a million things to ask him, if he really was going to stop talking. Finally, I said, "How?" and then, louder, almost shouting, "How? How am I going to do that?"

He opened his mouth, but nothing came out.

CHAPTER 14

T HEY WENT at our coal room by room, threw up pillars, worked it out of the walls, made some more pillars, made some more rooms, pulled out more coal. They blasted it out of the seam with dynamite, threw it onto conveyer belts, rolled it to the tipple, poured it into trains. Fires used to burn all the time in the coke ovens carved into the hills, and all of Banning was a cup of light and singing noise. But before the fireshots and the metal hitting metal there were hundreds of millions of years of everything being quiet. Coal is trapped sunlight that got caught up in the leaves of gigantic swamp ferns, leaves that made shade when Pennsylvania had dragonflies with thirty-inch wingspans. When you burn coal, that trapped sunshine is what makes the heat, that old, old sunshine locked up for all that time, coming loose.

When they first found it, there were thirty billion tons of coal in our bituminous fields spread out over three big seams— the Upper Freeport seam, the Lower Kittanning seam, and the Pittsburgh seam. And it's our seam, the Pittsburgh seam, that's the biggest; its coal lies in four- to six-foot beds. A lot of it has been carried up out of the ground by bare hands, scorched out with dynamite and hammers and picks; its dust everywhere on the outside of the miners and then later inside of them too, in their lungs, in their blood, in all their memories of the world.

In my father's dreams, lakes were always filled with water black as oil, snow fell in black flakes, and the sun sometimes rose black and spread dark instead of sunshine. He thought he was in such terrible love with my mother for his whole life not because of her good looks, but because of how dark her eyes were, almost black.

After she took up with Zoli, when she couldn't sleep, she'd wake me by putting shoes on my feet. It'd be the middle of the night or nearly morning, I'd feel something pressing on my soles, and when I looked up, she'd be tying my shoes. I'd get up and follow her. I didn't say much on these walks, but she did. That was when I learned about the coalfields and how the coal was inside my father's dreams.

Standing in front of the boney one night by the Bluebird pit, she told me about how when she was a kid, she would toboggan down the piles on sheets of tin. It was always her and Marko and my dad. They would try to get the coal dust off her before she went home, but Slats always knew and gave her hell for ruining her clothes. My mother told me a lot of stories then. I know now that she was getting ready to go away, and the stories were what she was going to leave me with.

The night Great-grandfather spoke his last words in my ear, I felt my mother putting my shoes on. I sat up and saw that my room was empty and silent. I put my shoes on anyway. I sat on my bed for a while and listened to the town, its noises floating along in the air—people walking home talking, someone's car going past, the hum of machines at the Plate Glass.

I couldn't tell if Slats was asleep or not, but to be sure I didn't get stopped, I climbed out the window. I was probably still halfway asleep until I walked into the club, into its smoke and shouting and lights. There was a band playing one of those old sad Croatian songs that my dad liked so much. I saw Walter right away. He was standing behind the bar. I might have said something to him, asked if he could come with me, but it seemed to me that all I did was walk into the club and look at him and then we were running through the Monkey Dumps. The vines were swaying in the breeze, making the shadows move, and Walter was all the time just in front of me, his yellow hair shining.

At Zoli's, Walter found a piece of metal wire on the ground and he tried working the back door. I tried the windows. They were still locked up tight. I went around to the front of the house and that's when I caught sight of the outline of a man standing on the edge of the Monkey Dumps. My breath burned in my throat. I thought it was Zoli. He came closer.

"Marko?" I said.

Walter came running up behind me. "Where?" he said.

"Marko?" I said again.

"Dad," Walter said, "hey, Dad."

I thought Walter would be in trouble for leaving the club, but Marko didn't seem interested in him. He was staring at the house. He looked like if the breeze picked up, he'd fall over.

"Dad," Walter said. "Hey, Lessar here doesn't believe about how you did that show, how strong you are."

"Lessar? Jimmy? Where?" He looked around.

"No, not him. Lucas. The other one's not around anymore. Remember the blowup? How they didn't find nothing of him but his foot in his shoe?" Walter looked at me. "Sorry," he said.

"Show him the poster," Marko said.

"He already saw it."

"Show it again."

"How am I going to show him a poster? We're in the woods in the middle of the night."

He kept staring at the house. "Another time then."

"Show him how strong you are," Walter said. "We need to get into Zoli's house. Break something open for us."

"Zoli? Is he in there? You in there?" he shouted. "Mirjana?"

"No one's in there," Walter said. "No one's in there with nobody."

Cold air ran down the hill out of the Dumps. I could hear pieces of a song. The cold seemed to sober Marko up a little. He nodded. "Okay. We'll get inside."

"I'll find something to help you pry open a window," Walter said and ran away from us.

Marko pulled open his coat. "Look, Uncle. Always the heaviest rock he could find, he puts here. It's no problem for me. Then he takes the big heavy hammer and lifts it up and up, and then it comes down on me again, and then again until he breaks the rock. In the audience, the people yell. But it's easy for me . . . You know how I got to be so strong?"

"You ate iron shavings."

He squinted at me. "No. Of course not. I ate regular foods . . . Where's Zoli?"

"We're trying to get inside and find out, remember? Walter told me you thought he was locked up in Bedford, grieving over my mother or something, but I—"

"Walter told you that?"

"Maybe there's something in there that says where he went to, and that's where she'll be."

"I don't know why Walter tells you that. That's not what I said. I said Mirjana, *her* grief, from losing Jimmy. Maybe she is there at Bedford. Mirjana grieving, maybe she had to go there."

I felt like I must have heard him wrong. "What?"

"I found her sometimes, two, three times, walking alone, nothing there, not herself. Nothing like herself—"

"What are you talking about?"

Walter rushed up behind us, "Shut up, Dad!" he shouted. "You're too drunk to talk."

"I was trying to tell about how I became so strong."

I said, "How could she be there? Why would she be up there?" My voice was shaking.

Walter said, "Keep your mouth shut, Dad. Just help us get inside the house."

"How I did was I carried the sadness of losing Mirjana, losing her to Jimmy. The rock, the hammer, these are no problem—"

"Cut it out," Walter said. "I'm tired of you telling that story." He picked up a rock and cocked back his arm.

"It made me strong," Marko said.

Walter threw the rock. It hit Marko in the chest. Marko said, "See now, Lucas, rocks and things are no problem for me." He leaned over and picked up the rock. His lighter fell out of his shirt pocket, onto the ground. "Mirjana," he shouted at the house. "Zoli, you son of a bitch. Come outside!"

It was me who picked up the lighter and held it tight in my hand. Marko went on talking, shouting for Zoli, tossing the rock up in the air and catching it.

"He's not in there!" Walter said. "Shut up." He picked up another rock.

It was me who walked over to the carport and found the pile of rags and gasoline canisters.

I stood looking at the house. Just like Great-grandfather said had happened to him, ghosts climbed into my mouth and made it hard to breathe. I thought about my mother and my father. I thought of how Great-grandfather was leaving us piece by piece, first his dogs, then his animals, then his voice. I thought about the pear tree standing up in the empty field, scraping the sky with its black branches and broken bottles.

It was me who dipped the rags in the pools of spilled gas around the near-empty gasoline canisters, then tossed the canisters onto the porch.

Walter threw a rock, a window broke, then a second window broke. I don't really think it was possible that the music from the club was as loud as it seemed, but it felt like once the windows were broken, that music was roaring all around us, and that maybe it was the music, not the rocks, that was breaking the windows. I found a couple of sticks and wrapped the rags around them. Someone was singing "Samo Nemoj Ti." Someone was saying, "*Ti si rajski cvijet.*" You are a flower from heaven. "*Tebe ljubiti ja neću prestati.*" I'll never stop loving you. The music was so loud and so beautiful, I was sure the house would explode, and the town would fall apart.

It was me who lit the first rag with Marko's lighter and held the branch like a torch. I broke the third window and threw the torch inside and then broke another window and threw in another torch. Later, Marko would say he'd done it and everyone would believe him, because everyone in Banning knew, everyone except for me until that night, that Marko had always loved my mother. But it was me who took the lighter and fixed it so the flame would hold after I let it go and tossed it at the gasoline canisters piled on the porch. I was the one who stood still and wouldn't run away even though the fire was coming closer and closer, so I could listen to that music roaring in my ears while I watched the house light up and let it wrap me in heat and noise. It was me.

PART TWO

CHAPTER 15

G REAT-GRANDFATHER WAS wrestling bears in a traveling circus when he decided to come to Banning. He'd wanted to go to America and had left his village walking. One night, he came upon this circus and saw a man nearly taken to pieces by a bear. He didn't know the first thing about bears, but he needed money to get to America, so he offered to take the man's place. He wasn't as big or tall as most bear wrestlers, but he was quick on his feet, and he always gave the crowds a terrific show of how terrified he was. He wasn't pretending; he really was terrified. To calm himself, he talked to the bears, told them stories about his village in Russia.

The circus went all through the Austro-Hungarian Empire. As he went from place to place, he saved his money and kept his plan to go to America a secret. Then the circus came into the places where people were speaking Hungarian. Most of the time, he had no idea what they were talking about, but something in the sound of it, when he heard it, his heart did nothing but break. Though he couldn't be sure, it seemed to him, from the sounds of their words, that the Hungarians were always talking about things they wanted and couldn't have. In a room filled with their talking, the air would be so heavy with wanting that he'd have a hard time moving under the weight of it. Lying on his pile of blankets at the circus, he would hear the Hungarians passing by, talking, and he would almost weep. Sometimes he did weep.

He learned how to say a few things in Hungarian. He kept talking to the bears, and since he believed Hungarian to be a language of strung-together wishes, when he spoke it, without being able to help himself, his secret about wanting to go to America started to work its way out of his mouth. Sometimes the audience overheard. People wanted to help, and every so often, they handed him slips of paper, with names and addresses of people they knew in America. There were many Hungarians in Banning then.

But even after he'd saved enough for the ship and had pockets full of names, he still couldn't make himself leave. He knew it was only a matter of standing up and putting his things in his bags and beginning his walk to the sea, to a boat, but he couldn't manage it. He wasn't sure what he was waiting for. At night, he'd take his blankets and his rolled-up mattress out into the forest and lie down under the trees. He'd wait for the thought that would release him from the life he had and let him make his way into the life he had an idea was waiting for him someplace else. He'd look past the trees for the bright outlines of Ursa Major, the Great Bear. But nothing happened, no big idea came, only sleep.

The circus closed for a few days on the outskirts of Vienna, and Great-grandfather walked into the city. There was a festival and the Hapsburgs had opened the doors of the Imperial Chapel to the public. Great-grandfather patted the dust from his sleeves, wiped his shoes off with his handkerchief, and walked up the stairs into the chapel. Candles were burning, and sunlight was coming through the colored windows. He wanted to stand still, watch people come and go, and lean his head back so that he could see all the way up to the reaches of the ceiling, but he got swept along in a crowd. When they stopped, he found himself standing for a long time in a small room, not understanding what everyone was looking at. There was a set of shelves, and all along them rows of small urns. A man explained to him, in a whisper, that they were in the Heart Crypt, and that here, in front of them, were the hearts of the Hapsburgs, each one in its own urn.

"Their hearts?" Great-grandfather said.

The man nodded. "The dead Hapsburgs, their hearts."

Some of the urns were small, some were grander-looking, others were newer, shinier. After a long while of staring at them, Great-grandfather thought he could hear them beating. He put his hand on his chest and found that it wasn't the noise of their hearts beating that was filling his ears—it was his own. He understood, just then, maybe for the first time in his young life, that someday his heart too would be taken from him, and that there was nothing he could do about this, nothing even a Hapsburg could do.

That night, he gathered together the slips of paper that people had been handing him, the names and addresses of people in America. He copied them onto a single sheet of paper, whispering their names as he wrote them. There was a name that he liked from the minute he copied it, liked the way it sounded and the way it looked on the paper, Katalin, Great-grandmother's name.

The next morning, he started his walk to the sea. As he walked, he memorized the names on his list. He repeated them over and over. When he was tired, he would say, at each step, that name he liked, Katalin. On the ship, all the way across the Atlantic, he held the name in his mouth.

He knew what she looked like before he met her—that's what he told people—from saying her name for all those miles of walking. So that when he saw her, standing in the Banning company store looking into a barrel of black powder, he could walk up to her and introduce himself and know exactly what she would say when he asked her name.

My mother told me this story, and in the days after Great-grandfather's voice left him, I heard pieces of it again from the great-aunts and great-uncles. My mother thought the reason the sound of Hungarian made Great-grandfather sad was that it was Great-grandmother's language and he missed her. If you told her that didn't make any sense, that he couldn't miss her—they hadn't even met yet—she would say Great-grandfather's love for Great-grandmother didn't have anything to do with time. That's how the great loves were, the same as the Luna mine fire—that fire didn't seem to understand how unreasonable it was, blazing away for all those years for no reason anyone could point to. It didn't care about time, or about making sense—it only cared about burning.

The great-aunts and great-uncles flooded the farm after Great-grandfather's voice went away. They brought boxes packed with food and liquor. They stood around his bed with worried faces, whispered in the corners of his room clinging to each other; or they cursed and broke bottles against the side of the house. Every so often, Kaya would sing.

It wasn't long after she'd sung one of her songs that two of the great-uncles got into a shouting match and ended up outside swinging at each other. We all followed them. They'd been drinking, and it had snowed, so whenever one of them threw a punch that missed, he slipped and fell over. The rest of them weren't so much breaking up the fight as they were yelling at the great-uncles to get back in the house so we could all get out of the cold. Slats made me go inside and put my coat on and bring her a sweater.

The great-uncles wouldn't let up on each other. Slats kept asking, "What in hell are they fighting about anyway?" No one seemed to know. "You should have a topic if you're going to fight this hard."

I brought her the sweater and she pulled it on. I was standing behind her. She turned around a few times and looked me up and down. "How come your coat stinks like smoke?" she said.

"How should I know?"

"What do you mean how should you know? It's your coat. Where you been wearing it?"

"Nowhere."

"You didn't go down and take a look at that fire, did you?"

"No."

"You stay away from there. Whoever was mixed up in that is going to be in some real hot water."

"What do you mean?"

"I mean with the police. Frank D'Angelo was already down there poking around. You better tell me if you know something." She looked at me for a minute, then she pulled her sweater tighter around her and got back to yelling at her brothers.

I went in the house and smelled my coat. It did stink. The other great-grandchildren came pouring into the room. I had to tell them a hundred times to leave me alone before they finally did.

In a closet, I found the old coat of Benci's that I'd worn out to the barn on Christmas Eve. It was a big old black coat with a fur-lined hood and wide pockets. I put it on and pulled the hood up. It went down over my eyes some, but I could still see. It made everything around me quiet, like being inside a cave.

There was a grocery bag in the bottom of the closet. I put my smoke-smelling coat in there, and I stuffed the grocery bag under some shoes and boots.

When I went back outside, two cars I'd never seen before were coming down the driveway. They were big ancient cars, long as barges, one black and the other deep blue. Halfway to the house, they pulled over to the side and parked. The car doors opened, making a creaking sound. At first, it seemed like a flurry of black cloth, or smoke, was pouring out of the cars, but then there were flashes of pale skin, faces and hands, and I saw that they were priests, Orthodox priests with long black cassocks and beards and those tall black hats. They gathered up their books, closed the doors, and walked toward the house, their black cloaks brushing against the snow.

There were seven of them. Everyone, even me, knew what it meant when they came to you in sevens—they were bringing you the last oils of forgiveness to free you up of the sins you'd done on earth, before you left it. I pulled off my hood and looked at Slats. The great-uncles stopped cursing, put their fists down, and stepped away from each other. Everyone seemed to freeze to the spot they were standing on. No one went out to greet the priests.

In the space after the singing, the yelling, and the fighting, a heavy silence opened up. I'd been trying to figure out all day why there was so much more fighting and cursing than usual, and I finally understood that they'd been trying to drown out the quiet of Great-grandfather's voice being gone.

The priests got closer. Slats looked around at everyone and said, her voice low and cold, "Who sent for them?"

One of her sisters said, "We might try a doctor before a priest."

A brother said, "We'd have had to tie him down."

Benci walked out to greet them. He was the oldest, so it was his place to, but the way Slats looked at him, I knew she thought he was the one who'd asked them to come. He led them up the stoop, into the kitchen. Everyone walked past me and followed them inside. I could hear the priests' hard shoes knocking against the stairs on the way up to Great-grandfather's room.

A big wind blew across the farm and shifted the top layer of snow. I buttoned up the coat, dug my hands into the wide pockets, and watched Great-grandfather's windows fill up with people and shadows.

Eli came rushing outside. He hadn't been out with us during the fight and must have been inside with Great-grandfather when the priests came into the room. He came and stood next to me. We both looked up at the window. He smelled like the cold the deep woods give off.

"How come you aren't up there?" I said.

He shrugged. "Maybe if I don't watch, then it doesn't happen."

"What doesn't happen?"

The screen door slapped shut loud and it gave me and Eli both a start. Benci came out of the house, almost running. He got into his truck. I said, "He must have been the one sent for the priests."

"First, he should have made discussion with the others, the brothers and sisters, your *dedka* too. Make some agreement so that everyone is not so surprised."

"You ever hear of a Banning Two?"

He raised his eyebrows. "He tells about this to you?"

"He said a ghost was making him have this cough, a guy from Banning Two."

The wind kicked up again. Snow twisted around our ankles. He pointed to Great-grandfather's window, "In our religion, when a soul leaves a body, it must travel through some twenty tollhouses. At each one, you must face your accusers. They have records of your actions that you made. You have to pass through these, try to pass through these. They are up there, in sky." He looked up. "That's what they teaching us anyway. Our old friend has some fear, I think, that when he must do this, there will be some of his old friends. Maybe this is why he is thinking there is some ghost. Maybe has some fear."

"What would they be accusing him of?"

"Regular things that happened in life. The accusers are there to say that you did this, you did that, you failed at whatever you were trying to not fail as . . . as a brother, as a friend, as a son."

We watched Benci drive off into the fields. Up in the window, the great-aunts and great-uncles had their backs pressed against Great-grandfather's windows. Their heads were bent over; they were praying, I guessed, or looking at their shoes.

"What about the Two? Banning Two?"

"I haven't heard him talk about it for a long while. Always before with me, this was his way of talking about our friends that weren't with us anymore. He would say, 'Oh, you remember that guy? He is working now over in Banning Two.' Why? I don't know. He liked to think, I guess, that they hadn't gone so far away."

Another of the great-uncles came outside. He walked down past the barn, up into the fields. "Luca," Eli said. "You were a help to him before. Maybe he is look for you now, for more help. I think you must go inside."

I pointed to the great-uncle out in the fields. "He isn't in there. You aren't in there, either is Benci. Why do I got to go in?"

He started to walk away up the drive. He turned around after a while and saw that I was still standing there waiting for an answer. "That's what I'm telling you," he said. "It's you."

Inside the house, a mumbling run of prayers in deep unfamiliar voices hummed along the walls. Slats was sitting by herself at the kitchen table. "Guess it's official now," she said. She was concentrating on her hands in her lap, rubbing one with the other, over and over.

"What is?" I said.

She gave me an empty look that I didn't see on her too often.

Everyone was lined up the stairs or in Great-grandfather's room. I took the steps two at a time. In his room, his white bed and white sheets and white skin seemed to be swallowed up in the ring of the priests' black cloaks. I got close enough to see his face. He was looking at the priests in a way I thought you shouldn't, squinting, waving them away.

The great-aunts whispered to me that the priests brought holy oil that had been blessed by the Metropolitan all the way over in Moscow. They read Gospel readings to him. They blessed his eyes, ears, nose, mouth, hands, and feet. They asked God to forgive the sins he'd made with those parts of him.

The head priest put the open Gospel book on Great-grandfather's head and said another prayer. I looked around at all of the family. Some of their mouths were hanging open. They looked surprised. I didn't know them to be the kind of people it was easy to surprise. When bad things happened—someone getting shot, or all of a sudden dropping deathly sick or disappearing—they'd shake their heads, click their tongues, maybe cry, but they never looked the least bit surprised. Maybe what we thought was that it was impossible that Great-grandfather would ever die. But then the priests were there, and it was as if they'd carried his death into the house and set it down in front of us, and the longer they stayed in the room, the more certain it seemed.

The priest took the book away from Great-grandfather's head, Great-grandfather looked around the room at all of the family. And then he looked right at me, like he was looking all the way through me, or inside of me, to see what I was made of.

Surprising myself, I said to the priests, "You got to leave." No one seemed to hear me.

"Hey," I said, louder this time. "You got to get away from him."

"Shh," the great-aunts said.

Great-grandfather was still looking at me.

"Tell them to leave you alone," I said.

He tried to whisper something, but nothing would come out of his throat.

Slats came into the room. "Lucas. Quiet down. Be respectful."

"They got to go away. If they go away, then—"

"Be reasonable, doll. Let them do their jobs."

"Sorry," one of the great-uncles said to the priests.

A great-aunt said to one of them, "He's just—" And then, looking away from me, "His mother—"

"Leave him go!" I yelled.

The great-uncles came at me. One of them wrapped his arms around my chest and pulled me out of the room and down the stairs. Slats shouted, "That's too much. You don't got to do that." The great-uncle kept pulling at me until we were all the way down in the basement. He set me against the wall and shook his head at me. "Learn your place," he said. He went up the stairs and shut the door behind him. The lock made a loud clacking noise sliding into place.

CHAPTER 16

T HE WINDOWS in the basement were up near the ceiling and covered with snow, but light still made its way through, a spread-out light, like smoke. It was quiet. I pulled the hood of my coat on and tried to make it even quieter.

My father had told me that when George Washington first came to western Pennsylvania, he took a boat down the Ohio. He carried a matchcoat and a bottle of rum, gifts for the Indian queen Aliquippa. He looked for Frenchmen in the trees. My father seemed to think the story told us all we needed to know about George Washington. He had smarts, and had charm—bringing a gift for Queen Aliquippa. And he had some sand to be running the river like that, the woods full of Indians and Frenchmen likely ready to cut his throat.

Back then, my dad told me, Pennsylvania was a big stretch of forest. A whole state made of trees and trees. It must have been so quiet, especially down by the river in the places where the water hardly moved. I thought of what Washington's boat looked like from up above, the water snaking through the hills, and the hills a carpet of trees.

He told me that up in the north part of the state there was a little pocket of virgin forest still there, a stand of tall white pines and old hemlocks tucked inside the Allegheny Forest. It was called Hearts Content. He thought we might get our act together sometime and take a trip up to see it, have a walk through those old trees. We got out a map of the forest once and looked for it, but we couldn't find it. He said we could just pack some sandwiches and go driving around until we found it. How could we miss it? The trees would be giants, he thought, and so old.

Down in the basement, I wondered for the first time if it was even a real place. Maybe it was just something he dreamed up, a kind of place where all the lost things were, like Banning Two. It had just the kind of name my dad would put together for a made-up place, the kind of phrase he might slip into a song if he forgot the real words—Hearts Content.

The lock popped on the basement door and one of the great-uncles shouted down, "All right, you're allowed out of the dungeon."

Slats came to the door and said to him, "Think this is funny? I don't hear anyone laughing."

"I'm laughing," he said.

"My own brothers," Slats said to me, coming down the stairs. "They're afraid of those priests because they don't go to church." She came over to me, reached out and put her hands on the sides of my face. "You okay?"

I pulled away from her and walked through the piles of clothes to the far end of the room. She went back to the stairs and sat down on the bottom step. "We used to get sent down here when we were little," she said. "That's what would have happened to them if they'd disrespected someone. That's why he brought you down here. They don't have any ideas of their own. Don't you worry, you'll be avenged. When I go back up there, I'll raise complete and total holy hell."

I didn't say anything.

"You all right? Those priests' dark outfits put a scare into you?"

I moved over toward a set of old rain jackets that were pegged to the wall and saw, under them, glinting in the bare light, a rusted pair of ice skates. I took them down off the wall.

She said, "They obviously scared the shit out of Benci. Did you see him race out of here? He's probably halfway to Florida."

"Whose skates are these?" I said.

She shrugged. "Come over here and sit down."

The skates were white with black heels. They were narrow. The pegs and eyeholes for the laces were rusted almost to black. I hung them back up.

"Will you come and sit down? Please? You're making me nervous in that coat with that hood on. You look like a hangman."

I stayed where I was. "You ever been out to Bedford?" I said.

"No," she said, but I saw her flinch a little. She turned away. She started rubbing her hands one over the other, like I'd seen her doing before upstairs. I walked closer to where she was sitting. I had that feeling, like I did every so often in school, when something I couldn't make out was starting to set itself straight. Or when I could see that a balloon someone was working on was about half a breath away from blowing to pieces.

She stopped rubbing her hands and turned and looked at me. "I got half a mind to get you locked up in a place like that for what you just did upstairs."

"Marko said maybe she's up there."

"Marko?" She looked at the floor. ". . . Maybe those priests scared me a little too."

My mother used to say that Slats had the doctor take out her tear ducts when he took out her gall bladder. She never cried, but she did just then, for a second, a quick burst, more like a sneeze.

She pointed to one of the clothes piles, "Get me something."

I picked up an old pair of pants and handed them to her.

"These are scratchy as a shingle. I'll bleed to death."

I went to get her something else, but she put her hand on my arm. "Just . . . it's okay. These are all right. Just sit down. Sit still here next to me, all right? Everything around here's happening so fast."

I sat down. She kept her hand on my arm. Wind shook the windows. The floor creaked above us with everyone's footsteps. Kaya yelled down for Slats to come upstairs and help her cook. "Cool your jets," Slats said.

"I'm trying to make that apricot roll the boys like, but I don't think I know what I'm doing," Kaya said.

"I *know* you don't know what you're doing," Slats said.

Kaya laughed.

"I'm making a conversation with my grandson," Slats said. "They don't deserve that apricot roll anyway."

Kaya walked away from the basement door. Slats stared ahead of her for a long while. Then she said, "You know, when we were growing up, he used to stand in the middle of the living room with his arms stretched out, and then we could hang on to him, two of us on one arm and two on the other. He would raise his arms up and down. It was hard to hold on, but what a kick, like a ride at the county fair, only it was in the living room. He was so strong. I had no idea. I thought everyone could do that, and that I would do it too when I was as big as he was. Turns out I can hardly hold two grocery bags at the same time."

"What about what Marko said—"

"I'm trying to tell you something." She wrapped her hands around my arm. "I'm trying to tell you that it's hard to keep going sometimes, hard to be strong all the time. Sometime it happens that you find out you can't hold two grocery bags at the same time." She had another sneeze of tears and said, "Don't you say nothing to those people upstairs about me crying." She wiped her face on the old pants and threw them on the pile. "They'll think I'm going soft and they won't know what to do with themselves." She started up the stairs.

"What about my mom?" I said.

She kept walking.

CHAPTER 17

K ING WAS TAPPED OUT.
    Rumors had been running around for a long while that
it was spent, that it was too dangerous, that they could never
get the air clean enough. After my father got killed, it seemed
that people said those things more often. On the nights when
my mother couldn't sleep and she'd make me go out walking
with her, we sometimes ended up at King. As much as I didn't
like getting woken up in the middle of the night, I liked to
walk over there and make sure the mine was still up and running. I thought that us going over there, looking after it, was
helping it stay afloat. I didn't like the idea of the places he'd
worked getting sealed shut, the whole thing called off. I didn't
know about her, but I wanted King to keep running, on and on,
forever.

    The company had posted notices around town letting us know
when they were going to pull out the stump that held up the pit's
roof. Benci and I saw them when we were driving to the school.
Slats had made him stay with us through the night at the farm.

In the morning, she called in sick to the Plate Glass and had Benci take me to her house to get ready for school.

Benci didn't work a mine, but he said that when they yanked the stump there was going to be about 150 feet of earth caving in on itself. He said we didn't have anything to worry about, that the notices were for people that had creaking porches, or pretty china plates, or nervous ways of thinking.

Coming down the road to Slats's house, I saw there was a police patrol car parked in her driveway. "What in hell?" Benci said. He slowed down.

Mr. D'Angelo was sitting on her front porch swing.

I slid down in the seat. "Keep going."

"Let's find out what's going on."

"You got to keep going."

"Maybe her house got broken into or something. You don't need your books or anything? Why are you all slid down like that?"

"I got the books. Or they're at the school already."

He gave me a hard look and started to wind down the window.

"Benci, don't say anything to him. Keep going."

"You do something?"

"I got to get to school. I got things to do there."

"I think you're telling me a story."

"I'm not. I got a test."

"You're definitely telling me a story," he said, but then he sort of smiled at me and wound up his window.

When we got to the school, he said, "Whatever you done, you know that D'Angelo is kind of a hard-ass. Be careful."

I nodded. I went inside and waited until I heard his truck pull away, then I went out the back. I took the bus to Brilliant first. Once I got there, I couldn't really figure out how to get the rest of the way to Bedford, and I didn't want to ask anyone. I stood at the bus stop watching people come and go. I saw a pack of student nurses in blue capes. They had student nurses in a couple of hospitals, and I thought they probably had them out at Bedford too. I took the buses they took. When they finally got to where they were headed, it seemed like it was in the middle of nowhere. There was a patch of low buildings across the road from the stop and as soon as we got off the bus, the nurses disappeared into those, their capes fluttering behind them.

A few other people had gotten off the bus too. I followed them. They went up a hill and then turned onto a road. Once we got to the crest of the hill, I kind of caught my breath; there was the yellow smokestack that I knew, but aside from that, Bedford wasn't at all what I'd pictured. From far away, it always seemed like it was just the one red building with that smokestack poking out over the hills, but it was practically a whole town. The big red building was in the center, and spread out all around it were sets of smaller buildings, and barns, and wide fields with animals scattered over them, and tractors, and office buildings with wide shining windows.

Once we got up the long driveway to the entrance of the big red brick building, the people walking ahead of me went off in all different directions. I saw a sign pointing the way for visitors and I followed it inside the main building. It smelled like food cooking, but not a good smell, more like a pot of meat someone had forgotten about boiling and boiling away.

I walked around in the hallway until an older man, a guard with salt-and-pepper hair, said, "Can I help you?"

"I'm looking for someone," I said staring at the floor tiles.

"If you're looking for them down in those cracks, we're going to have to keep you in here." He put his hand on my shoulder and pointed me to an open doorway. "You got to go into the office and talk to the big gun."

In the room, a large nurse with a sharp, clean white hat sat behind a counter, tapping on a humming electric typewriter.

Walking behind her were more nurses dressed like her and student nurses with blue capes, and behind all of them, there were rows of filing cabinets, and shelves and shelves of glass jars full of pills.

"I'm looking for someone," I said.

She didn't slow down in her typing. "Not a visiting day today," she said. "Visiting days are Sundays."

I was all turned around about what day it was. I kept staring at her.

She stopped typing and looked at me. "It's a school day today, in case you didn't know it." She went back to typing.

I felt all spent. I'd hardly slept the night before at the farm. I couldn't picture getting on the bus back to Banning. And when I did get back, Mr. D'Angelo might still be waiting for me on Slats's porch. There was a chair behind me. I sat down.

The nurse looked up at me. "Just come back on Sunday."

I stayed where I was and watched the doctors and nurses coming and going in the hallway, and the people pushing carts and wheelchairs. She got up from her desk and left the room. A while later she came back and stood in front of me.

"You going to wait for it to turn Sunday?"

I looked past her, out to the hallway. "Maybe if she's in here, she'll walk by."

"Walk by? We got close to five hundred people in here." She went back behind the counter. "I don't even know how many people work here." The guard who'd led me to her came in and leaned against the wall. "How many people you think work here, Red?" she said to him.

"Let's see." He pretended like he was counting. "Too many," he said. The nurse laughed like it was the best joke she'd heard all year.

I stayed where I was, watching the hallway. I'd probably been sitting there for an hour or so when a young girl and a lady—

her mother, I guessed—came in from outside. The older lady went up to the nurse, leaned nearly all the way over the typewriter, and started talking to her loud and fast.

The girl sat next to me. She pulled a cigarette out of her purse. It was a clove cigarette, and as soon as she lit it, the room smelled like cinnamon and burning flowers. She didn't look much older than the girls in the high school.

She leaned toward me. "I'd ask you if you want one of these, but she makes me pay for them myself." She nodded toward her mother. "I have to keep watch over them like they're the crown jewels." She was wearing a denim jacket with a sheepskin collar. She had green eyes with freckles scattered under them and a lot of long, black curly hair.

I shrugged.

She kept looking at me. "Seems like I know you. Are you from Luna?"

My throat was all dry. I was too tired to talk and was half asleep. I shook my head.

"Did you ever come to Luna to get an animal stuffed, you know, something you shot or a fish you caught or something?"

I shook my head again.

"Huh. You look familiar is all. My dad's the taxidermist, in Luna." She took a long breath of her cigarette. "He doesn't work anymore though, you know, now that he's cracked."

I opened my eyes wide, to keep from falling asleep, but I guess she thought she'd scared me.

"It's okay," she said. "He's not like that man who killed his wife with a blender, out in Mineral. That guy's in here too though, you know. I've seen him—"

"Helen," her mother said. "You're going to disturb that boy."

"He's already disturbed, Mum. What do you think he's doing here? He's checking himself in, that's what. He was just telling me about it. Came to fill out all the papers."

The nurse leaned back from her desk. "Would you mind putting out that cigarette, young lady? It doesn't smell right."

The girl's mother said, "That's what I tell her. Smells like burning garbage."

She took the cigarette out of her mouth and looked at it. "I got a lot of precious smoke left here." She stood up. "Come outside with me."

I didn't move.

She said, "I don't like walking around here by myself. I might see someone crazy, you know, like dear old dad. Just walk me outside."

I stood up. When we were sitting down, she'd seemed taller than I was, but we were the same height.

"I shouldn't talk about Dad like that," she said when we got outside. "He's all right. Strictly speaking, if you were to make a study of it, the only cracked thing he does lately is talk to my brother Billy. Always telling him to stop hanging around the gas station with his friends. Or that he's going to have his fingertips stained for life if he doesn't quit rolling those cigarettes."

I followed her down the steps and over to a rambling post fence that faced a long, story-high barn. She smashed her cigarette in the ground and tapped on it with her shoe. She took another one out of her purse and lit it. "Billy got shot in Vietnam. So he's dead. It's no use telling him anything anymore." She shrugged. "He was always putting things in his mouth, Billy was. Cigarettes, lollipops, toothpicks, chewing tobacco. And whenever I think of it happening, I think of the guy pointing the gun at him and then him grabbing the gun and kind of sticking it in his mouth . . . What do you think? Think that's how it happened?"

My father had been just a little too old to get called up for Vietnam. Maybe if he would have gone over, it would have happened the same way it did at King, or almost the same way—he could have stepped on a mine, or walked under a bomb. It was better that it happened at King. Vietnam was so far away from us, but we could go over to King whenever we wanted and sit by the mine pond. We could walk over the hills and know he was under them, just under our feet. I didn't know if it would be the same with the mine closed.

"They're shutting down King," I said. It came rushing out of me like I was spitting up something I ate.

"Are they now? That's sad, isn't it?"

"It's tapped."

"Is that right?"

"It's the last one left in Banning."

"Well, that's too bad . . . The last what?"

"Mine. King's a coal mine. What'd you think I was talking about?"

"You're worked up about a coal mine? Thought it was a movie theater or something. You sure you aren't mental? You won't catch me getting worked up over a coal mine. We don't live too far from the mine in Luna. That's why I have to smoke this cigarette. I miss all that smoke when I'm away from it. This is, like, portable. Billy used to say that all the time. He made perfect cigarettes, rolled them himself, no kidding, just like a machine. I still have one he gave me before he went away. He left me a whole batch, but I smoked about all of them, couldn't help myself. I saved just the one. It's a good one though." She opened up her pocketbook and pulled out a lip-stick case with big Chinese flowers painted all over it. Inside was the cigarette. She smiled. "See, his fingers touched this." She looked at it for a long while. "Anyway, I'm Helen," she said. She closed the case up and put it back in her purse. "Helen Jameson."

"I'm Lucas Lessar."

"That's a good one. I like that alliteration." She looked over toward the fields. "They grow pigs down there," she said. "Like on a real farm."

"What's alliteration?"

Someone shouted inside the building. A door slammed. She stood up straight. "That'll be Mum," she said. "Every so often, she gets seized with the idea that we should come out here and spring Dad. Only it's the state that put him in here, so it's going to have to be them that lets him out."

"The state?"

"The state, you know, Pennsylvania." She smiled. "How old are you?"

"Thirteen."

"Thirteen? I thought you were older. You still got to get through high school. You're better off checking yourself in here, if you ask me. I just graduated last year. Mum made Billy and me go to the Catholic high school in Brilliant with the monks. I had the creeps the whole time. I had the creeps for four whole years. But I learned how to speak French and read Latin. Isn't that nice? Isn't that going to get me far in Luna?"

"What do you mean the state put your dad in there?"

"Well, who put your friend in there? Or whoever it was you came out here for."

It got colder all of a sudden. I put my hands in my pockets. "I don't even know if she's in there."

"Is she cracked?"

"No."

"Why would she be in there then?"

"I don't know. Someone said she might be."

"You're supposed to come on Sundays if you want to visit."

"I'm here now though."

"You are." She looked at me for a minute. "You want one of these cigarettes, Lucas Lessar?" She took a pack of cigarettes out of her purse. It was a new pack and she spent some time packing them, knocking them against her leg. A tractor started up in a field nearby. I watched it work its way across the field.

"You know," she said. "I been in there about a thousand times. Dad started cracking up two minutes after we found out about Billy . . . What's your friend look like? Maybe I've seen her."

"She's like a regular lady, with dark hair."

"She nice-looking? Or is she a big mean steam engine like Mum?"

"I don't know . . . My dad, other people, they used to say she was pretty, and that she looked like Hedy Lamarr."

"Who's that?"

"She was a movie star. In old movies."

She turned around. The guard was standing outside the big doors. She shouted to him. "Hey, Red, you got anyone in there looks like Hedy Lamarr?"

"Don't I wish," he said.

She tapped a cigarette out of the pack and handed it to me with her lighter. "You know what you're doing, right? You're not going to drop dead or anything are you?"

I'd smoked cigarettes before, though not the kind she was smoking. I said, "I know what I'm doing." I lit it and took a few breaths from it, but then I started coughing. I coughed and coughed.

She shook her head. "What are you doing, Lucas Lessar? You said you wouldn't die on me."

I looked away from her. I could feel my face turning red. I held my breath to stop the coughing.

"Billy didn't like these kind of smokes either. He just rolled straight tobacco from the grocery store. I'm talking about him so much, I'm starting to sound like one of those girls that's practically in love with her brother. I wasn't like that before. I mean, I liked him all right. He was always trying to do something kind of big time. I liked that about him. You know, like

167

he was saving up so that me and him could go over to France and talk it to some actual French people instead of to some dumb monks from Pittsburgh . . . How do you know her anyway?" she said. "The dark-haired lady?"

It was hard to talk without coughing. "I just know her."

"You know, Red is kind of a bleeding heart. He let Mum bring a record in here one time to play some old ugly song for Dad. Wait here."

The cigarette was still burning in my hands. I tried smoking it some more. It was the middle of the day by then. More people were coming and going, the smell of meat boiling was stronger. A group of patients came out of a barn and went into a door on the side of the big red main building. The patients, all of them, wore the same kind of outfit; the men were in dark blue jumpsuits, and the women were in dark blue dresses that looked to be made of the same material.

I'd choked my way through the whole cigarette by the time Helen came back. I threw the butt over the fence.

"You didn't get any pleasure out of that, did you? Waste of a perfectly good smoke." She lowered her voice, "Red over there said he might be able to help you out. I sold him a big story about you. Said you walked all the way out here in the freezing cold from Banning looking for this lady, and that she was the love of your life. He says he can't get at the record book, the names, but it's lunchtime. You can get a look at a whole slew of them."

From the cigarette, the inside of my head felt like it was lined with sparks. "Okay," I said.

She held her hand out for me to shake. "I have to go see how Mum's doing, how deep she sunk her teeth into that nurse." She held on to my hand for a while. "So long, sailor," she said, walking away.

* * *

I followed Red into the same side door where the patients from the barn had gone. A couple of swinging doors later, we were in the kitchen. It was crowded with big ladies in hairnets and men in tall white chef's caps, and huge pots, and tubs of mayonnaise and spaghetti sauce as big as beer kegs. "Who's this?" one of the ladies said, pointing at me.

"Can you believe it? My nephew. Had some wrong idea to visit me at work."

He asked after her family, and her headaches, and her new shoes. While he was talking, he pulled one of the chef's hats down off a hook, handed it to me, and pushed me toward a door. I turned around and looked at him and he nodded. I went through it.

The room had green walls and big windows and spreads of long tables. Patients in the blue uniforms leaned over their trays. A couple of people stared at me. I put the hat on. They looked away.

I walked around the room, close to the wall. It smelled of boiled meat and cleaning chemicals and restrooms. A lot of the patients looked just like anyone you'd see at the store or walking on the sidewalk, going about their business; other people had waxy skin and empty stares; and others couldn't seem to help fidgeting with their food or their hair or their clothes. A few people seemed to be so tired that they couldn't pick up their feet when they were walking; they slid them along the floor.

It was the place itself, though, more than any one person, how big and strange smelling it was, that made me feel that Marko couldn't have been right about her being there. When we went out to eat, she would pick a diner if she had to, but she liked best a nice place in a department store with quiet music playing and ladies in smart shoes coming and going, carrying shopping bags with creased edges and tissue paper sticking out the top.

I wanted to find her more than I wanted anything, but when I was looking around the room, with each face I looked at and saw it wasn't hers, I felt relief running all through me. As much as I needed to know where she was and that she was safe, to find her there would have meant that she'd changed so much she would practically be a different person.

I felt someone tapping my shoulder. I spun around.

It was Red. "Oh," I said. "Hi. The guy who said she was here was wrong about it, I guess."

"No Hedy Lamarr?"

I shook my head and handed him the chef's hat. What I had to do, I knew, was listen to the note she'd left me. Stop looking for her. Trust that she would be coming back like she said. Take care of my schoolwork. "I got to get back," I said.

"All right. Hold on a minute—I need to talk to one of these nurses real quick," he said. He went away and came back a few minutes later with one of the student nurses. He nodded for me to follow them.

We walked out of the dining room and down the hall through a set of doors, and then another set. I saw a sign for the office; we were headed back that way, toward the exit. It was all I could do not to break into a run to get out of there. Just as I was about to make a list in my head, like my dad used to do to settle down, the word *California* slipped into my mind and hung there like a stubborn wish. I whispered it to myself, and I kept my eyes on the nurse's cape, waving like a flag in front of me.

We turned a corner, the nurse stepped over to the side—my head was still swimming a little from Helen's cigarette, and for a second, I had the feeling that the floor had moved so that I'd stepped out over a piece of empty air.

There was my mother, sitting in a chair next to a window, smoothing her dress.

CHAPTER 18

WHEN I SAW HER, I remembered something that happened after my father died. The two of us had taken
charge of his tomato patch. He'd always worried about keeping
the deer away. His last idea was to put hair out there. The deer
weren't supposed to like the smell of human hair, so they would
sniff it, he thought, and slink back into the woods. He told us
to ask whoever cut our hair if we could have it when they were
through with us. He was really the only one that remembered
to do it though, so the bag was full of his hair, and just a little
of my mother's. We had a pretty-good-sized bag of it by the
time the tomatoes started to come up, but by then he wasn't
living anymore. One night, after we'd seen a ten-point buck
walking around in the yard, my mother said we should put
that hair out in the garden. I said we should cut up a hose into
pieces instead; the deer would think they were snakes. I told
her I thought that would work better, but that wasn't really
what I thought. I just didn't want to touch his hair.

I watched her from inside the house. The porch light was on

and it lit up the garden. At first, she went at it slowly, being careful about where she put it. Then she got impatient and started to throw it around, tossing it up in the air, letting it stay wherever it landed. When she came inside, she poured herself a glass of water and sat down at the kitchen table across from me. Under the lamp, I saw that all over her shirt were short pieces of black hair.

She saw me looking. "What?" she said. "What?" She looked down at her shirt and then back at me.

At Bedford, seeing her, I had the same feeling I did then. I should have thought to get rid of that hair, or thought to keep her from worrying over those deer, or thought of something to help her—but up against her grief, I was always outsmarted.

"Your friend here's come for a visit," Red told her.

My mother stood up and grabbed my hand. The student nurse pulled up a chair for me. "A visit. Not even Sunday. That's nice, isn't it, Mrs. Lessar?" she said, like she was talking to a baby. I didn't sit down. My mother looked at me and looked at me and looked at me.

Red leaned over and whispered in my ear, "I'm going to have to escape you from here before the head nurse shows." He backed away but stayed nearby. Someone down the hall called for the student nurse and she left us there staring at each other.

Finally, I said, "I know you told me not to go around looking for you . . . " I ran out of breath. I wasn't sure what I was going to say anyway. I looked at the floor.

She put her arms around me. Then she stepped back with her hands on my shoulders and looked at me again. She touched my coat, ran her hands over the inside of the hood, and looked at the tag. Her hands weren't like before—they felt tiny, light, like small birds. She said, her voice cracking, "So where'd you get this?"

I had a lump in my throat that I had to work to swallow

down. She ran her hand over the scar under my eye and said, "Tell me everything."

I tried clearing my throat. It didn't help much. It was hard to talk. I said, "Why are you here?"

She stepped away from me and sat down. I sat down too. We didn't say anything for what felt like a long time. I wondered if there was a way to ever get enough sleep to fix how tired she looked. Her hair wasn't floating around her head like it usually did, like it was supposed to. It was hanging flat, and looked almost wet, greasy.

I said, "I got it out of the closet at the farm, this coat. Great-grandfather said it used to be Benci's . . . " I cleared my throat again. "The animals went away from there, even the dogs. Great-grandfather says I got to do something, have to fix it, but I don't know what to do. I don't know anything about farms or animals or—"

"Remember when Frank D'Angelo quit the police and moved into that lawn chair in his yard?"

I nodded.

"I went over there one time and said to him, 'You can't do this, Frank. You're giving my son wrong ideas about it being okay to act like this—'"

"You coming out of here with me? I figured out all the buses—"

"I would always think—when I saw him over in that chair— I would think, I would never let that happen to me. I would never fall apart like that in front of the whole town..." She took a deep breath and said, so quietly I could hardly hear her, "But I guess I did."

"What do you do in here?"

She pushed a couple of tears away with the palms of her hands. "I take some pills. I talk to the doctors and nurses."

"The state put you in here?"

"No, no, honey. That's what I'm trying to tell you. I put my-self in here. Slats and I came out—"

"I knew it! I kept saying so. I knew she knew. Why wouldn't she tell me? Why didn't you tell me?"

"I told her not to. I didn't want you seeing me like this. Or her. I told her not to come back here after she brought me up . . . It's like when my dad died, I wouldn't go to the viewing. I didn't want to remember him like that, stiff as a plank with his arms at his sides. I wanted to remember him how he was when he was mowing the lawn, or laughing at a joke, or . . . I don't want you to think about me in this getup . . . I didn't want you to know. I told her not to tell you. I'm sort of surprised she was able to keep it to herself for so long. Must be a record for her . . . But if she didn't tell you, how did you know?"

"Marko."

"Marko? How'd he know? She told him?"

"He didn't know for sure. He doesn't know for sure. He kind of—he guessed it."

"Marko," she said. "Well, he always did know me and Jimmy all the way through."

Red stepped closer to us, "We got to think about making a break for it."

"When are you coming out of here?"

She didn't say anything.

After a few minutes, Red tapped my arm. "You're going to get me in some trouble, and yourself too. They might not let you come back."

I got up to go. She reached out and squeezed my arm at the elbow and stood up. Red pulled at my shoulder and then we were walking down the hall away from her.

"About the farm," my mother called out. "Talk to Eli, maybe talk to Eli."

"But he's not a farmer."

She held up her hand in a wave, held it still.

I turned around at every step to look at her.

Everyone always said she was beautiful. I guess, looking back, it's possible that I only heard the good things they said about her, or that people might be likely to say that kind of thing to a young boy in a small town. But I don't think so. I didn't really know it until I was watching her disappear as I got farther away down that hallway at Bedford, but I think they said those things because they meant them. They were right— she was beautiful.

By the time I got the whole way back to Banning, it was almost dark. Walking to Slats's house, the line of streetlamps ahead of me started to flicker. I stopped to watch them pull themselves all the way on, and then I saw it—a long green car with a black top crossing from one side of the street to the other— the Skylark.

CHAPTER 19

Z OLI TOLD HIS FRIENDS at the Plate Glass that the night he decided to come back to Banning, he woke up thinking his pillow was on fire. He was sleeping in the back seat of the Skylark. It was bone cold. Frost was gathering on his windows, but waves of heat were pulsing all around him, like a flame coursing over his skin. He got out of the car and made a few laps around it to make sure it wasn't smoking. It was so cold he could see his breath, but his clothes were soaked in sweat.

The first thing he saw coming into town was a column of smoke. He thought the pear tree was still burning, that maybe it was some kind of magic tree after all, like Mirjana's grandfather, that crazy old Russian, had always claimed. Then he thought no, it wasn't that, it was a fire at the Plate Glass, the wires in the front wall finally burned up like he always said they would. Then he decided it wasn't a fire at all; it was just a mirage, just a fear left over from waking up with that heat on him.

He said that when he finally saw it, his house burned to the ground, the firemen standing around talking to each other, he wasn't surprised. He wasn't anything. He sat on the hood of his car and watched them walk through the soaking and blackened ruins, kicking things over.

He'd parked back in the woods and listened to the firemen. They didn't know he was there. "She's all cashed in, this little house," one of them said. "Someone's going to pay. From what I know of Zoli. Even if he started it up himself."

When they were through, they rolled up their hoses and drove away. Zoli came out of the woods and walked through his place. It was a little blackened bit of a house now. Everything was smashed. He found a few pieces of broken plates. He picked them up and carried them to his car. At the Plate Glass, he spread them out on one of the big tables at the factory and showed them to everyone.

The office girl had called Slats to tell her the news, that he was trying to get his job back, and that she'd seen him with her own two eyes practically blubbering about his lost dishes.

Slats was waiting for me when I got in the door. Before I had a chance to say a word, she told me the whole story about Zoli, all the while looking out the windows, checking the doors. She stuck her hand under the couch a couple of times to make sure the knife was still there. "Now don't worry. I already told my brothers. I called up Marko too, told him to watch out over at your house, you know, in case he sees Zoli around there. He's going to come over and get the key so he can go inside and check on things."

She stopped talking and looked at me. "You're white like a sheet. Are you all right? You know what else the girl in the office said? She told me she saw Frank D'Angelo hovering around here when she was getting out of her car this morning. I couldn't figure out what he would have wanted from me, but then I started to think that, hey, maybe it's not me he's looking for. You know what I'm saying to you? You do something to get yourself in trouble?"

"I found her," I said. "I saw her."

There was a chair behind her and she sat down in it like she was falling over.

I said, "Why didn't you tell me?" I felt like water was roaring through my ears. I could hardly hear myself talking.

"How is she?"

"You should have told me."

"She didn't want you to know, doll. She made me promise, not just that I wouldn't tell you while she was away, but that I wouldn't tell you ever. In your whole life. And don't you look at me like that . . . She thought she'd be gone just for a week, but then, I don't know what happened. It got away from her."

"How long is she going to stay up there?"

"And then she told me to stay away, and I thought I better listen to her, do what she wants. Not like some people."

"You could have told me."

"She made me swear on an actual Bible, I'm not shitting you. A real Bible—"

There was a knock at the door. Marko and Walter were outside. Slats and I went out on the porch and she gave Marko the key. There were saying goodbye, walking away, waving, when Zoli pulled up in his car and parked across the street at the Plate Glass. He had his old glass goggles on, propped up on his head, the kind he used to wear to work in the factory. I guess he was going in to make another pitch to get his job back, but he saw us. He turned around and stared. He looked hollowed out, like he hadn't eaten anything the whole time he'd been away.

I was almost relieved to see him—at least now I knew where he was. I didn't have to worry about him popping out of the woods at me everywhere I went. Everyone else was quiet. I yelled to him across the street, "Where you been?"

"Where've I been? Here and there. How about you? What've you been doing?"

"School."

"Kind of," Walter said under his breath. "Sometimes."

I kicked him. Slats was holding on to the railing of the porch, gripping it tight, watching Zoli, and she hadn't heard Walter, but Marko had, and he gave me a hard look.

Zoli took off his goggles and put them in the car. "You know about what happened to my house?"

"What do you want?" Slats said.

He crossed the street and came into the yard. He stopped at a strip of dirt next to the porch. There was a thin lead pipe sticking out of the ground near him. It was a post for Slats's roses, but since it was winter, there was nothing looping around it, no thorny stems or wires to hold up the stalk. He rested his hand on it. "Hey, Marko. Walter. How you doing, Slats?"

"I'll be doing a lot better when you get the hell out of here."

"I thought maybe . . . I don't know . . . When I saw my house, I thought maybe your brothers had been looking to get back at me for what happened at your dad's place."

"They don't do those kinds of things."

"Oh, they're like good upstanding citizens or something, not like me? Is that what you mean? What do you think, Lucas? Think they done it?"

Marko said, "All right, Zoli, how about you leave Lucas here alone."

"He knows though. Look at him. That soft mama's boy face of his gives everything away. He knows where Mirjana is. I bet too that he knows which of those brothers burned my house down." He pulled the pipe the whole way out of the ground.

He lifted it up in the air a little and it looked, for a minute, like if it hit you, you would hardly feel it, but then it swung back down to the ground and knocked against his boot and made a loud thud; it was heavy.

"You can't help me out, Lucas?" Zoli said. The lines in his forehead creased together, like he was worried. He opened and closed his hands around the pipe.

It was cold outside, freezing almost, but sweat was gathering all around my collar. I pulled it back away from my neck.

Mr. D'Angelo came driving down the street in his patrol car. He pulled into Slats's driveway, got out of his car, and said, "All right now, Zoli. I told you I was looking into it. I'm looking into it."

Zoli ignored him. "You can't help me out, Lucas?" He pointed the pipe at me.

Mr. D'Angelo said, "Okay. Okay—"

Marko said, "You know, Zoli, I only wish you were inside your shitbox house when I set it on fire—"

"Dad," Walter said. "What are you doing?"

"Marko?" Zoli said, and started to walk up the porch steps toward him.

Slats said, "Hey, you want your job back, you better not do anything more stupid than usual."

Mr. D'Angelo put his arm out in front of Zoli and stopped him.

Marko said to Mr. D'Angelo, "I did it. All right, Frank. You can lock me up, or whatever you have to do." He looked at me. "But get him away from Lucas here."

Mr. D'Angelo said to Zoli, "Let's be peaceable. You let me look into it. All right? I'll make sure everything ends up fair and square, but you got to keep away from these folks. Stay out of trouble. Can you do that? Can you agree to that?"

"All right. All right."

Mr. D'Angelo pointed at the pipe. "Get rid of that thing and get on back to your car."

Zoli opened his hands and looked at the pipe. He shrugged. "It's mine. I put it in there with Mirjana when we were trying to help Slats's flowers."

How I would wish later, still wish, even now, that someone had taken that pipe away from him just then. But he took it with him and walked across the street. He tapped it against the gravel, then he put it in his car. Just before he got in himself, he twisted up a half smile and looked at Marko.

CHAPTER 20

Next morning, Walter was waiting for me outside the
school. He grabbed my arm and yanked it behind my
back and pushed me inside the building.

"What are you doing?" I said.

"My dad said to make sure you stay in school all day."

"I'm here, aren't I? I'm not going anywhere. Let me go."

He let go. Before he'd grabbed me, I didn't have any plans to
cut school again, but I dropped my bag of books and tore out
of the building and the schoolyard and down the hill. He followed me. I cut off the road, through a gully full of brambles
and sharp-cutting dead branches. I was wearing the big coat
and I pulled my hood up so I wouldn't get scratched. I could
hear Walter cursing and knew they were getting him. Still, he
wouldn't let up on me. I could hear his feet pounding on the
ground just behind me. We ran and ran. I thought my lungs
were going to pop open in my chest. Finally, I heard him say
"Fuck it." We both slowed down, then stopped.

Walter had brambles sticking out of his coat sleeves and a

mess of scratches on his face. He leaned over and put his hands on his knees, catching his breath. We dragged ourselves out of the woods, up to the road, and I saw that we'd run the whole way to the edge of town. It was warmer than it had been in a long time. I opened my coat up.

I sat down on the shoulder and so did Walter.

"It's like, hot out," Walter said. He took his coat off.

I said, "What did Mr. D'Angelo do to your dad?"

"Told him to come down to the police station and fill out some papers later."

"That's it? What else is going to happen to him?"

"I don't know. Maybe nothing. He seemed more worried about what's going to happen to you. He was all worked up about you missing school." He kept saying, 'If Jimmy knew how much school he was skipping, he'd flip over in his grave.'"

"He isn't in a grave," I said.

A few cars went by. We were far from the school. I could see the sharp tip of the bell-tower poking between the empty branches of the trees. I said, "They're pulling out the stump today at King."

He wiped at the cuts on his face. Behind him, I thought I saw a bus coming, way down the road. He spread out his coat and pulled some nettles out of it. He looked back toward the school. "Oh man, you know how fast I'm going to have to run to get back there in time?"

I wondered what it would sound like when they pulled the stump. Benci predicted something like a homemade earthquake. The town would wobble back and forth for a second and that'd be it, the last sounds out of King. Whatever it was going to sound like, I didn't want to hear it. "Let's get out of here," I said.

"What do you mean?"

"We're already in trouble. We'll never get back up there in time."

184

He didn't agree with me, but he didn't walk away either. When the bus came, I jumped up and waved for it. The driver stopped and opened the door. "Come on, Woj," I said. The driver gave us both a hard look. "He's injured," I said, pointing to Walter. "I'm taking him to the doctor."

We stayed on the bus until it got to Luna. I found out where the Jamesons lived from a phone book in the post office. "Where are we going?" Walter kept saying.

The Jamesons' house was at the end of a long empty lane lined with pine trees. To the side of the house was a little shed with an old peeling sign that said Taxidermy. The house itself was big and faded yellow brick. There were a pair of dead starlings pressed between the storm and outer windows at the attic. Walter pointed at them. "Are you roping me into some kind of haunted house situation?"

I knocked on the door. No one answered. Walter said, "When my dad finds out, he's going to kill me, you know. He might kill you too." I knocked some more. "Then my mother will kill us all over again."

Helen opened the door. She looked different than she did when I'd seen her before. She was wearing makeup. I'd wanted to ask her about Bedford, but when I saw her, I forgot what I was trying to do.

"Hi," she said, and seemed to be waiting for me to say something.

Walter said, "You got dead birds up there." He pointed up. "In your attic window."

"Is that right?" she said. "Thanks for coming by to say so."

"You can see their bones. Bird skeletons. You probably got bird ghosts in your house."

"We probably got ghosts from all the animal kingdom in here."

Her mother came to the door and looked at us. Helen said, "Mum, they grow the strangest boys over in Banning. We should make a study of it."

Her mother shook her head and walked away.

Walter looked behind Helen, into her house. "Can we come inside?" he said.

"Woj, shut up," I said. "This is Walter," I told her, "Markovic."

"Believe you me, Walter Markovic, you don't want to come in here." She picked her purse up from a table and pulled on her denim coat with the sheepskin collar.

"Why?" he said.

"You'll get the creeps." She pulled the door closed behind her and came out on the porch. "You'll get them so bad, you mightn't recover," she said and sat down on the steps. "It's nice out here today, isn't it." The sky was cloudless, all blue.

Walter said, "I won't get the creeps. I live almost on top of the Bluebird toadholes."

She lit one of her flowery-smelling cigarettes. "The what?" she said.

"You don't know about the Bluebird toadholes? They're behind my house. There's a couple of miners trapped down there from a slate fall. You should come out to Banning. They're famous."

"Sounds like a nice place to go, a regular vacation spot."

"If you put your ear over the hole, you can hear them crying like babies."

"Is that right?" She tapped the ashes off her cigarette into the yard. She looked at me. "We're not in a library, you know. It's okay to say a few words, here and there."

"He's always like this," Walter said. "Don't worry about him. 'Gloom and Doom' Lessar."

She smiled. "You know, Walter, what we got here in Luna beats crying ghosts any day. We got our own *un feu infini.*"

"What?" I said.

"A fire that won't go out. *Un feu sans limites, un feu sans fin.* You learn your French at Catholic school and you'll learn all manner of ways to talk about fires and hellfires and things that don't end."

Helen's mother opened the door and said, "I'm going to steam the upholstery next. You helping me or what?"

"Give me two minutes, Mum," Helen said. "Okay? Upholstery cleaning will commence directly."

Her mother closed the door. Helen said, "I think this false spring has Mum all overcome. It's like she wants to wring out the house and dry it on a line." She crushed her cigarette out on the porch, stood up, and nodded for us to follow her. We walked past the taxidermy shed, through the backyard to where it ended at a stand of woods, and then we walked into the woods. There wasn't a path, but she seemed to know where she was going.

Walter asked Helen, "What kind of animals are in that taxidermy shop?"

"Strictly speaking, dead ones," she said.

"How about, are there any of that kind of fish with like a sail on its back—marlins. Or how about sharks?"

"Sharks? Walter, we are clean out of sharks in this part of Luna. The shop's closed; it's pretty empty."

"One time this guy tried to sell us one of those marlin fish to hang above the bar at the club. I liked it, but my dad didn't think it fit the décor right."

"Décor?" I said. "There's no décor there."

"That's how he wants it. If he bought this marlin, he figured he'd have to get like fishing nets on the ceiling and pretend portholes on the walls, and a couple of sea shanties for the jukebox— you know, to follow through with it. It'd kind of never end."

"Sea shanties?" I said. "What are you talking about, Woj?"

"You know what I mean, Lessar, sea shanties. Where are we going anyway?"

Just as he asked it, we were all of a sudden standing in a clearing. It was ringed with tall trees, and their branches, reaching together, made a kind of roof over the place. At the edge of the clearing, there was a log on its side. Pressed into the dirt near it were a couple hundred cigarette butts.

"Hey, this is nice in here," Walter said.

"Isn't it?" Helen said and sat down on the log. She put her hands in her pockets. "It's even better in the summer. When it was hot, Billy and me used to sleep out here. It's like natural air-conditioning." She pointed up at the ceiling of trees.

I sat down next to her.

"Who's Billy?" Walter said.

"Just my old brother," Helen said, taking her cigarettes out of her purse. She gave one to Walter and lit one for herself. "You don't get one," she said to me. "If you choke to death, Walter and I will have to drag you out of the woods. That'd be a real burden on us wouldn't it, Walter?"

"It would," he said. He lit the smoke and I waited for him to break down coughing, but he breathed it in and then out, like he was born smoking clove cigarettes. At school, Walter never seemed right; it was almost like he was too young for our grade. He never understood what he was supposed to be doing. He was always in some kind of trouble, and having the wrong answer for the teacher's questions. But from working at the club, he could do other things—add up long drink bills in his head, refuse to serve drunks four times his size, and, apparently, smoke and talk to girls older than him like it was the easiest thing in the world.

He said, "The guy had the marlin in the trunk of his car and we went out there to look at it. It was shiny and all blue and purple and green. I got kind of instantly hypnotized. You don't get to see something like that too often, right? We should have bought it. If we'd have bought it, we could have looked at it all the time. I could go home and look at it right now."

Helen was smiling. "And that would be nice wouldn't it?" she said. "I'm sorry to say there's no marlin in there, Walter, but Daddy did leave the bobcat."

"Where'd he get a bobcat?"

"Right here. I don't mean here, sitting on this log, but somewhere in these woods—"

"Can I see it?" Walter said.

"Sure, go ahead. The door's locked but you can climb in the window. It's open."

"All right," Walter said, and walked out of the clearing.

When I could tell he was out of earshot, I said, "How can I get my mother out of there?"

"Oh, I didn't know it was your mum. You didn't say."

"How long do people stay in there for?"

"All different kinds of time."

"What about your dad?"

"I don't think we should use him as our sample. Even when he wasn't cracked, he was a hard case. When you saw her up there, how was she making out? Does she seem better than before?"

"She's different."

"Better?"

"No. I don't know. Different. Tired. Real tired."

"Resting can help, and some of the medicine makes them tired so they have to rest, even if they don't want to. Strictly speaking, her seeming tired isn't a hundred percent a bad sign. How tired? Was she all input and no output? Was she doing the Thorazine shuffle?"

"What's that?"

"It's a strong medicine that gets them tethered to the terra firma, you know what I mean? Some people, they sort of shuffle instead of walk when they're taking it. It makes them too tired to lift their feet, I guess."

"No, she wasn't doing that. What'd you mean about your dad being a hard case?"

She looked at me for a minute. "I mean, well, can you promise you won't get the creeps and run out of the woods while I'm in the middle of a sentence?"

I nodded.

". . . He's been up there for years and years. And he's been in and out of places like it since me and Billy were little."

"But I thought it was just because of what happened to your brother."

"That's the story I've been selling lately. It's not too far from being true, really. If he wasn't already cracked, that would have done it to him anyway."

"I didn't know you could be in there for that long."

"Some people live out there till they die, even. I think they got a cemetery up there, behind the cornfields." She put her hand on my back. "Lucas Lessar," she said. "Your hands are shaking." She lit a cigarette and handed it to me. I put it in my mouth and shoved my hands in my pockets. After a while, she said, "I don't know about getting her out of there, but when you visit her, you could try some things to get her feeling better."

"Like what?"

"Mum sometimes brings Dad things from his old shop. Lets him sniff some formaldehyde, look at some paint brushes. Or you could maybe try to do something a little more big time."

"Like what?"

"What's her favorite thing? Something that always makes her happy?"

". . . I don't know." I choked a little on the cigarette, but she didn't seem to notice. I could hear Walter coming back, tromping through the woods. "I got to get her out of there," I said.

She said, "Do something big. It's hard to think that way around here, but you know, I try to anyways, and I think you should too, Lucas. Okay?"

I didn't know what she meant, but I nodded.

Walter stepped into the clearing, "He found that bobcat out here in these woods? That's crazy, how big that bobcat is. I like how he made it have its mouth wide open like that. You can see all of its teeth. But it makes it sort of terrifying too, right, like it's going to chew you up."

"Well, it is the crown jewel of Jameson taxidermy."

Walter asked for another cigarette. He lit it and walked around the ring of trees. "You got ice skates?" he asked Helen.

She said, "You an ice-skater?"

"I'm taking lessons," Walter said, which couldn't have been true. "You want to go skating sometime? I got a rink. I made a rink."

"You did not make a rink," I said.

"You ever see bobcats out here?" he said.

"One time, when Billy and I were out here, we saw one. We sat up and looked at it and it looked right back at us."

"What happened?" Walter said.

"I think it hypnotized us," she said. "Instantly."

Walter walked out to the center of the clearing and lay down. He put the smoke in his mouth and spread out his arms. "So this is how Lessar lives," he said. "My dad is always worrying over him. Always saying we got to look out for him. I'll have to tell him it's not so bad—Lessar's just cutting school, going from town to town, sharing smokes with Catholic girls."

We stayed there until we'd gone through her whole pack of cigarettes, and then we stayed some more.

Walter and I sat in the very last seats in the bus on the way back, across the aisle from each other.

He said to me, "You like that girl?"

"She's like a grown person, already out of high school."

"She's pretty, right? Don't you think?"

I didn't answer him.

"I like that coat she has with that nice collar—that's a good kind of coat. I'd like to have a few dollars and get a coat like that for my mother."

"Woj, your mother's like two and half times bigger than her."

"So what? I'll get a big one. And then I'll get the man's version for me."

"You want to have matching coats with your mother? Hah. What about your dad? Then you could have a whole family in the same coat."

He thought about it for a minute. "No. He don't get one. He wouldn't keep it nice." He laughed at this, and then seeing him laugh, so did I.

I looked out the window for the rest of the ride, at all the towns flying past us. Coming into Banning, the bus twisted between the boney piles, the last sun of the day lit up the skins on the sycamores. There were a few clouds out by then, but they weren't the low, mean clouds we were used to in winter, the kind that fell over us like a heavy lid. They were pure white, tall piles. I inched down in my seat so I could see high up and watch them knocking into each other.

I walked with Walter back toward our patch of houses. When we got close to the Markovics' place, I saw that there was something glittering all around the Nash. Marko was standing next to it. Walter broke into a run. Closer up, I saw that it was glass and that all the windows on the Nash were smashed. Walter walked around and around it. "We can fix it," he said to Marko. "It's okay. We just need new windows. We can get some new windows in here."

Marko looked at Walter and drew in a long breath. Later, when I would think about Marko, I would remember him as he was then. He looked to be pulling parts of himself up from his feet with that breath. He was standing a little taller than he usually did. You could tell it was hard for him, that he'd rather just drop down on the ground. He put his hand on the side of his face and ran it over the stubble on his cheeks. He ran his fingers through his hair, tried to pat it down. He took a long look at Walter. "It's okay, son. It's okay. This car, we are maybe done with this car."

Walter opened the door and used his coat to sweep the glass off the seats. He stopped a few times, turned around and looked at me. When he was through trying to clean it up, he ran at me, grabbed me around the middle, and knocked me down onto the gravel. "It's your fault, you piece of shit."

"Goddamn, Woj."

Marko grabbed his arm, but he yanked it away. "We were trying to help you. You didn't have to light that place up. That's why he came after us." He wailed at my head. "You should have told him it was you who did it, so he'd break something of yours." I saw blood on my coat. He'd hit my eye.

"Get the fuck off me," I said.

Marko came down on both of us. He wrestled Walter away from me. "It's okay, son. It's okay. It's all right."

I stood up. My ribs creaked in my chest. I went across the street to my house and climbed up through the window on the concrete blocks I'd left there the last time I'd gone inside. I looked in the bathroom mirror. Walter had dragged me over the gravel and my face was cut up. I couldn't tell yet what was going to happen to my eye, but above it I could feel pulsing. I broke a bunch of ice into the kitchen sink and grabbed some up with a rag. I lay down on my bed.

Outside, Walter and Mrs. Markovic were shouting at each

other. Marko was quiet. Mrs. Markovic and Walter started inside their house, their shouts getting muffled.

I sat up and looked out the window. Marko was staring at the Nash. He kicked the tires and spread the broken glass around with his shoe. I laid back down and held the ice to my eye. When I closed my eyes, flickers of colored light bloomed in the dark. I was dizzy.

I could hear the sounds of glass smashing apart. I jumped up and looked out the window. Marko was sliding a crowbar along the bottoms of the windows. Zoli had left the windows jagged, sharp pieces sticking in the air. Marko was trying to make it a clean break.

I lay back down and listened. When that sound was coming from the Plate Glass, or when it was coming from anywhere, really—old houses, broken-up mines—a kind of thrill would run all through me. But the noise of Marko finishing off the Nash, sweeping the glass onto the ground, made me feel like I'd swallowed a cup of needles.

To get away from the sound of it, I left the house and walked up the street toward Slats's. I turned around and looked back at Marko and his car.

Then I looked at my house. I started to walk backwards, like my mother and I used to do, until I could fit my house in the palm of my hand.

"Let me see your face," Slats shouted when I got to her yard. I couldn't even see her yet. She was looking for me through her kitchen window.

Inside, I said, "How'd you know about it?"

"I got special powers, and also, a telephone."

I sat on the edge of the bathtub. She put some peroxide on my cuts. It sizzled and stung. When she was through with me, she started in on her own cuts with the iodine. She said, "It'll turn out okay with the Markovics, don't you worry. They always stand by you Lessars."

"Who said I was worried? I don't care about them."

"Okay then."

"Can you think of something that always made my mom happy?"

"That's some kind of question. Sheez. Let's see. You, for one. Almost always, except for when you're being a stubborn shit, like you can be. I don't know. Lots of things made her happy. That's maybe why everyone liked her so much." She put the back of her hand on my cheek. "I was just kidding about you being a stubborn shit. I mean, you are one, I wasn't kidding about that, but she even liked you then. You even were making her happy then. Why that's so, I couldn't tell you. It's an actual mystery."

It turned out that we hadn't missed the sound of them pulling out the stump at King. They did it in the middle of the night, a rumble slipping into our dreams. I sat up and held on to the windowsill until it was over.

In the morning, I walked over to the pit to look at it. It was a ghost of a mine. All the doors were open on the offices and the lamp houses. They were dragging things away on trucks. The pit was still open. I walked right up to it and looked inside. It was the darkest thing I'd ever seen.

People said there were helpers that lived down in the mine tunnels, the gypsies called them *pchuvushi*. They were supposed to know which way the seam went, how to follow it, and they helped out when the very first miners started digging for it. Some people thought they showed up dressed in mining clothes, holding lamps, except they were small, half the size of regular men. Other people thought they showed up only as pieces of light. If you worked in a pit, they wouldn't let you get twisted up in the tunnels. You could follow those flashes of light back to the room you worked or the mantrip that would pull you back up the slope.

Walking away from King, I wondered if those helpers had broken loose now that our last mine was shut down, wondered if they were drifting through the woods, on their way out of town.

CHAPTER 21

T HE OTHER PERSON in Banning who used to wrestle bears in the Austrian circus was named Jumbo, and he was tall, with wide shoulders and thick arms. He was as old as Great-grandfather, but age hadn't thinned him out. He still looked like he could wrestle a bear if he needed to.

It was hard to picture Great-grandfather doing anything alongside Jumbo. There were only a few pictures of him from back then: his wedding picture and one of him standing stiff as a board next to the farmhouse, holding his hat. He didn't look, in either one of those, like he was ready to stand alongside Jumbo and take on some bears. I always liked the picture of him by the farmhouse though. You could see, if you looked closely, that the photographer was trying to make things professional, so Great-grandfather is standing on what is supposed to be some kind of black tile, but the frame of the photograph stretches past that, and you can see that at the edges of the tile the ground is white. He's standing on a few pieces of tile thrown down on the snow.

He doesn't look it, but he must be freezing, standing there in his thin suit jacket.

He never looks like a bear wrestler in any of my memories of him either, and when he started to get sick, or when he thought that ghost had taken up living in his lungs, he started to look less and less like he'd last a second with a bear. I wondered even that he'd ever worked in the mine. His fingers thinned, and the knuckles looked huge. His two hairs got longer and longer, and they blew around on his head nights when he was feverish and we opened the windows to cool him off. He slept all the time. Sometimes he gave me searching looks. "What?" I'd say. "What am I supposed to do?"

The night I went to tell him about my mother, the room was full of great-aunts and great-uncles. I sat next to him, leaned over, and whispered, "*Dedka*, I found her. I've seen her."

He gave me a long look. The skin around his eyes was turned out a little, red. He gestured to me to open the windows. He wasn't warm, or feverish, so I didn't understand why, but I did it anyway. It wasn't all that cold, that warm, almost-spring air was still hanging around, but, slowly, and I saw him watching, the great-aunts and great-uncles that were sitting in the room caught chills and went downstairs.

It was just me and him. He sat up and waved for me to keep talking. I said, "She's a little sick, so, she's in like a hospital. But she's coming out. I'm going to go get her and then I'll bring her here soon to see you and everything." I didn't have any idea how I was going to do any of the things I was saying—they just fell out of my mouth.

He got up out of bed and started rooting through his dresser. "You should probably lay back down," I told him. He covered his ears like he couldn't hear me. He got dressed in his brown overalls that he wore when he was working. He fished a coat out of the closet and then looked out a few of his windows. The only way downstairs was the steps that led to the kitchen. He went over a few times to the top of the stairs and listened. They were all down there, talking, their spoons and forks clattering on the plates.

He popped open the window in the bathroom. "What are you doing?" I said. He'd hardly been out of bed since he'd gotten sick, let alone out of the house. The window opened onto the roof of the front porch. He climbed out there. Even though he was wearing heavy farming boots, he seemed light on his feet. He climbed over the side.

I followed him. The roof was at a steep slant and it was a lot harder to walk on than he made it look. I sat down and pushed myself over to the edge. He was standing down in the yard looking up at me. He was crouching so they wouldn't see him out the window. "You got to get back in here," I said.

I looked over the edge. There were wooden square pillars that held up the roof; he must have slid down one, but they were all splintered. I didn't want to cut up my hands. I hung on to the edge of the roof, dropped my legs down, then swung out and let go. It was a far drop.

"You got to get back inside," I said. He didn't listen to me. He walked away. I followed him. We walked along the fence. He saw the hole where Valentina had chewed her way through, when she'd made her escape. He made some gesture to me that I was supposed to fix it. "How? With what? I don't know how to do anything needs doing out here . . . Who needs the fence anyway? There's no animals here to keep in."

We went over to the woods that led to Eli's house. We didn't cross into the trees though, just walked all along next to them. He stopped and, for a long stretch of minutes, stood looking into the woods and then up at the tops of the trees. I said, "What are you doing? We got to get back inside before Slats finds out you're missing."

We kept going. He walked so fast and with such a sense of trying to get something done that a couple of times I had to practically run to catch up with him. The color was back in his face. He touched the fence at each of its corners. We walked out to the pear tree. He took a long look at that too.

When we got back to the barn, he felt his way around in the dark for a few minutes and then he led me to his workshop. It used to be some animal's stall, but he'd set it up nice, all clean with working lights.

There was a big table and a wall above it covered with tools. He put all the tools out on the table and inspected them. They were all well used, molded at the handles, even the metal handles, by the long years of his hand gripping them. He turned on the sharpener and worked at a pair of sheers that had rusted.

"I'll be right back," I told him. I slipped into the house and then down into the basement and hunted around until I found those ice skates I'd seen before. I took them back out to the barn and handed them to him. He hardly seemed to notice. He was just sharpening things and polishing things up quick as he could. He moved forward, but then he stopped just as he was about to touch them to the sharpener and handed them to me. He showed me how to hold them and how to slow the sharpener down or speed it up. The skates flew out of my hands and banged against the wall. Air popped in and out of his throat; he was laughing at me. He shook his head and gave them back to me. The same thing happened again. I got it right the next time though, and cleaned the skates up pretty well. They looked ready to cut through bread.

There were some long pieces of plywood out in the barn. He

handed me a saw and showed me where to cut them. "Cut them? What are we doing out here? Building something? Can't we do it in the daytime when it's not pitch-black?"

He pointed again at the place where he wanted me to cut the boards. After what felt like forever, we finished them up. He picked them all up himself in one quick motion and went outside. I followed him.

We went back up to the fence and slapped the wood over the hole. The wood we'd cut fit perfectly from post to post somehow, even though he hadn't measured anything.

He slipped two hammers out of somewhere in his pockets and put a set of nails, one after the other, in his mouth, the sharp ends sticking out. He put a few in my mouth too. And then we set to work, nailing the boards up. He'd cut up exactly enough pieces of wood to go from the ground to the top. It was all fixed.

A car started up near the house and this seemed to wake both of us up out of some kind of dream. We walked back toward the house. It was Kaya leaving. We watched her car pull away and go up the drive. He gestured to the house. He seemed to think we should get back inside.

When we got to the front porch, he hoisted himself up on the splintery pillar and then up onto the roof. I followed him. I thought we would go inside once we got up to the roof, but he wanted to sit out there. He sent me inside to get him something to drink. "What do you want?"

He pointed back toward the pear tree.

"You want pear brandy? I thought you said we should save it?"

He waved that idea away.

I snuck some up from the basement and brought it out to him. One by one, we watched the great-aunts and great-uncles get in their cars. Slats wasn't one of them; we always left last, or stayed overnight with him. They slid up the drive in their wide cars. As each one drove away, Great-grandfather raised his bottle to them and then had a big swallowful. His spirits got even higher. Benci was the last to leave. He came out of the house, walked around his car, looked up at Great-grandfather's windows, and then got in his truck.

Great-grandfather peered inside the bottle at the pear. He hit the neck of the bottle with a short hard tap against the side of the house and broke it off. Then he pulled the pear out and took a bite of it. It was soft and dripping, like a sponge. He held it out to me. "No thanks," I said. "That pear's probably been in that bottle for a hundred years." He worked at the pear with his long fingers. I couldn't tell what he was doing.

And then he held out his hand to me—it was full of seeds. He opened my palm, put them in there, and closed my hand around them.

CHAPTER 22

S LATS AND I got to Miss Staresina's wedding late in the afternoon when it was already spilling over with women in long-sleeved dresses and high-heeled shoes, their hair fixed, their perfume mixing with the smell of smoke and food and liquor. The men were in dark pants and good shirts and shined shoes. Marko was cleaned up and shaved, his hair newly cut. Mrs. Markovic wore a shiny blue dress with ruffles that showed at the edges of her apron. The whole town was there.

I found Walter behind the bar. "I got these skates," I said and held them out to him.

He grabbed them and turned them upside down to look at the blades, then he shoved them back at me.

"I'm giving them to you," I said. "You can have them."

"Those are girl skates, Lessar. Maybe you can wear them."

"They are? How do you know? They're big though. I mean, they might fit you all right."

"I don't want anything from you."

"How can you be picky about it?" I said. "You got nothing."

He walked away. A man sitting at the bar said, "People with nothing got a right to be picky."

Slats was next to him, mixing salt and pepper into her beer, stirring around the ice cubes. "They most certainly do not," she said. "That's pure nonsense."

The man laughed.

Slats didn't smile. "It isn't funny." She called after Walter, "You take those from him, you hear me?"

I stood there for a while, waiting for him to come back, and then I set them behind the bar.

Miss Staresina favored gypsy songs and she'd hired a band I'd never seen before. They had different instruments than the bands that played the regular Croatian music. They had a violin, a couple of smallish guitars, and a single drum that a man played by sliding the heels of his hands across it. They all took turns singing the songs, going through a couple of languages and back again.

The people dancing were all sweating, their clothes clinging to their skin. Marko was walking around the room opening the windows. The band wasn't taking breaks because everyone was throwing money at them and stuffing dollar bills in their shirt pockets. These were people from Banning who didn't have much money, and who a lot of times kept watch over what they did have with knives and bared teeth.

Slats bought me a Coke, set us up at a table near the bar, and then went to get a closer look at the band and the dance floor. When she came back, she said, "They've all lost their minds."

A state trooper walked in and took a long look at all of us. He talked to a few people, and one of them led him over to Marko.

"Oh, Marko," Slats said. "Jesus Christ in heaven."

"What?" I said.

"It's about that fire."

"What about it?"

"If there's a trooper here, Marko's in pretty deep."

Marko wiped his hands and held up a glass, offering the trooper a drink. The trooper didn't take it. Then they walked outside together.

The music was loud. The band was singing one of the regular wedding songs—"May you live for hundreds of years," they sang. "May your sons grow like trees."

"In deep, like what? Going to court or something?"

"Or jail. Or having to pay for it."

"Pay for it? How would they do that?"

Miss Staresina was going from table to table, a trail of flower girls pulling her along. When she came to our table, she said "Hello, Mrs. Jankovic," to Slats, then put her hand in my hair and tugged it. "You'll come up for the dance, Mr. Lessar?" she said. Before they sold off the cake, they'd have a dance, where everyone would get a turn to have a shot of whiskey and dance with the bride for a dollar.

"Sure he will," Slats said.

"Think he'll start coming to school too?"

Slats looked confused. "He hasn't been coming?" she said, but the flower girls were pulling at Miss Staresina's hand already, taking her to another table.

"What's she talking about?" Slats said to me.

Mrs. Markovic went outside. I got up from the table to follow her.

"Where you going?" Slats said.

"To see what's going on."

"No you're not. You're going to stay where you are and explain to me what she was talking about. Sit down."

"She probably has me mixed up with someone else is all. I'm going to see what's going on."

"That trooper won't like people snooping around. You stay away. Marko can take care of himself. Most of the time anyway."

"But I want to know what's going to happen."

"I'll tell you what's going to happen. I'm going to clean your clock if you don't tell me what that teacher was talking about."

I sat down. A big drumming sound pulsed through the room. More and more people came inside. Every once in a while I'd catch a flash of Miss Staresina's dress, see her tilt her head back laughing, put her hand on someone's arm or back. Even if some of the songs were too slow to dance to, people stood up anyway and wandered around on the dance floor, just to be closer to the music.

Mrs. Markovic came into the club. Marko chased after her into the kitchen.

I got up again.

"Now where do you think you're going?" Slats said.

"To get us something to eat. I'll be right back." She tried to grab my shoulder but I'd already stepped away.

There was an opening in the wall, a kind of window without glass near the bar so that you could order things from the kitchen. Inside there were sets of roasters, two wide stoves with griddles, a big sink, and a refrigerator. I watched through it as Mrs. Markovic did something I'd never seen her do in all the thousands of times I'd been to the club—she untied her apron and pulled it off. While she was patting down her dress, she said, "That's enough, Marko. I've had enough. You know how it is. You know how it was with the rock on your chest. You take it and you take it and you take it, and then there's a day you get to the end of what you can take." She put on her coat. She brushed past me on her way out of the kitchen. Marko stood still watching her. Then she did another thing I'd never seen in all the times I'd been to the club—she left.

I went into the kitchen. Marko watched the door as it slammed shut behind her. "Marko," I said. He looked just like he had in the refrigerator that day, blinking, like he was buffeted by surprises from all sides. "What did that trooper want?" I said.

"Trooper?"

"That state trooper. What did he want?"

Walter came to the window. "She wants the dance to start now. Where's Mom?"

Marko found a tray and covered it with shot glasses, then filled each of them to the top with whiskey. He told Walter to watch the bar. He handed the tray to me. "Take care of the bride, okay, Uncle?"

I walked outside of the kitchen, slow and careful, trying to make sure the whiskeys wouldn't spill. People were already forming a line around the dance floor. A song started. A bridesmaid shouted at me to get it going.

In the line were people who used to work at King, people from the Plate Glass, from the club, other teachers from the school. Miss Staresina didn't do much more than give them a turn around before letting them go. Pretty soon, I had to shout for Marko to get more whiskey. Every beat on the drum was like a hitch, a gear, in the room's machine. It seemed like everyone I'd ever seen in my whole life growing up in Banning came up to have a dance.

The wedding was the same as all the others we'd had—no invitations on heavy paper, everyone just knew about it, and they all showed up at the club to buy some wedding cake and have a shot and a dance with the bride. I knew from the pictures that my parents' wedding had been just like it, only my parents had gotten married in the summer, and at some point in the day, my mother made everyone, even the band, walk out to the meadow she always liked down the street. Just as it was getting dark, my father realized his ring had slipped off his finger. He called a halt to the music, and everyone hunted around in the grass for it. The grass turned cold. The sky got darker. Stars came out. And finally, Marko found the ring.

When the line to dance with the bride was through, there were just two full shots left on the tray. Miss Staresina had one. Her new husband had one. I thought they were set to dance, but she thanked me for helping her out, took the money I'd collected, grabbed my hand, and pulled me out to the dance floor.

Even with all the windows open, it was hot and my head felt like someone was pumping air into it, making me lighter and lighter. A good song started up, and the next thing I knew, we were spinning around. I felt like we weren't even in the room; we seemed to be floating above everyone, like she was carrying me in the folds of her dress. It was then that I saw Zoli standing just inside the door, a winter cap pulled down over his eyes. He was hiding himself, but I knew his slouch, the way he leaned against the wall. The door banged shut. He straightened up and pulled off his cap.

Then it was over—the song, the dance. Miss Staresina planted me in a seat next to the dance floor. She and her new husband went out to the middle of the floor and stood still, holding each other, waiting for the next song. His hair was flopped down in front of his face. He'd taken his jacket off, and his tie was undone. She was smiling up at him like she was looking at the sun.

The rest of us, though, we were watching Zoli. Great-grandfather told me once that over in the old country, people died from love all the time. "Think of the music from over there," he'd said. "All songs are about love that is going to some wrong person. Love that is too nice for you, you don't deserve. Love that makes you tie bricks to your feet and walk into river."

He said things were more organized in America—people didn't die from love.

Zoli had shaved and gotten his hair cut, and seemed cleaned up, but he still looked all carved apart, down to muscle and bone. He'd walked through glass for my mother without hardly getting cut up. He'd probably lay down on a railroad track for her or step in front of a truck, and in my mind, neither of those things could hurt him. He'd always seemed practically invincible to me. But being away from her, left all to himself, worrying over where she was, I don't know, it looked like it just might take him under. Maybe Great-grandfather was wrong, maybe you could still die from love, even in Banning.

He ordered a beer, paid for it, and got change. Marko treated him just like a regular person. "Haven't seen you around," someone said at the bar. I couldn't stop staring at him, like when you come across a half-crazy dog and everyone says, don't look at his eyes, but you can't do nothing else but look.

He moved over to a far corner of the bar. He kind of leaned over his beer, keeping to himself, like he didn't want any trouble, but something wasn't right in the room. I remembered my dad explaining to me that when certain kinds of particles were floating in the coal dust, nearly anything could happen. Someone could light a spark by slamming his lunch pail down and it could blow the whole tunnel apart.

Zoli took something out of his pocket and laid it on the bar in front of him. I stood up and tried to see if I could tell what it was. He held up a piece, showing it to the guy next to him. It was one of the blackened bits of broken plate that he'd taken from the fire.

A skinny girl with a violin took a turn at the microphone. She looked to be about my age, but when she started to sing, it filled up the whole room. She was singing in a language I didn't know, but that sounded familiar. One of the men with a small guitar stood next to her and played softly, just under her voice, like a whisper, like he was standing in the yard across the street and not right there in the room with us.

Slats came over and said to the lady next to me, "Hey, you got to move, all right. I need to have a meeting of the minds here with my grandson." The woman didn't put up a fight for her chair. Slats sat down. "Do you think she's trying to break my heart on purpose or it's just something she's doing by accident? It's Hungarian, you know, same as what my mother used to talk in. Do you know how much hot water you're in with me?"

Once she said it was Hungarian, I started to recognize a few words. I heard the word *szép*, "beautiful." "What's she singing about?"

"Someone she used to know," she leaned forward and listened closer. "Or a place she used to go to? I don't know, it's just what people always sing about, something they lost . . . Zoli's in here, just came in." She looked toward the bar. "I think it's probably better if we go home."

We got up and walked toward the door, but it was too late. Whatever the song or the close air or the liquor was doing, it had already worked through the crowd. You could feel it happening, the way you could sometimes feel rain coming, the second before you were trapped in it.

I was used to missing my father by then, but a new way of missing him took a hold of my throat. He would have known what to do to make the wedding keep rolling along like it was supposed to. He might have stopped that girl from pouring that mournful song all over us, stepped close to the microphone and made some kind of joke. He would have gone behind the bar and gotten Marko and Walter away from Zoli. And Zoli would have finished his beer and put his cap back on and slunk out the door, and the party would have kept going on until it was so late that the sun would already be worrying the edges of the hills, and people would have wrapped their pieces of wedding cake in thin paper napkins and headed home, never knowing that the night could have ended any different.

Marko seemed nervous. He was pouring someone a drink, then he turned around to put the bottle back, but he did it too quickly. He thrust his hand out and punched the bottle against the row of bottles instead of into the empty place where it belonged. The bottle he was holding was bigger and made of thicker glass, and the smaller bottles just sort of popped, broke apart. Liquor ran down the counter, all over the place. Marko said, "No one light any cigarettes around here."

"You worried about starting a fire?" Zoli said.

Marko ignored him. Zoli asked him again. A few people walked away from the bar. Other people turned quiet. It all happened so fast. Zoli was at the end of the bar, so all he had to do was get off his chair and turn around the corner and then he was behind the bar right next to Marko. He picked up a broken bottle by its neck, and asked Marko again, "You worried about starting a fire?" He jabbed the ragged edges of the bottle at Marko's chest. It didn't look like he'd gotten to him, but then Marko turned toward us and his shirt was running red.

Slats was holding on to my arm. Walter took off like a shot out the door. Marko stumbled out from behind the bar and then past us, outside to the parking lot. Zoli followed him. People were trying to talk to the two of them, but it seemed like they were in a kind of bubble, just the two of them, like they couldn't hear or see anyone else. Marko looked at his shirt. Zoli went to his car and then he came back with that pipe he'd taken from Slats's house.

I still wake up sometimes remembering the noise it made when Zoli hit Marko with that pipe. He hit him full on across his chest. Marko fell back, onto the ground, and then Zoli took to kicking him with his boots and hitting his sides and his legs with the pipe. It wasn't like other fights I'd seen in town. Everyone was rushing around, trying to get a hold of Zoli, calling for the police, for a doctor, for an ambulance. They knew right away what I couldn't quite understand. But that noise, the flat muffled noise of the pipe hitting Marko and something breaking inside of him, finally made me understand—Zoli was going to kill him.

Marko held his arms up in front of his face. I felt frozen to the place where I was standing. My voice was stuffed inside my throat. Watching, I started to figure out something that the town had gotten wrong, maybe Marko wasn't in love with my mother. Not in the way they thought, maybe not even in the way he thought. It was something different, the way he always was looking out for the three of us. Never asking for anything. Drinking too much. Sleeping in that shack. He was like some kind of broken-down knight. I knew too that if something happened to him, that would be one more thing of my father's that wouldn't be around anymore. With my mother away, me and Marko were all that was left in Banning of my father—his son, his best friend. We were it.

And every time the pipe hit Marko and made that sound, I knew it should've been for me. I knew I was letting him down, and wherever my father was, I was letting him down too. I felt my voice come rushing up from the center of my chest. "It was me," I shouted. "It was me."

Zoli was swinging the pipe back to take another hit at Marko. I threw myself in front of him. Zoli stopped. "Get out of the way, Lucas, okay?"

"I did that to your house."

He squinted, "Maybe if someone put a gun to your head, you could do something that gutsy."

"It was me."

"Move out of the way." He looked at his hands. There was blood on him. He seemed like he was surprised to find it there. He stood still long enough for the men to grab a hold of him. It took him a few seconds, but he got away from them. Mr. D'Angelo came tearing down the street in his patrol car. He and Walter got out. The crowd made way for Mr. D'Angelo, and he went straight at Zoli with his club. He hit Zoli's arm with a sharp hard tap and knocked the pipe out of his hand.

Zoli lunged at Mr. D'Angelo with his fists, throwing punches where he could. Mr. D'Angelo kept twisting around him trying to get a pair of cuffs on him. He couldn't though, not by himself. Men from the club had to take hold of Zoli's arms and then they had to pin him to the ground. Someone held his head down with a boot while Mr. D'Angelo snapped the cuffs shut. They dragged him to the patrol car and sat him up in the front seat.

They came back toward us. I turned around to look at Marko for the first time. His eyes were closed. There was blood all over him, all over both of us now. "Marko? Marko!"

Mr. D'Angelo put his hand on my shoulder and moved me away from Marko. "I got to get him to the hospital. All right, Lucas?"

Three men from the club picked Marko up.

"Aren't you going to arrest me?" I said to Mr. D'Angelo.

"Why would I do that?"

The men started to carry Marko to the patrol car. His arms were hanging down, his head was tilted back, and his eyes were closed.

"For setting the fire at Zoli's house. I did that. It was me he should have come after."

"No, son, that's not right. You don't have that figured out right. What Zoli did, he shouldn't have done to anybody."

They laid down Marko in the back seat of the patrol car. Mr. D'Angelo got in the car and drove off. Walter chased after them. He ran after the car until I couldn't see him anymore.

Slats took me back into the bar, to the kitchen, and wiped Marko's blood off me. After all the noise of the screaming and the rushing sounds going through my ears, it was strange how quiet it was in the club.

Miss Staresina and her new husband were sitting at the bar and she looked like she'd been crying. The band decided to reorganize themselves. The girl that had been singing in Hungarian, the skinny girl about my age, she started out on a real quiet song—she didn't even turn on the microphone. She almost seemed to just be singing it to herself. At first, they weren't words, she built the tune of the song by humming, la la la la-a. And I knew what was coming. I braced myself. It was the song I used to think protected my father in the mine, "Samo Nemoj Ti." She sang in Croatian this time, not Hungarian, but it still sounded like a language of strung-together wishes. "*Ti si rajski cvijet. Tebe ljubiti ja neću prestati,*" she told us. You are a flower from heaven. I'll never stop loving you.

She didn't sing the song the whole way through, just a few lines over and over. My face burned with embarrassment that I ever thought something so small as that song could keep us safe, could keep us all together.

CHAPTER 23

THEY TOOK MARKO to the hospital in Brilliant, and then they had to take him to a hospital all the way up in Pittsburgh. None of the doctors at either place could get him to wake up. Walter and Mrs. Markovic stayed overnight in the hospital. No one seemed to know if Marko was going to be okay or not. Mr. D'Angelo put Zoli in the county jail for beating the life out of Marko and for resisting arrest. And the whole town held its breath waiting to find out if the police were going to have to charge him with murder.

It was Sunday, the day after the wedding. I was standing in the driveway waiting for Slats to take me up to Bedford when I heard metal banging on metal in the Plate Glass, yelling, then the sound of the metal getting dragged across concrete. I thought I heard Great-grandfather's voice floating out the windows. It was inside the scraping sound, not words or him calling out, just the pitch of his voice, its notes. I knew it was just a trick of echoes, but for a minute it seemed like the sound was a living thing, loose and gliding through the trees. I thought I could bring it back to the farm, if I could just get a hold of it, catch it between my hands.

Slats stayed in the waiting room and sent me to convince my mother that she should let Slats see her, and then we could all three visit. But when I saw my mother, I said, "I'm taking you out of here." She hugged me and pushed two chairs together. She sat down and patted the seat next to her, for me to sit. But I wanted to get out of there. I said, "We'll tell them it's time for you to go back. Me and Slats'll help you at home. We got Great-grandfather doing better. Me and him went outside and fixed a piece of fence."

"He's sick?" She looked worried. Her voice was quiet, and her words came out slower than they should have.

I sat down. She looped her arm through mine. "No," I said. "Me and Slats fixed him . . . We're practically doctors."

She smiled, but she closed her eyes too, for a second, like she might fall asleep.

I said, "Do they give you that medicine that makes you shuffle when you walk? Thorazine?"

"How do you know about that?"

"I told you, I'm practically a doctor."

"Ha. No. They didn't give me any of that. Not yet anyway." She took a big breath and said, "Listen, I got to tell you something. Everything happened so fast when you were here before . . . I'm sorry about all of this . . . And . . . Isn't this something, I've been planning this out for days, what I was going to say, and I just . . . Well, it can wait a minute." She started to tap her foot back and forth, like she was nervous. "How are you, L?" she said. "Did you go talk to Eli about the farm? Did those animals come back?" She nodded a little toward the window. "Tell me how things are out there."

". . . Something happened to Marko."

"What?"

But there was too much. If I told her about him, I'd have to tell her about what I'd done to Zoli's house and what had happened to Great-grandfather's pear tree. I didn't know how to start. I said, "How come we only save pictures of people, and not other things about them?"

"Like what?"

"Like how they sound when they talk. How come people don't try to save that, you know, on a record or something. Their voices."

"You can't just make a record. You need a special machine." Outside the room, people were walking up and down the hallway. Visitors, patients, nurses, doctors. "I guess you're right though," she said. "I mean, it'd be nice to have other things, but people do tend toward the concrete. They like to have a picture, not something like a voice."

"Remember how Dad used to say we should go up to visit that place where the old-growth trees are still living, Hearts Content? Maybe if we went up there, that'd be like saving something, not like a picture, but, you know, doing something he wanted to. I don't know. Do you think it's a real place, even? Me and him couldn't find it the one time we looked at the map. He could have made it up. Great-grandfather told me about this place, Banning Two. He talked about it like it was real. But I found out that he made it up. That's what he calls the place where his friends went to, his friends that are gone, you know, dead."

"Hearts Content. Sounds nice. If Jimmy made that up, he did a good job of it. You have to like the sound of a place like that, don't you, L? But what were you going to tell me before? What happened to Marko?"

I still had the feeling that if I started tell her, I wouldn't be able to stop talking. I said, "Slats brought me here. She wants to see you. She's downstairs."

217

She unlooped her arm from mine and put her hands in her lap. "Well, see, that goes back to what I was trying to tell you before. I don't know that I can do this, have you seeing me. Like this." She opened her hands and looked at her palms.

"She doesn't have to come up," I said. "I'll tell her I forgot about her."

"I don't think you understand about me not wanting you, or her, up here—"

"We wouldn't have to take the bus back, if you left with us. She's got Brown Lu here." I was talking really quickly, my words running together. "We could just drive away. If you don't want to go back to the house. We could go wherever you want. Even we could go up to Hearts Content. Find out if he was just handing us a story. We'll drive up to the Allegheny Forest and . . . " I stopped talking and caught my breath.

"Oh, Lucas . . . I'm sorry."

I knew that meant she wasn't coming with us. I looked out the window. I said, "I heard they grow pigs out here, like on a real farm."

"If you get better, they let you go outside and do farm work."

"Really? Sounds backwards. Seems like if you got better, they'd let you go to the movies or something."

"I don't know. I think I might like it, but you have to be feeling better first, so, well, I haven't been out there."

"I think Great-grandfather's farm is coming apart. He told me you used to like to swim in that pond of his. Is that true? I'd never get in that water. It looks like old coffee."

A ruckus broke out in the hall; it sounded like a couple of chairs falling over.

"I haven't done that since I was a kid. It was the only pond I knew though—I probably thought they were all that color."

"Mom, how long are you going to be here? I heard some people stay in for like years and years."

"Sweet, I need you to try to listen to what I'm telling you about coming here—"

Two guards and a nurse ran past the room we were sitting in. They were carrying between them what looked to be a big set of sheets. "What's going on out there?"

"They're frozen, those sheets. They stir them in tubs full of ice."

"What are they for?"

"The people that are real worked up, the nurses use the sheets on them."

"Why?"

She took a long breath. She didn't yell at me very often. She'd leave my dad to do that kind of work. Or sometimes when he wasn't around, she'd call Slats over. But the few times that my mother did yell at me, she did what she was doing just then, that long inhale. She looked right at me. "I mean, what I've been trying to tell you is that I'm decided about it. I don't want you coming up here, L. Not anymore, okay? I want you to stay in Banning. Keep getting yourself through school, and getting those good marks like you've always done. I'll see you soon, but not here, okay? I'll see you another time."

"Why?"

The guards walked past the door again, going the other direction, and they had a patient with them. They were holding him up, one on each side of him. He wasn't yelling or anything, but he was long and lanky and he kept twitching away from them. They had to pull him down the hall.

"Because you shouldn't be seeing these kinds of things. You shouldn't see that man like that. You shouldn't see me like this. I got to protect you in the only way I can now. It doesn't mean I don't love you to the ends of the earth, but, just, you take care of things at home, take care of Slats. Even if I do have to stay for years and years, I don't want you coming back here." She covered her eyes. "I'm sorry, Lucas. I'm sorry." She got up and walked out the door. I went after her.

She started down the hallway. In the other direction I saw Helen and her mother chasing after the guards and the man the nurses were going to use those icy sheets on. Helen's mother was shouting at the guards, "Now come on. He's all right now. He's okay now." It was Helen's father.

The guards barreled through a set of swinging doors. The doors swung back and knocked Helen's purse out of her hand—all of her things went flying. I went over and crouched down on the floor with her and helped her put everything back in her purse. She looked up at me like she didn't remember me, or didn't know me, then she took off after her dad. Before I stood up, I saw, under a chair, her lipstick case, the one with Billy's cigarette. She'd missed it. I grabbed it and yelled after her. "Hey!" I said. "Hey!"

By the time I turned back to my mother, she was gone.

CHAPTER 24

T HE FARM WAS CROWDED with great-aunts and great-
uncles that night. They milled around talking about Great-
grandfather and their bosses and their kids and how they needed
to hose down their aluminum siding and re-pave their drive-
ways. The other boys had found some of Great-grandfather's
old mining equipment stored away in the cellar and they kept
asking me to come look at it. But I stayed in the kitchen with
Slats, where we sat without talking and stared out the windows
or into our glasses of Coke. She hadn't said a word since I'd
told her about what happened with my mother, and all the
way from Bedford to the farm, she'd made little almost-crying
sounds. I couldn't stand it. I'd pulled my hood forward over
my ears.

Kaya said to Slats, "You all right?" She pointed at me, "You
two don't look right."

Slats didn't say anything.

Kaya said, "Well, we all got things to worry about here
but . . . " her voice trailed off and she looked up, toward the

stairs. We all turned to see what she was looking at. Great-grandfather was standing there, smiling. He was wearing blue workpants and a collared white shirt. His face was shaved clean and his two hairs were brushed back. It was the first time they'd seen him out of his pajamas since Christmas.

"Daddy?" Kaya said, like she couldn't quite be sure it was him.

He came down into the kitchen and then went into the dining room. We followed him. He still couldn't talk, but he could whisper a little, and he could throw his arms all over the place to let us know what he was thinking. He was in terrific admiration of all the liquor that had been assembled while he'd been recovering. Usually, at parties, we'd have a card table set up for the bottles of whiskey and vodka and pear brandy, and a few jars of moonshine cherries. They'd been bringing by things to eat and drink since he'd gotten sick, so they'd have something there while they sat in the living room, taking turns to go up and sit with him. There was so much liquor collected by then and so many plates of apricot roll and cookies, that they'd done away with the card table altogether and started using the dining room table—it was covered.

Great-grandfather opened a bottle of pear brandy and poured himself a shot. Everyone took this as a sign of his recovery and they started to drink the pear brandy too. They started talking, louder and louder. Great-aunts and great-uncles who hadn't been there earlier in the night showed up, and pretty soon the house was ringing with arguments, stories, songs—just like it always used to.

Benci though, he kept quiet and he stayed in a wide chair in the corner of the living room, watching. I went over and sat next to him. He handed me his cup of whiskey. I don't think he knew what he was doing, but no one at all was paying attention to either one of us; they had their eyes fixed on Great-grandfather. It was a whole family, a huge, loud noisy family, breathing a ragged sigh of relief.

I drank the little that was left in the cup. He took it back and poured himself another one and then another one. The whiskey hadn't made me drunk but I felt like I had a lit match stuck in my mouth. I went to the kitchen and drank from the faucet. Slats came over and said, "I got an idea. Why don't we go over it, what she said up there. You know? Maybe she meant something different from what you think she meant. You tell me again all the things she said."

I shook my head and went outside. Great-grandfather was out there with some of the great-uncles standing near the porch. They didn't see me. I stepped away from them, out into the dark, and watched from there. They were passing around a bottle of Great-grandfather's pear brandy. I didn't understand why he wasn't worried about saving it anymore. They were all drinking it like it came out of a tap, making up toasts for each other. Great-grandfather looked like he did the night we'd walked the farm together. His cheeks were red. He kept breaking into choking laughs at the great-uncles and the things they said. The light from the porch shone in his eyes.

I'd put the pear seeds he'd given me in one of Slats's bank envelopes and put the envelope in my coat pocket. I felt them to make sure they were still there.

I walked down past the barn and up to the pear tree. I remembered the book I'd seen at the feed store. All there was to do for a tree with fire blight, it'd said, was to watch over it, look out for the branches that hadn't been ruined, and cut the rest. I guessed that the same thing might not work for a tree really torched with fire, but I went ahead and wiped what was left of the snow from the low branches and pulled at the burned bark.

Pear trees turn colors three times a year. The leaves change in the fall and spring like other trees, and when they blossom they turn all white and get to looking like big pieces of puffed cotton. I wiped down more of the tree, using the sleeve of my coat. It seemed to me that if Great-grandfather and I were going to get things right at the farm, like he wanted, we'd have to start with the tree, but I couldn't see any live parts left. No matter what I did, how much I wiped it down, the black of it glistened, stubborn and dead.

I didn't know it until I looked back at the house, but my eyes were blurred over. I was crying. I felt in my pocket for the envelope of seeds. The ground was still too frozen really to plant anything, but I didn't know what else to do. I dug a couple of lousy divots with my shoes and put seeds in them and covered them over. I wanted to wake up in the morning to some full-grown pear trees, bottles already on them.

I knew that if I went in the house, I wouldn't be able to get away from Slats. It was still a little warmer than usual and I had my big coat with the hood, so I climbed up into a deer stand from where I could see and hear and watch the party. I wished that I had a cigarette and I remembered that I did have one. I pulled Billy's out of my pocket. I thought of the way Helen had looked through me, like I wasn't even there. I'd probably never see her again anyway, since my mother didn't want me going up there anymore. I went ahead and put it in my mouth. I could feel the paper start to sort of disintegrate right away. It had a strange taste, the melting paper, the old tobacco. I checked all the coat pockets for some matches, but there weren't any and I didn't feel like climbing out of the deer stand yet. I kept it between my teeth for a little while, then I put it back in the case.

The noise of the party was warm, and comforting, like some kind of heavy blanket. I fell asleep right there in the deer stand.

I dreamt I was in a busy train station. The man behind the

ticket window asked me where I was headed. "Hearts Content," I said. He handed me a ticket. I held it tightly. I walked out onto the platform and opened my hand to take a look at the ticket. Only, there was no ticket, there was a butterfly, and it flew up into the air. In the sun, it flashed white then yellow then orange. It wouldn't stop flying around me, and then I understood that I wasn't supposed to take a train, I was supposed to follow this butterfly.

We were outside the train station, then we were in the woods. There were more and more trees as we went along, and the woods got darker, but the path held out, faint, harder and harder to see. I kept my eyes half on the ground and half on the butterfly.

I tripped on an old carbide can. It was in the middle of the path. Since it was something I always did when I found one, I got some snow, put it in the can, smashed the lid down hard, and ran back away from it. When it blew, thousands of birds I hadn't even noticed were there before, flew out of the trees around me, black birds, crows, barn swallows; they covered the sky.

Great-grandfather came out from behind one of the trees. "*Dedka?*" I said. "Where are we? What is this place?"

He came closer to me and I saw that he was bone pale, and had stubble all around his cheeks. "Lucas," he kept saying. "Lucas." He pointed behind him and I saw that the birds had been blocking my view, and that beyond the trees were mine buildings—a lamp house, a tipple. "Banning Two," he whispered. "It's Banning Two, where I am."

"*Dedka!*" I shouted, and my shouting woke me. I opened my eyes. I must have been sleeping there for a while. It was still dark, but there was light at the edge of the hills. Benci was standing at the foot of the tree, saying, "Lucas." I sat up. "Lucas," he said again. I looked down at him. And I knew, sure as

CHAPTER 25

FROM STAYING AT SLATS'S HOUSE, it had gotten so I knew just about every sound that came out of the Plate Glass. The machines switching on early in the morning. The rhythm of the factory doors opening and slamming shut at different times of the day. The ping the straps on the trucks made after they'd slid a sheet into place.

I'd started to think that the second something went wrong with a piece of glass, I could hear it. It seemed like I could hear the beginning of the break and each sound that followed—the fissures opening the sheet; the shards hitting the concrete floor; the long-handled broom they used to gather the glass, getting pushed across the floor.

In the days after Great-grandfather died, I kept wondering if, when we died, could we feel every part of us loosening and falling like that? Had Great-grandfather felt all the steps he took going away from us? Did he know it the second that something started to go wrong in him? Had my father known when something started to go bad in the fireshot? Would I know when it happened to my mother? To Slats? Would I know when it happened to me?

Great-grandfather died in his sleep. Slats would be telling me about something else altogether and then she would just stop and look at me and say, "He died in his sleep." When she had to call friends of the family, she said to each of them, a few times a piece, "He died in his sleep."

She turned to me after one of these phone calls and said, "Why do I feel so terrible? What's wrong with me? He had a long life. What else did I want for him? To see actual angels come and carry him into the sky?" She shook her head.

I didn't have a suit to wear to the funeral. Slats had to borrow a shirt with a collar and a jacket for me from one of her brother's grandsons. The jacket was too big and the shirt was too small. It didn't make sense. I put my big hooded coat on over it anyway.

Slats wore her nicest shoes. The nail was sticking out of the heel of one of them. She asked me to fix it, but I couldn't move around in that shirt, and I said no.

She tried taking me up to the front of the church to sit next to her and the great-aunts and great-uncles, but I didn't want to sit anywhere near the priests; they were the ones who'd carried Great-grandfather's death into his house and left it there.

The service started. I went and sat next to Eli. "What are they supposed to be like, those tollhouses you were telling me about?" I said.

He shrugged. "I don't know anyone to come back from them. Ha."

The lady in front of us turned around. "Shhh," she said.

I whispered. "I told you I was no farmer. I couldn't do anything to help that farm. It's like how you were supposed to be a magician, but you couldn't do it."

"I am supposed to be magician?"

"That's what he said, Great-grandfather. Your dad was some kind of famous sorcerer, and he tried to make you one, but you were lousy."

"Famous for magic? My father? I don't think so. Maybe for crazy. How can he be famous? He makes only one trick. Always the same. No variety."

"What was that?"

"You won't believe, but people would give him money to write wishes on small papers."

The lady in front of us turned around and shushed us again.

"What kind of wishes?" I said.

"People say to him what they are wanting. Then on papers he writes first who he is, his name, then his father's name, his father's father's name, to make known who he is. Then he explains what it is that customer needs. You want for something or not for something. He would write this. Then he takes paper and buries it in ground. He tells them putting them in the ground makes the wish happen. But he says to me that he must put them in ground because they are so much nonsense, people want things only that they can't have, impossible things. They should feel shame."

"What did they ask for?"

"To have someone that is not in love with you to love you. Someone who is dead to not be dead."

It was getting hot in the church, or maybe I was wearing too many clothes. The candles were hot. They were burning too many candles. Up ahead, I could hear Slats walking around, her wrong shoe with the nail sticking out. Click, quiet, click, quiet.

"Did it work?" I said.

"Maybe sometimes. From coincidence." He sat up a little out of the pew to get a look at the coffin. "I don't know," he said, when he sat back down. "Sometimes there's nothing else to do anyways, you might as well make a wish on a small paper. Have to try out something. Better to do that than have all of your wishes caught insides your throat."

The walls of Great-grandfather's church were covered with *ikonas* with gold backgrounds. All the painted saints had small mouths because they kept quiet, and large ears because they were good listeners to God's words. They had eyes as big as dishes so they could see fully the works of God.

I guess they said things about Great-grandfather at the funeral. I only remember the saints staring at me with their gigantic eyes. The works of God, I thought. That's us, we're the works of God. It wasn't the kind of thing I'd ever thought about before. My palms were sweating, all the middle of me was sweating. I unbuttoned my coat and my suit jacket. My shirt was changing colors, the sweat darkening it in patches.

I turned around to see what was behind me. I saw Jumbo, the other bear wrestler from the Austrian circus. I went and sat next to him. "*Ochen' zhal*,'" he said.

People had been telling us they were sorry all day. I wasn't sure how to answer. "All right then, Jumbo, *spasibo*," I said.

I liked Jumbo, after a few minutes, though, I felt like he was so big that he was giving off heat, like a turbine engine, like the machines that poured the glass at the factory. I went back farther, away from him, to the last row in the church, an empty row. I laid down on a kneeler. I thought it'd be cooler by the floor. I looked up at the colored windows. I tried to pray for Marko. They still hadn't gotten him to wake up. I tried to follow along with the prayers, but I couldn't get any words to stay still in my head.

I heard Slats's wrong shoe getting closer and closer. They were all walking out of the church. I got up and followed them. Outside, I couldn't understand why I was so hot, the warm weather we'd been having was gone and there was snow everyplace again.

All the people around me were wearing coats and hats and scarves, their breath freezing in the air above them.

The next time I paid attention to what was happening, we were all inside the house like we always were for Christmas Eve or other parties. The great-aunts in aprons carried things into the house from their cars, or from visitors' cars. There were brightly painted plates and different kinds of food, all over every inch of every table. Everything was the same, except that everyone was wearing black, and they were all dressed nicer than usual. The great-uncles were busting out of their suits, their ties weren't right. And everyone was doing what they usually do at those kinds of parties, except that Benci sat away from everyone in that corner chair, drinking whiskey. Everyone, actually, seemed to be drinking more, and drinking with more of a sense of purpose; more like they were mowing a field than that they were trying to have a party. Everything was just like Christmas Eve except that people were crying and talking in low voices, and except for how Great-grandfather wasn't there to tell us his story about coming to America.

And everything we ate was the same too, except that when we made the *kutya*, we didn't put any honey or poppy seeds on it. We ate it plain, because it was a funeral, and that's how you're supposed to eat it at funerals. It sat in my mouth like thick pieces of paper, and I didn't want to swallow it, because if I swallowed it, I thought it would mean that Great-grandfather really was all the way dead and gone away from us. I went outside and spit it in the trough where the cows used to eat.

I was standing outside by myself, heat coming off my skin. I took off my coat and the borrowed suit jacket and hung them on the antenna of Brown Lu. I walked out toward the fields, where it looked colder; the snow was piled in deeper drifts.

The sycamore trees were so white that the woods looked like

they were made of bones. I walked up past the pear tree. The sky looked like a piece of slate, and low clouds slid across it.

I guessed that Great-grandfather was up there, or his soul, or whatever of him got to go up, trying to get past his accusers. But, I thought, maybe none of those things happened, maybe you just dropped over into darkness and then into the ground, and then silence, like the men trapped in the Bluebird pit.

I walked into the woods. Maybe I walked for hours, I don't really know, but the woods got messier, the trees got bigger. A few times I thought I heard someone walking behind me, but then I'd stop walking and find that it was just the noise of the wind working on the trees, or my walking unsettling the leaves.

I came over the crest of a hill, and when I stopped, everything fell quiet. But then, out of the quiet, came that other sound I'd heard outside the Plate Glass, Great-grandfather's voice, or the sound of his voice, the texture of it, racing around in the trees.

I had the feeling of him being scattered all around the property, and so I had the feeling he was with me. The wind blew at the dead leaves and old snow. It seemed like things were picking up speed in the sky. The clouds were twisting, gray then black then gray. They churned like sheets holding twisting bodies. I looked down and looked up again, and they changed. The sky was crowded with what Great-grandfather told me was up there—the angels and the devils the Archangel Michael had kicked out of heaven. I touched my eyes to make sure they were open, that I wasn't asleep, because I knew it didn't make sense, but I *could* see them. They had bodies like men, but terrible teeth, and shining wings that looked like they were made out of hammered metal. Their teeth scratched as they tore into each other.

I put my head down and kept going. I thought getting some wind on my skin would help me cool down. I broke into a run.

Branches were hitting and scratching at me. The trees turned a white so clean I had to squint when I got close to them. I ran until I found a deep drift of snow, and then, I lay down in it.

Great-grandfather was sitting next to me. Are you going to be living up in that pear tree now, *Dedka*? I asked him. Sometimes you used to call That One *dedushka*, "grandfather." Does that mean when it was living, that it was someone's grandfather, your grandfather? I never asked you. I can't imagine you having a grandfather, old as you were when I knew you. But I guess you did.

Are you a ghost now? An angel? Or just under the ground? Why didn't you tell me what would happen to you? Is it going to be too quiet there, like the bottom of the Bluebird mine? When your soul was twisting up through the air, did you have to fight through those packs of angels and devils? What am I supposed to do now? In all this snow? Nothing's colder than this, can't imagine there being anything colder. No, that's not right, I can imagine something—those sheets I saw at Bedford. Those are colder.

Then we were walking together, me and him. In front of us there were double wooden doors, a stone wall. He pushed them open, and inside it was the orchard—the orchard of the Slovenian monks. There were the pear trees, the bottles on the branches. Sun was shining off the bottles, the pears were bright inside of them. And there were leaves on the trees, on the hundreds and hundreds of trees. A forest made of glass.

I don't remember much else from the time I spent wandering through the dark hallways of that fever. Always with me was the feeling of being hot or of freezing. I went back and forth from one to the other without climbing up or down through other temperatures. The sheets seemed to be soaked in mustard plaster, burning my skin, or made of ice. And always, Great-grandfather was next to me.

Close to the end of it, I woke up in his house. The room was dark. I sat up. I touched the sheets. They felt regular, not hot or cold, just soft and warm. Slats was asleep on the floor next to the bed, trying to fit all of herself under her coat. Eli was in the room too, sitting in a chair, asleep. He'd been drawing; next to him on the floor were a few sheets of paper, some twigs he'd turned to charcoal.

Great-grandfather was gone.

The room was cool, the windows were cracked open. I was in the room where, on Christmas Eve, I'd spotted Zoli splashing gasoline all over the tree. I picked up one of the sheets of Eli's blank paper. I started to write a letter to my mother, to tell her everything that had happened. I didn't get very far. It seemed hopeless to try to explain everything. I crumpled the paper and took another piece. I wrote,

My name is Lucas Lessar. I'm named after a dead great-uncle who was named after a dead baby. I'm the son of Mirjana and Jimmy Lessar. I'm the grandson of Raisa Jankovic. I live in Banning. I am writing this all down on this piece of paper to ask for the Tot-to to come back to the house here and look after us like Great-grandfather said it used to.

I folded the paper and put it in my pocket. I went outside. That last stubborn piece of winter seemed to have melted away. I must have been sick and asleep for a long while. I kept my eyes on the ground while I walked. I was afraid to look at the sky. I was afraid I was still in the fever, that this was just another piece of it, and that those angels and devils I'd seen before would still be up there fighting each other. I walked up to the pear tree. I was pretty weak, and it took me a couple of tries to get a foothold on the tree good enough to climb to a place where there was a kind of opening, a hole. I pushed my note inside.

Climbing down, I could feel under my hands, a couple of branches that were still living, maybe coming back for the spring.

When I got to the stoop of the house, I grabbed the door handle, closed my eyes, and tilted my head back, facing the sky. If those angels were still there, I knew it would mean I was still locked up in the fever after all.

I opened my eyes. And it was just regular sky, clean and black. The farm was quiet. I looked out over it. While I was sick, it seemed to have shrunk, everything looked smaller, fragile even.

I let go of the door handle and walked back out into the yard. I leaned over, tore up some grass and some dirt, and put it in my pockets. I tore up some more grass and I put it in my mouth. And then dirt too. I chewed it and swallowed it. I walked back inside.

PART THREE

CHAPTER 26

I T USED TO BE that before Christmas Eve dinners Great-grandfather would throw some of the *kutya* up to the ceiling and see how much of it would stick. If a lot of it stuck, it meant we'd have a good spring on the farm, but if it fell down in quick clumps, we were in for it. After Great-grandmother passed away and Slats took over the dinner, she did away with all that. She thought it was a useless thing to do and she didn't like cleaning it up afterward.

The only times I paid attention was when the *kutya* fell someplace it shouldn't have—dropped onto someone's dress or hair—and I hardly noticed when we stopped doing it alto-gether. But when I was climbing out of my fever, I wished we had done it at Christmas. It would have been good to have some idea about what was coming. And if it had been a lucky hit at the ceiling, it could have been some assurance to lean on, even if it was something as slight as a smudge of porridge on the ceiling.

* * *

After I was well enough to leave Great-grandfather's house, Slats gave it a cleaning and we locked it up and left. Benci took Valentina to his place so he could look after her. Slats kept me home from school because of how sick I'd been. We stayed all the time in her part of Banning, where I seemed to sleep most of my days away, sometimes on the couch, other times out on the fake grass on her porch. All Slats did was work and read magazines and take my temperature, and talk about Great-grandfather. We never went to the club, or out to see any of the other great-aunts or great-uncles.

I kept two things with me all the time: Helen's lipstick case with Billy's cigarette tucked inside, and the picture I'd found on my mother's desk that said *J and L at county fair* on the back. I still couldn't find my father in the picture. While I was wasting away those days sleeping and listening to Slats talk about Great-grandfather, I tried reading the picture like a map. Going over each square of space to see if I could find my father. In the picture, I'm holding the reins like I'm in charge, turned a little to the camera with a royal-looking smile that I must have outgrown.

Zoli had broken a good number of Marko's ribs and one of those ribs had poked a hole in a lung. He had also crushed his knee and the doctors wanted to put a pin in his leg to hold things together. Marko was knocked out cold for days and days, and when he finally did come to, he had to stay in the hospital for nearly a month. Slats drove out to the hospital to see him, but when she did, I stayed behind at her house.

"You ought to call the hospital and say hello to him at least," Slats said. But I couldn't get myself to. I was afraid of what he might sound like, broken like he was, or what he might say to me.

* * *

While I'd been sick, Zoli had scraped together enough money to bail himself out of the jail. Slats told me he'd hovered around the farm, driving his car up and down the driveway every once in a while, until she'd called Frank D'Angelo. After that, Mr. D'Angelo took to following Zoli everywhere he went. He wouldn't leave him alone. By the time Slats and I moved back to her house, Mr. D'Angelo had driven him half-crazy.

The last thing Zoli did before he left town was tear around all the streets of Banning in the Skylark. Something had gone wrong with the muffler or the engine, and it was almost as loud as Benci's truck. We'd only been back to Slats's house for a day when he did it. I was sitting out on her porch swing, half asleep. I could hear his car in the streets behind her house. I knew I should get up and go inside, but I was still feeling weak and doing everything in almost slow-motion, and the next thing I knew—there it was, the Skylark, sliding past the house.

I sat as still as I could, but he saw me up there, slowed down, and stuck his head a little out the window. He had to practically shout for me to hear him over the muffler, but he didn't use the voice he used when he wanted to scare the crap out of me. He said, in a kind of serious voice, like it was important business, "You take care of yourself, all right? And your mom."

I knew that in the next minute he could change his mind and be up on the porch with his hand wrapped around my neck. I didn't breathe again until he drove away. I didn't feel any better when the sound of the car got quieter and quieter and then disappeared. And I didn't feel any better the next day or even the next, when we all figured out that he wasn't coming back. I mean, I'm still afraid of Zoli. Even now the hair on my neck stands up every time I see a green Skylark with a black top.

* * *

As soon as I was feeling well enough, I went to Luna. I handed Helen the lipstick case when she came outside. She opened it. I thought she'd be happy, but she looked like she might cry. We sat down on the steps of her porch. She was quiet for a while, and then she said, "You spring your mum out of there yet?"

"No."

"You sound gloomy, like you're giving up."

"I don't know what to do."

"Me either. I don't know why I'm telling you not to give up. Just seems like no one ever gives advice saying you should give up. You got to try and think of something. It'll be a big idea, maybe it won't even fit inside your head." She laughed and lit a cigarette. "We're going away, me and mum. Dad's in a real fix. So they're letting us try another place. It's up in Pittsburgh. Mum's got a sister lives there."

"When will you come back?"

"You think I should just smoke that cigarette of Billy's and get it over with? I had five heart attacks trying to think of where it was. I was about to steal some of Dad's medicine to get myself calmed down. If I smoked it, I wouldn't have to worry about it anymore."

"No. You should keep it."

"For how long?"

". . . Maybe keep it until the fire goes out in the mine."

"In other words, forever," she said, and smiled.

We didn't really say much of anything else to each other, but I didn't want to go and she didn't ask me to. We stayed out there for a long time, until the only light was the charged end of her cigarette. Of course I didn't know it then, but it would be years before I would see her again. We would be standing on the street in Brilliant. She would be the same, all that black hair. But I would be different, taller than her, and she'd hardly recognize me. "It's me, Lucas," I'd have to tell her. "Lucas Lessar. It alliter-ates, my name. You used to like that about me."

When Marko came back to Banning, they had to bring a hos-pital bed to his house. They cleared out the living room and put the bed in there, right by their front picture window. Slats made them a casserole and asked me to carry it over.

"You should take it. You cooked it," I said.

"His wife's so busy she doesn't have time to turn around. They probably don't have a thing to eat."

"You take it."

"You know those Markovics always come around for you Lessars. You got to do the same."

"Just go. I'm too tired."

"How come when I need you to do something, you're tired, but anytime you want to go someplace, you got plenty of en-ergy?"

"I really am tired now, though. You're making me tired."

After she left, I went up through her attic to the roof and looked out toward the Markovics' house. I looked out over the hills to see if I could see the smokestack at Bedford poking out, but I couldn't. I went back down into the house, found a magnifying glass in Slats's desk, and went to work all over the picture again. I liked the way everything looked all stretched out of shape under the glass, even the trees. I was getting a kick out of moving it over the horse's face, looking at his long eyes. Then I saw, down near the horse's hind legs, a pair of boots, the cuffs of work pants. My father. He was standing back there hiding himself from the camera, but he must have been holding me up.

The next morning, I took the picture with me and walked over to Marko's house. The curtains were opened, and he was in the hospital bed, almost like on a display. He was all bruised, his eyes were shut, his face was a kind of pale green. Walter must have been at school already. I saw Mrs. Markovic in the kitchen, cooking. When I looked back at Marko, his eyes were open. He held his hand up and waved for me to come inside.

When I came to the door, Mrs. Markovic wrapped me up in her big arms and kissed my forehead. I felt all choked up, just like I did last time she did that. I shut my eyes tight to keep them from watering.

Marko held out his hand for me to shake. He sat up a little in his bed. I stood next to it. I didn't know what to say to him. I pulled the picture out of my pocket and showed it to him.

"It's you?" he said.

I cleared my throat. I turned the picture over and showed him my mother's handwriting, *J and L at county fair*. "See, he's back there." I showed him the boots. "I found him."

He held it away from his face, "Jimmy. Huh. That's something."

"That pin in your leg, can you feel that it's there?"

He was still looking at the picture. "It's just like him, kind of hiding, but there, still there. He'll never leave you, you know. It's like now—we can't see him, but he must be around somehow, helping us."

"Marko," I said. I cleared my throat again. "Sorry."

"For what?"

"For what happened to you."

"The pipe comes to me with the crazy at the other end of it, see—that's proof Jimmy's around helping. If it was you against that pipe, we might have no more Lucas Lessar." He looked at the picture again. "Jimmy was with me many times when I made my show, my strongest man show. So, he knows about how I can get banged around, but not broken." He looked back at me. "You will come here again, sometime to see me, okay?"

"I think Walter pretty much hates me."

"Don't worry about Walter. I'll take care of Walter. You come back."

Slats thought I was recuperating, but in the mornings after she left, I started to go out to Bedford to see if my mother had gotten better enough to work on the farm. Red explained the whole system to me, how the people that were doing well came out in the mornings and went down to the barns. He showed me which doors they came out of and where they went to. She was never there.

I remembered when Mr. D'Angelo was sitting out in the lawn chair growing his beard, that my mother had said he was doing a penance, one he made up himself. So even though I didn't want to go over to Marko's, when I came back to Banning from Bedford, I'd make myself visit him. I got an idea to go back in the shed and get his box of *Famous Monsters of Filmland* magazines. We started working our way through those, reading the articles, looking at all the crazy things for sale in the back pages. Some days he had a nurse that came to crank up his hospital bed, and she brought him a cane so he could practice walking on his knee with the pins in it. Those days we'd walk from the front door to the Nash, with all its broken windows, and then back. I would leave before school let out, so I wouldn't run into Walter. Then I'd go back to Slats's house, where she would watch the news and read magazines and drink her beer with salt and pepper poured into it.

It seemed that pretty much the whole spring would spend itself like that, but then Slats got a phone call from a man who'd heard about how our animals had gone missing. He called to say that a cow had shown up at his place, trying to stick her head through his fence, and that maybe it was one of ours.

We drove out there to have a look. Neither of us could say for sure if she was Great-grandfather's cow or not, but no one else around had any missing, so we took her. We had no way of hauling her back. We had to call Benci. He didn't have a truck big enough for her either. He put a rope around her neck and walked her back to the farm. Slats and I waited for him there, sitting in her car with the lights on. She didn't want to go in the house. I kept looking at it though; it was so strange to see all its windows dark.

"What are we going to do with her?" I said.

"Leave her here, send Benci out to feed her."

When Benci showed up, Slats got out of the car and had a long look at the cow and patted the side of her face.

When we got home, she went back to reading magazines, and I went back to sleeping. A few days later, though, we got a call about a pair of sheep. Benci hauled them in the back of his truck. I had to sit back there with them to make sure they didn't jump out on the road and break their necks. We took them to the farm and Slats had a long look at them in the light from the headlamps, then we drove to her house.

One afternoon after I'd been to Bedford and it seemed like my mother would never come out of there, I went to see Marko. We tried walking out of his yard, onto the street. I told him, "You were right. About my mother. She's where you thought."

He stopped walking. He winced at the pain in his knee. "You saw her?"

I nodded.

He looked worried. "How is she? She's okay? How's she doing?"

"I don't know. I can't visit her anymore. She says for me not to."

"Huh. Well, maybe she just wants to be alone until she feels better. Some people like to be alone when they don't feel good. Not me, but some people."

"I got this friend and sometimes she would do things for this guy she knows up there, and it'd cheer him up. She'd take him old things he used to like from his house. You know. They played him a record one time. Can you think of anything that used to make her happy?"

"How about . . . you know what she always liked were those couple of songs in the jukebox by Stevo, the flugelhorn player from Mineral, and his brass band. How about we go to the club. We'll unplug the jukebox and take those songs from there. You can take them up there for her."

But looking down the street at how far it would be to walk to the club, and at Marko's face, all twisted up with pain, I knew it'd take us a week to walk that far. It seemed too small a thing anyway, a couple of old records. Another idea came to me, "Do you know him? Stevo?"

"Sure."

"Let's take his band out there and make them play a song for her."

"In her hospital room?"

"They got this song they always play at the end of their shows. We'll make them play that one."

"Ha. Lucas, don't you know there's like fifteen, maybe twenty people in that band? Also, those guys, they are too much. How they play that music. If the doctors see them, they'll lock the whole band up in there and never let them out . . . The record will be good. She'll like the record."

"It's not enough, that idea. It isn't big enough."

Walter showed up on the porch one day when I was sleeping. He woke me up by stepping on my shoulder.

"Jesus, Woj," I said.

"My dad says I'm supposed to come over here and smoke the peace pipe with you. I'd rather break your knees and crack your ribs."

I didn't say anything.

He looked around the porch. "Let's do something."

"All right." I sat up and rubbed my shoulder. "What?"

"Let's go out and see that girl with all those cigarettes."

"She had to go visit her aunt in Pittsburgh or something. She's not there."

It was a warm day. It was still spring, but it was one of those days when you can feel everything leaning into summer. People were running lawnmowers, driving past on motorcycles. I could hear, someplace far off, a set of dogs barking at each other. "Let's go to the farm," I said. "My great-grandfather's farm."

"How are we going to get there? Walk? It's sort of far."

"I walked there all the time in the winter. It's not that far."

"All right, Lessar."

I stayed still for a while, closing and opening my eyes, listening to the lawnmowers. The air felt different than it had in the winter. It wasn't just that the cold was gone, there was a sweet smell lingering around, cut grass, new flowers. I remembered the night Great-grandfather reached out from under his covers and rubbed the air between his fingers, feeling the cold of it. I reached out and did the same thing.

Walter kicked me in the leg. "We're going anywhere you'll have to stand up, you lazy shit."

Walter was right—it was far to the farm. I couldn't keep up with him. He said, "This is worse than going for a walk with a hundred-year-old lady."

"Shut up."

We crossed through a bank of silver maples. In the winter, the trees were always dark and gray. You could only really tell in the spring and summer why they were called silver maples; the undersides of their leaves held a shimmer. It was like walking through a box of tinsel. I grabbed a handful of leaves.

"Walter," I said. "Do you know Stevo, the guy from Mineral with the brass band?"

"The flugelhorn player?"

"You know where he lives in Mineral?"

"No."

"Does that Nash still run?"

"Don't need windows to run."

"Think your dad's all right to drive it yet?"

"So, let's see, Lessar, are you trying to tell me that you want to drive around in a trashed car with no windows looking for a flugelhorn player? You still got that fever or what?"

At the farm, I showed Walter around the fields and the pond. He kept looking at the house. "He still up there?" he said.

"Who"

"Your crazy great-grandfather."

"What's wrong with you? He died."

"Someone's in there. Look." He pointed at the kitchen window.

It was Eli. He opened the window. "Are you the new farmers? Is empty here. All empty." He came out and the three of us walked the property. Eli showed me all the places where things were growing too wild, or weren't growing at all yet.

"You seen Benci around here?" I asked him.

"No. He's not so good at his job of oldest son. So now no one is doing that job and house is empty and animals are here alone. Maybe together, me and you can do for him his job? What do you think?"

"I don't know what that means." I looked inside the barn. There was another cow there. "Hey, where'd that come from?" I said.

We all went into the barn.

Eli said, "She shows up the other day. From where? I don't know."

"It's one of the ones from here?"

"Maybe. Could be she was one of the ones that leaves here and then she finds a way back."

"Like a homing pigeon," Walter said.

"Except she is cow," Eli said. We all stared at her.

Later, Eli had me fill some of the holes, the craters, that Great-grandfather had dug looking for oil and water. He had Walter start to tear down the chicken pen, which was listing and needed to be taken down and then built up again.

At the end of the day, it wasn't warm enough to swim, but Walter jumped in the pond anyway.

I found out from the phone book where Stevo the flugelhorn player lived in Mineral. One night when they had a big order to fill at the Glass and Slats had to work through the night, I called his house.

"You at your house?" I said.

"*Molim?*"

"Hi. You busy?"

"Who is this? What are you want from me?"

I didn't know what to say. I hung up. I went over to the Markovics' house and talked Walter and Marko into driving out to Mineral in the Nash. Once we were in the car though, I knew I didn't know what I was doing. I didn't have any money to give Stevo or a way to tell him what I wanted from him. "Forget about it," I said. "This is so stupid."

Marko had already gotten the car started up. He was in the front seat, pressing on the gas, warming the engine. I was in the back seat. He turned around and looked at me, then he looked behind me, at my house. "No. It's not so stupid, Uncle," he said.

He explained to Walter where we were going and why. When we got to Stevo's house, he got out of the car with his cane, and a while later he came out with Stevo. Then we went a few blocks down the road and got a trumpet player. We were missing the drummers and tuba players and the rest of the trumpet players, and the other flugelhorn players. "What about the rest of them?" I asked Marko.

"This is what we have."

"We can't go up there with just the two of them."

"But this is something. It's what we have. This is what we can do. Okay?"

At Bedford, we had to park out on the road, climb over the fence, then walk through the woods and the fields.

Stevo stopped and said, "Markovic, you haven't given us even close to enough money for this kind of trouble. I think maybe we turn around."

"You're already out here," Walter said. "Just come on. We'll pay you extra at the club in beers or Slim Jims or whatever."

"Slim Jims?"

"Yeah."

Stevo shrugged. "Okay, Woj. Many many Slim Jims though. A feast of Slim Jims." Then he saw the building and figured out where we were. "This is some serenade place, huh." He whistled.

I led them over to the window where, best as I could remember, I'd seen my mother on visiting day. "Play that song you play at the end of your show."

He started playing a song, but not the right one. "No. Stop," I said. "It starts out different, starts out sounding like someone climbing up some stairs. Then it speeds up." I hummed it. It didn't sound like it should have at all. He tried again and it was the right song, but outside, and just him alone, it was a small sound and it got picked apart by the breeze. It was nothing like listening to it in a small room getting your ears blown out. I walked away.

He stopped playing. "What?" he said. "What's problem now?"

"She'll never hear you."

He looked at his horn. He took a deep breath and went at it again.

How'd he make that noise come out of that horn? I couldn't figure it out. It was like there was nothing inside him but lungs. He played for a while and stopped and the trumpet started up, and then the best part came, when they played together. Stevo started to pound his foot on the ground, and the horn got even louder, and it seemed like there were twelve of them instead of two.

It wasn't a song about something cheerful, or about being happy—it *was* those things. It was like the difference between someone telling you what it was like to get shocked and you yourself taking a hold of a piece of cowpuncher between your teeth. You didn't think about electricity then, you were electricity.

He dipped into some old sad song. "No," I said. "No, come on. Play the other one again." He wouldn't stop. I kicked his shin.

He pulled the horn away from his face. "I don't feel happy here, so I can't play happy songs," he said. "You can't, you know, control me. I am artist."

"You're an artist?" Walter said. "Ha. You play the flugelhorn."

Marko said, "Jesus, Stevo." He took ten dollars out of his wallet and put it in Stevo's coat pocket.

Stevo shrugged. "I feel a happy feeling all of a sudden." And then it came out again, the good song.

I walked back and forth along the building, looking up at all the windows. It seemed like everyone in the whole hospital came to see what was going on, except my mother. A nurse and a couple of guards and orderlies came running outside toward us. Red wasn't one of them.

"What is going on out here?" the nurse said.

Stevo stopped playing and kind of saluted her. "We're lost," he said. "Lost musicians."

"What's wrong with you. You know where you are?"

"We took some wrong turns, I think," Stevo said.

The guard said, "We got people in here with real delicate situations. You better get out of here before I call the law."

Stevo and the trumpet player walked ahead of me and Marko and Walter through the woods. Walter said, "I thought I saw her. I'm pretty sure I saw her."

I shrugged. "I don't think so."

Marko did something he'd never done before, but that my dad used to do every once in a while—he put his hand on my shoulder and planted a kiss in my hair.

A few nights later, when Slats was looking through her magazines, breathing in a set of long sighs and every so often letting loose a short burst of crying, I said, "You know, we could live out there."

"Out where?"

"At the farm. It doesn't seem right it's empty. It's a big house."

"I think that fever did some permanent damage."

"We could work the farm, like Great-grandfather did, sharpen up the tools. You don't have to live right up against the Plate Glass just because you work there."

"I don't have to live out there just because it's empty."

"He left all kinds of things planted. Even though he's not around, it's like they can't help themselves, they're starting to grow anyway. Eli can show you."

"We'd be in over our heads with that place."

The more I thought about it, the more I liked the idea. "We should move out there."

"If it'll inspire you to give up sleeping so much, maybe we can go out more often, check on those animals."

"We could live there. We could start collecting dogs."

Slats made me go to school for the last two weeks of it, even though the principal and Miss Staresina had decided that I'd missed so much of the year, I'd have to do the whole thing over again.

After it was all through, on a morning of full-out summer, I went out to Bedford and stood at the fence where'd I'd smoked with Helen. It was too hot to move. I think the student nurses must have gone away already for the summer. I didn't see any of them. Everything felt quiet, like it does on those kinds of too-hot days. Finally, I saw one group of people come out of the building and go down to the barns. When they got closer, I saw it was all men with buckets.

I thought of giving up. Don't come out here, even if it's for years and years, she'd said.

There was another group of patients behind the men. I couldn't see them at first because the men blocked them out, but it was a group of women. One of them was walking at the edges, just a little away from the rest of them. I walked along the fence, closer to where they were. I couldn't be sure if it was her or not, but I started waving. A few of them waved back at me, but not her. Then they all disappeared into the barn.

I decided to wait for them to come out. I fell asleep in the grass. When I woke up, I kept watch through the fence.

When they finally did come back out, this time the women were in front. I'd been right. It was her. I jumped up and waved.

It wouldn't be until much later in the summer that she would finally come home from Bedford, but there she was, carrying a bucket, wide awake, her hair pulled back in a ponytail. She didn't wave to me, but going back up the hill to the building, she turned around and held out her hand; and she started walking backwards, until, I guess, she could fit me in the palm of her hand.

through the night there, and that she still liked the things she'd always liked about the place—climbing up the ladder on the side of the corn silo, swimming in the pond. I wouldn't go in that heavy brown water, but I would stay close while she and Walter swam. The *vodianoi* was down there after all, Great-grandfather would have said, hoping to snatch them away from me. No matter how deep they went in that dark water, I could always see Walter's yellow hair, glowing like a light.

Though it wasn't the kind of thing either of us were used to doing, or were very good at, my mother and I spent the summer mending the fence like Great-grandfather had shown me, and, with Eli, building a chicken coop.

Sometimes when we're all in the house, sleeping and dreaming, I get out of bed, feel my feet on the wood floor, and walk, quiet as I can, downstairs and outside. I don't walk all of Banning like my mother and I used to do. I just walk out of the kitchen and stand on the hill that slopes down to the barn. I watch the pear tree and listen to the breeze knocking at the bottles. With my back to it some mornings in the sun, I'm sure it's no spirit that lives in the tree; it's just the tree itself, good and generous. Or I'll think it's no spirit, but is my father somehow, him thinking about me. Other times, when it's more perplexing—noisy one minute, quiet the next—I'll think it's Great-grandfather. Then I'll think that no, there's nothing in the tree, those ghosts live right in me, taking their turns, making their spaces in all the hollows of my chest.

Sometimes, when I'm out there on those nights alone, I think about the land in the moments just before the very first miners came here poking in the ground, looking for which way the coal seam was headed. The hills rise up to meet them, ready, the trees shining, newly green. None of us have met yet; the people who came to live here and work the coal out of the seam are still scattered over the earth, living in our own countries, fighting in our own languages. All of the little houses that the companies threw down and that are slapped now with different-colored paints, they aren't here either. I think someday, soon probably, the brambles and trees will grow so thickly over all the mines that it will seem as if they were never there, and so the land might start to look again as it once did, but what it will never regain are those moments of perfect greenness, soft earth, hills ready to open at your feet.

It's not grand now, maybe, but I think it was then, charged with promise, everywhere you looked, charged with promise. I think of Great-grandfather carrying Great-grandmother's name with him, whispering it as he walked, holding it in his mouth all the way across the sea. I think of all the things people carried here to Banning. Those songs in the jukebox at the club. Those notes and words on the music sheets, instruments, the songs in their heads, all their hopes of what it might mean to get here and what would happen to them after.

"Will it be beautiful when we get to there, like the Hungarians says to me?" Great-grandfather asked me in his fever. I didn't answer him, but I should have. I should have said, it will be, *Dedka*. It'll be beautiful just like they told you. We won't be able to believe what our eyes see.

ACKNOWLEDGMENTS

For believing in this book and making it happen, I'd like to thank my teacher John Edgar Wideman, my agent Jin Auh, and my editor Kathy Belden. Thank you to the *Alaska Quarterly Review*, which published an early version of the first chapter; St. Albans School in Washington, D.C., which gave me a year to write the chapters that followed; and Yaddo and the MacDowell Colony, both of which gave me time and space to keep writing. Linda J. Ivanits's book, *Russian Folk Belief*, helped me make sense of some of the myths I'd heard over the years. For their help with earlier drafts, big thanks to Rilla Askew, Jim Foley, Noy Holland, Brian Jordan, Jacob Kornbluth, Emily Miller, Curtis Sittenfeld, Erin White, Leni Zumas, and my sister Jessica Priselac. I owe many thanks to Nadine Johnson and Mitchell Terk for their generosity and enthusiasm; to Brian O'Keefe for his high-quality friendship; to Alexander Chee and Laura Dave for years' worth of conversations about books and writing; to Josh Ditzion and my sister Sarah Priselac for putting a Harlem roof over my head; to Ralph Falbo and Dorothy Duffy for all their help and good stories; and to the wonderful, incomparable Elizabeth Powley for thousands of things and for reading everything (including these acknowledgments) a minimum of a thousand times. Thank you to all Sattlers and all Seliys, and their fearless leaders, Marge Sattler and Irene Seliy. For their support and all-around excellence, I am grateful to my sister Lindsey Seliy; my stepmother Laura Seliy; and my brother, David Priselac. Lastly, for being the best kind of parents a person could hope for, and for always teaching me it is important to take a shot, my deepest thanks go to Steve Seliy and Mimi Priselac.

A NOTE ON THE AUTHOR

Shauna Seliy grew up in Pittsburgh, Pennsylvania, and lives in Washington, D.C. She has received fellowships from Yaddo, and the MacDowell Colony. She is a former writer-in-residence at St. Albans School in Washington, D.C. Her work has appeared in *Other Voices*, the *New Orleans Review*, and the *Alaska Quarterly Review*. This is her first novel.